PADRE CISCO

*Conversations
with a
Desert Father*

MICHAEL McCABE

PADRE CISCO
CONVERSATIONS WITH A DESERT FATHER

iUniverse books may be ordered through booksellers or by contacting:

iUniverse
1663 Liberty Drive
Bloomington, IN 47403
www.iuniverse.com
1-800-Authors (1-800-288-4677)

ISBN: 978-1-5320-5359-7 (sc)
ISBN: 978-1-5320-5360-3 (hc)
ISBN: 978-1-5320-5358-0 (e)

Library of Congress Control Number: 2018910220

Print information available on the last page.

iUniverse rev. date: 09/07/2018

CONTENTS

Autumn

Winter

For
Becky Jane
"You make me want to be a better man."

"Abba, give me a word."
"What is your intention, my son?"
"To live out that word, Abba."
"So be it, my son."

PREFACE

"If it is not your story to tell, you don't tell it."
~ Iyanla Vanzant

I talked to Padre Cisco many times. To casual scrutiny, his stories at times can be obscure in meaning or roundabout in delivery. I am a cartoonist, and I hold my memory in images rather than words. While I cannot always attest to the specifics of the padre's stories, I can attest to their truth. Wisdom is wisdom regardless of its container; we recognize it when it appears.

The stories in books like the Torah and similar ancient collections tell not only of what happened long ago but also of what happens in each generation. The stories occur over and again in the life of each person. They are true, not because they happened but because they happen.

Often Padre Cisco would state some variation of "I don't know if the story happened this way or not, but I know it to be true."

This was an understanding of classical storytelling in ancient times in the Near East and the pre-colonial Americas. Storytellers would begin with a similar phrase. They knew their responsibility was to get the substance of the story correct if not all the details. If they varied too far, their audience would demand a correction. If you have read the same story or fable to your children or grandchildren and gone off script, you may have heard, "No, Papa" or "No, Mama, read it right." Such is my retelling of the padre's stories.

In my intent to tell the stories of Padre Cisco, what I did not anticipate was my discovery of the unfolding story of Rocky Stellar.

~ Peter Paul Stellar

PROLOGUE

The Man

"If you've heard this story before, don't stop me.
I want to hear it again."
~ Groucho Marx

I met Juan Francisco Angel O'Shaughnessy thirty years ago when he was teaching at Arizona State University. People knew him then as Dr. Frank O'Shaughnessy. We've kept occasional contact since. I am on his email list, but the connection has been more mine. I would get a message when he had a storytelling booking in the area. I attended when I could, as much to stay connected with him as to hear his latest stories. My wife, Gen, went sometimes, and Morgan and Alex would accompany us when they were young.

Padre Cisco, as he is known today, has a Gandhi-like quality about him in a rather Ben Kingsley sort of way. He is short, bespectacled, shaved bald, tan, and bandy-legged. He typically wears khaki cargo shorts, long-sleeved shirts, and Hoka hiking sandals. He wears a plain wooden cross on a leather thong around his neck. I asked him about it one time, and he said, "I wear it to hold myself accountable to my faith. I want people to know what they can expect of me. Sadly, because of people's experiences with Christians, some do not expect much of me."

He is seldom outside beyond mid-morning without a broad-brimmed hat. He's lived in the desert most of his life and is aware of its consequences. The sandals are a self-proclaimed extravagance, a consciousness if not obsession about taking care of his feet. Padre Cisco said to me, "What is the use of standing on your own two feet if they are crumbling beneath you?" He, also, says, "I am a vegetarian unless there is meat around." I have learned to take his maxims with a grain of salt.

From what I know of his career, the padre is likely in his late seventies but of indeterminable age from appearance. He is the descendent of Irish immigrants and a Yaqui shaman. His great grandfather on his father's side was a peasant farmer, who emigrated from Galway County, Ireland, in 1879 during the mini-famine. His grandfather was four at the time. The family traveled from Baltimore to Pennsylvania and eventually found their way to Laredo, Texas, where they farmed.

After graduating from high school, his father worked his way to Arizona and met Toloko Taa'am, *Turquoise Water* in English. Her name came from the deep, blue water near her birthplace. They married, and Francisco was born soon afterward. When America entered World War II, his father enlisted in the army. He served in Europe, surviving to live out his days in Eloy, Arizona, working on a cotton farm where he eventually became the irrigation manager. Francisco grew up roaming the farms and desert around that rural Arizona community.

Padre Cisco told me Toloko was the granddaughter, many generations back, of a Yaqui shaman, who traveled in the early

1500s across Mexico with the conquistador Juan Francisco de Coronado. The padre's parents named him for Juan Francisco.

Padre Cisco is the oldest of four children, two brothers and a sister. He is the first of his family to go to college. All four attained their parents' dream for them to finish college, and all work in professional positions. He attended the University of Arizona, studying history and anthropology, got a Master's in Education from Northern Arizona University, and took a job teaching in Phoenix. He fell ill and went to the hospital where he met Andrea, his nurse, who became his wife. He earned a PhD at Stanford art history and political science. He once told me the one advantage he experienced as a Yaqui, a minority within a minority, was that it got him into Stanford. He thought about working for the State Department or the Peace Corps, but events altered his vision. He and Andrea conceived their first child, and he continued teaching.

Padre Cisco came from a heritage of readers. Even his grandfather was literate though he had limited access to books. The padre told me his father was fond of quoting Mark Twain's aphorism, "The man who doesn't read good books has no advantage over the man who can't read them." Padre Cisco loves playing with words, keeping lists of homophones, inserting puns in conversation, creating new words, and writing what he calls his "fictionary." He grew up speaking English and passable Gaelic, and learned Spanish with a Tex-Mex influence. At times there is the lilt of brogue in his voice, though I believe he plays on it a bit when he wants to make a point. He lost his wife years ago, never remarried, and has three children living out of state.

Padre Cisco lives alone in a small house in the desert, harkening back to ancient times when thousands of Christians fled to the Middle Eastern deserts to live the lives of hermits and aesthetics. They were the desert fathers and mothers, the Abbas and Ammas, of the third through fifth centuries. Padre Cisco is ostensibly a modern-day desert father. While not an ascetic, he lives simply. Everything for Padre Cisco is multi-use; he chooses function over appearance.

This, however, is not the man, but simply the shape of the man. The man himself is an enigma. If I ask him for his point of view, he gives me information. If I ask for information, he tells me a story. If I ask for a story, he replies with a question. He answers questions with questions and my comments with lengthy gazes. There seems to be no end to his obliqueness. He laughs a lot and loves to laugh at himself.

He is a storyteller and wisdom teacher, though he says all he knows he learned from movies, novels, and the occasional song. He describes himself as an "unteacher," claiming that the term *teacher* is an elaborate subterfuge for preacher, which to the padre means one who engages in the vice of proselytizing. *Un* seems to be a favorite prefix: unteaching, unlearning, unknowing, unreaching, or ungrasping. He speaks of "engaging in unthinking;" now that is unthinkable (pardon me for that). His favorite prefix may be "un," but without doubt, his favorite word is "perhaps." Padre Cisco and the men around him seem to think and converse in a continual state of perhaps. He seldom speaks in absolutes. Whatever it is that he knows or how he chooses to share it, he has an uncanny ability to vex me. It can be unnerving, but I keep returning. I like him.

Winter

One
The Secrets of Selling Insurance

"Abba, you were invited to a conference."
"Yes, my son."
"Did you go?"
"No, my son."
"Why not, Abba?"
"So I would be present for you."
"But I didn't tell you I was coming."
"Yet, you are here as am I."

From the first time, I went to visit Padre Cisco, I've had a sense that he was expecting me. Typically, I call though I am still apt to drop in on him. During the early days, he didn't have a phone, but his kids pressed him to get a cell phone. Cajoled him into it would be more accurate. He spends time walking the desert alone. Given his age they worry about him. For a long time he only carried a flip phone. They wanted him to upgrade to a smart phone, but he said, "Mine works; what do I need beyond that? It rings and I answer it."

"Sometimes," they claimed. He relented when he learned he could use the phone as a hot spot for his computer.

The aroma of chorizo wafted from the house as I approached. I called out my presence, and he emerged from the kitchen wearing a benign smile I remembered from my time at the university with him. "Hello, Peter," he greeted me and opened the screen door, inviting me in. He reached out to take my hand, and we stood in the cordial embrace of shaking hands as he asked after my welfare and that of Gen and the kids. He offered me one of the two chairs in the "great" room, though I soon learned it was more than a chair. It was made of oak and had squared-off arms and legs with a solid flat back. It seemed large for the space. When I sat on the thin cushion, I found myself looking over Padre Cisco's head. He sat in a wicker chair festooned with a flowery round cushion as decorously inappropriate as most of his furnishings. I felt as though I were sitting on a throne. Padre Cisco asked if I wanted coffee. At my assent, "Black," he got up to get it from the kitchen.

Padre Cisco's house is near Three Points on Highway 86, southwest of Tucson. If you asked him, he would say he lives in the Rio Sonoita Basin between the Boboquivari Mountains and the Tumacacori Highlands, as though that would help. I wouldn't call his home remote, but it is certainly rural even by Arizona standards. It's about a half mile off the nearest road.

His house is made of adobe with red terra cotta tile roof except for the back, which faces southeast. Solar panels cover that side. The house is about six hundred square feet plus the basement. He contracted the foundation and three-foot-thick, ram-packed adobe walls. The contractor built the walls from the adobe dug out to make the basement. He completed the rest of the work himself. Padre Cisco describes it as his sweat equity project.

He is connected to the grid but powers his house and well mostly by windmill and the solar cells. He paid to have the power line from the highway buried so he would not interrupt the landscape. He has a radio but no TV, much less cable. He has a computer and Internet, but few of what we would call necessities in urban living. He cooks on a propane-fueled stove with a wood-burning backup outside, does laundry by hand, hanging it on a steel cable clothesline, and cleans the light brown polished cement floor with a broom and a mop.

I surveyed the room; it was simply furnished. A beehive fireplace with a niche holding a figurine of the Madonna filled one side. The walls are a latte color. A framed star chart hung on one wall along with a photo of the Milky Way taken from the Hubble Telescope. *Well I'll be...* Across from it hung an original of an early SoCal and Knuckles comic strip, "Nuke the Whales." That was their hippie and protest era. They raged against anything that didn't move freely, from caged minks to Republicans. I gave it to Padre Cisco just after he left the university. *I would have never thought I'd see that here...and framed.* A small writing desk sat below it with a lamp, a stack of books, and a laptop computer. A bookcase stood sentinel next to it with neatly arranged rows of books like soldiers waiting their call. There was a wrought iron pole lamp next to his chair. An overturned galvanized steel bucket sat between the two chairs. While sparsely furnished without a touch of style, the house was trim bordering on Spartan. There was no clutter, computer cords were bundled behind the desk, and the room was spotless.

"What brought you out here?" he said, offering me a hand-fashioned mug of coffee.

"Oh, I don't know. Gen suggested I talk with you. You know Gen. She's worried about me. She says I don't seem to be myself lately."

"Did you have waffles for breakfast?" he asked with a hint of amusement.

"No, I don't usually eat breakfast/" I'd missed the allusion.

"I have not eaten either; we should eat first. It is better to talk on a full stomach."

He set about fixing breakfast. He chopped and sautéed onions and small potatoes from his winter garden; and folded them along with the chorizo into scrambled eggs. He wrapped all of it in warmed, hand-made tortillas. Padre Cisco offered no small talk, working wordlessly as I stood to the side in the small kitchen. It was compact but efficient like the house itself and bore signs of how he lived. Iron skillets and pots hung from a rack. Drying herbs dangled among them like bats from a ceiling. More herbs and spices in small jars with hand-lettered labels sat alphabetically on a shelf over the stove. A timbered beam from floor to ceiling standing next to the stove had hooks and eyebolts screwed into it and held implements usually stored in drawers. Fruit, onions, and potatoes hung in baskets. He had nearly doubled the usable space.

He asked me to carry the glasses and table service to the living room. The plates and glasses were ceramic in the same handmade style as the mugs. When I asked about them, he said his mother had been a potter, and he still dabbled in it. I think he more than dabbled. He set the bucket to the side and moved the chair I had sat in to the center of the room. He flipped the back over onto the arms, turning the chair into a table. He called it a "tablechair." His great grandfather bought it from a Pennsylvania Dutch family and carried it to Texas. It served the small space well as a chair and when needed as a table. He retrieved two folding chairs from a closet. I set the table, he brought in the food, and we sat down.

He said a quick grace, "Holy One, thank you for the blessing of Peter's visit and for the opportunity to share a meal. He silently paused, said, "Amen," and we ate. We made small talk, catching up on the previous year. I wasn't ready to talk about my reason for the visit. We talked about the Sun Devils' football season, the possibility of coaching changes in Tempe and Tucson, the upcoming *Duel in the Desert*, and how acrimonious the fans had become in that rivalry.

I remarked about the ingenuity of the tablechair, and asked him about the wicker chair. It was the one item in the room decidedly feminine. He said the chair had been his wife's, and he sensed her presence when he sat it in. It was one of only a few times, I heard him mention her, but it was clear that in all the years since her death he had not let her go completely. I knew he adored her. In grad school, he would end our night classes by saying, "We must quit now; I want to get home to my bride."

"Is astronomy your hobby, Padre?" pointing over my shoulder at the Hubble photo.

"Yes and no, Peter. I pay daily attention to the sky, watching it move and change. I love to gaze at it just before the sun rises. I like to keep track of the seasons, the moon and such, but I am hardly an astronomer. I am not sure I would know which end of a telescope to look into. I would call myself a sky watcher. I keep the chart and photo to remind me of my place in the universe. It is a very small place though certainly larger than I need."

I thought it was very small, but then he probably wasn't talking about his house. I told him about Morgan and Alex's progress in med and law school and that we didn't hear from them often. We ran the gamut of topics, omitting religion, the weather, and politics.

We finished eating, cleared the table, and returned it to its service as a chair. He placed the bucket between the chairs. We sat down with coffee. Padre Cisco placed his cup there demonstrating its use. Without segue, Padre Cisco said again, "Tell me what brought you."

"I'm not sure, but I know that I need to talk to someone."

Padre Cisco's response was nothing more than a slight tilting of his head and the turning of his hand, bidding me to continue.

I gave the padre a thumbnail of my dilemma. I turned fifty-nine in August. Sixty is above the horizon. It's weird and unsettling. Birthdays have never bothered me before, but this one snuck up on me. It's different. I don't know what I am supposed to do. I lost my syndication. They wanted a younger artist to appeal to a younger demographic. I had talked with my agent about altering the strip, but this happened out of the blue. Sixty is supposed to be the new fifty, isn't it? My hair is barely turning gray. I'm not ready for the rocking chair. I've worked all my life. I don't have to work. Gen and I are more than financially secure, but I don't know how not to work.

My friends told me that this is a gift. My entire future is open to me. I get to relax, take up golf, or go on a cruise. Get real! I don't like golf, and I get seasick in a rowboat. I called Alex and Morgan and shared what had happened. She told me the same thing; it's a gift. She didn't hear a word I said. Sometimes, I wonder who raised her. Alex seemed to have some sense of commiseration. He at least he gave me more than five minutes.

"You wouldn't recognize those kids, Padre."

Alex is six-two and has grown a beard. It's more than one of those scraggly beards young men grow. It's full and dark like his hair. He has filled out. He doesn't have that gangly look as he did when he was in high school. Morgan looks like her mom. She has the tanned complexion and short, sun-bleached hair of a surfer. She's six foot and carries it well. She's aware she turns men's heads. She's another California girl.

"I would enjoy seeing them again."

"So would I, Padre. They are hard to corral. They are very independent, Morgan probably to excess. I love them dearly, but they can try a father's patience."

"That is their calling."

"I'm hearing no support here," laughing at myself. "I should get back to the work issue. I'm not ready to retire. Retirement has never been a part of my vision of the future. I just can't just see myself in my town car motoring safely down the freeway at 55 mph to the Social Security office and shuffling up to the window to check in so I can check out."

Padre Cisco sat quietly. I wanted him to respond. I wanted him to nod, agree, commiserate, say something, anything. What I got was...I don't know what I got. I wanted his sympathy. He was there. He was attentive, seemingly focused on what I had said, but he was mute. We sat there in silence for what became an eternity.

Why did I think this was going to make a difference? Maybe this was a mistake; I should go. Finally, the exasperation coming through my words, I said, "What am I doing here?"

"You seem to have a lot of questions." His response startled me.

"Yes, I do. I don't know what I am supposed to do. I'm out of work for the first time in forty years, know nothing but drawing, and I'm climbing the walls."

"So what is the deeper question?"

What is the deeper question? "What do you mean?"

"What is the deeper question?"

"I don't know what it is."

Padre Cisco shifted his weight up straighter. "Let us sit on that." He closed his eyes and inclined his head forward.

Seeing no alternative, I followed suit.

We sat there for five or more minutes. It took me a while to feel comfortable, first physically and even more so with my thoughts. My mind was awash with ideas, questions, and distractions. I thought about my career, a failed marriage, meeting Gen, the twins, trips and vacations. Morgan. *Meningitis. She could've died. I wasn't there for her.* Dad. *We've been at odds since I left.* I journeyed to New York to the awards banquet and my award. *Now they've put me out to pasture. I guess I had my fifteen minutes.* I relived a thousand moments in the span of those few minutes. Experiences soared through my head like comets, and I had no star chart on the wall to plot them. *The deeper question, what is the deeper question?* I tried to focus. *Was it worth it? You get your moment, and then they axe you. Is that it? Did it matter? Did I matter? Is that the deeper question? I drew cartoons, comic strips, and I'm done?*

I heard Padre Cisco in the distance, "When you are ready, come back to the present." Silently rousing myself back to the moment, I sat there in this strange self-inflicted circumstance. Finally, I said, "I'm here."

"So what is the deeper question?" I heard for the third time.

"Is my name the only thing that is stellar about me? Can I be proud of what I have done? Do I have anything to be proud of? Is anyone proud of me? Am I a good man? Was it all worth it? What am I supposed to do now?" The questions came rushing out of me, and the air seemed to go with them. I took a deep breath and experienced a sense of relief just having voiced them.

Padre Cisco sat silent for a few moments, and then a smile came over his face. "Peter, It just occurred to me that you have quite a *sixtuation* here."

"Do you mean situation, padre?"

"No, sixtuation is the word. I read an article by two young women approaching thirty. They referred to being in 'a thrisis.' I think if approaching thirty is a thrisis, then approaching sixty would be a least a sixtuation."

Padre Cisco picked up his cup from the bucket and asked if I wanted more coffee or a glass of water. I said, "I'm fine." What I wanted was a drink, and it was more than water that I wanted.

He continued as he went to the kitchen. "I keep a list of words I think might be useful some day. I call it a *fictionary*. I will have to add sixtuation. If you had lost your syndication ten years from now I might say, it is natural because you are approaching the sevenerance generation. I like that one. Let's see. I have no thought for the seventies, but the eighty and ninety-year-olds would face ninecessities and eventually centastrophies.

"It is just a frivolity. It started with my kids. *Gionic* I think was the first one. It was one of my children's words. It means big and powerful. That was from the era of the *Six Million Dollar Man* television show. *Kneepit*, the area behind your knee, was another. I think my favorite is *precrastination*, meaning divine intervention for putting off life's challenges until tomorrow. Come think of it that could mean I would be *prodestined*. This is good stuff. I glad you came today, Peter."

I realized Padre Cisco had changed the subject and diverted my attention, allowing for what I had just said to sit with me. He returned, took a gulp of his coffee, set his mug down, and said, "Let me tell you about my friend Michael Francis Lee.

He told me about growing up in the small town of Eloy and of making his way as a child of mixed ancestry. He said that he had to learn to fight if he was to have a chance to learn to read. One day by a bunch of boys who thought the Yaqui side of him did not belong there cornered him. He was in a losing battle until Michael decided the odds were not fair and jumped in to his rescue. The fracas was soon over. He and Michael went to the drinking fountain to tend to their wounds, and they began talking. Michael asked about his name, and Cisco told him it was short for Francisco. He said that the kids called him Cisco after *The Cisco Kid* on the radio. Michael told him his middle name was Francis.

Padre Cisco said, "From that day, we began a friendship that has lasted a lifetime. Out of that experience, I have always called him Michael Francis. About fifteen years ago, around the time he transitioned careers, he began referring to himself the same way. We both went on to college; I became a teacher as you know, and Michael Francis a successful business consultant and public speaker."

Padre Cisco described Michael Francis as anything but the corporate type, no coiffured hairstyle or Park Avenue suits, nearly as tall as me, pink-faced with wisps of white hair, and glasses hanging around his neck that gives him an aura of benevolence.

The padre said, "He is sort of a giant version of a puffy Albert Einstein minus the mustache. How he succeeded in the hard-driving frenzy of the corporate world is a mystery to me. Perhaps his gentleness allowed the Type-A CEO personalities to trust him. I trust him implicitly. Perhaps you will have occasion to meet him."

He paused, appearing to reflect on those bygone days of his youth, and I interjected, "I'd like to say that I got my nickname in much the same way, that I was a fighter as a kid; and I was nicknamed after Rocky Marciano. The truth is, my father was a diehard Cleveland Indians fan, and Rocky Colavito hit a grand slam the day I was born. The Indians beat the Tigers five to four. My dad started calling me Rocky that day.

"It seems only my mother and you call me Peter. Mom called me Peter Paul at times when I was a kid. That name had a different tone to it as you might imagine. On that note, what should I call you? Dr. O'Shaughnessy doesn't seem quite appropriate any longer."

"Some call me Padre or Padre Cisco. My friends call me Cisco. That would be fine."

"Okay, Padre Cisco."

"Just Cisco."

"Yes sir, Padre."

Padre Cisco nodded and told one of Michael Francis' stories.

A national sales organization invited successful insurance salesman to share his formula for success. He responded, declining the invitation. He told the chairman that someone else could give his speech and to not allow much time on the program for it. He wrote that the chairman should have the speaker tell them this, "While you all are sitting there at the conference learning the secret of selling insurance, I am at home practicing that secret – be present to my customers." He was not suggesting that people should avoid conferences; that was a big part of how he made his living. He had just returned from a conference for spiritual directors. He was just saying the big secret isn't a secret at all.

After many years of serving in the talking professions, he began a second career as a spiritual director and writer. In the days leading up to the conference, he held great anticipation for the opportunity to learn the *secrets* from the masters and was not disappointed. He had a sense of what he was seeking. He was still surprised.

"At our age," Padre Cisco said, "to be surprised is in itself is a joy. Michael Francis told me he learned his task was not necessarily to go to the conference, but to simply be there. Being present to the moment became his reason for attending."

"What does that mean, Padre? That is, if being present was his reason for attending, what did he do, or maybe the question is how did he spend his time *there*?"

"When I was younger, and traveled a lot, I would pick up a pebble wherever I went and bring it back. I particularly chose water rocks, pebbles from streams, rivers, lakes, or the ocean. Over the years, I collected quite a few. Have you been to the Petrified Forest, Peter?"

"I have. Gen and I took the kids there."

"Then you saw the signs warning tourists not to remove the petrified wood."

"Yes."

"As I grew in my understanding of my relationship to the world, I began to wonder about taking stones from their place in the water and bringing them to the desert. There seemed to be something wrong about that. There were no signs against it, but it seemed as though I was taking something from its rightful place. I quit collecting them. They needed to be where they belong. Beside that, the desert already had enough rocks." He laughed at that.

"I'm not quite sure I understand the relationship here, Padre."

"Well, Peter, Michael Francis's insurance salesman's story reminded me of my fundamental responsibility to remain present to others. Like the pebble, I am to be wherever I am and what I am in that moment. How I am supposed to do that out here is a curious question." He laughed at his own dilemma. "Perhaps I am to just be here when you arrive. Perhaps I should put a digital sign out on the highway: *Storyteller. Will talk for food.*" He laughed even more.

"For some time after I retired from the university, I thought I wanted to throw one more pebble into the pond. I wanted to see how many ripples I could make. At some point along the way, I understood I am not to throw the pebble. I am to *be* the pebble."

A pebble? How in the name of Moses do I become a pebble? Whether it was my body language or my expression, he must have sensed my quandary because he paused. When I returned to the moment he went on, "Presence is in itself an act of ministry. Woody Allen says, 'Eighty percent of life is just showing up.' That may be so, but many people only just show up. The other twenty percent is about presence. When the people who show up are actually present to those for whom they show up, they make a difference in people's lives. They are engaging in acts of ministry solely by being present. A friend Perry says, 'Ministry is not something you do; it is something you are.' Perhaps your presence in people's lives through your comic strip is a ministry. I would call it a ministry of distraction. Entertaining people provides distraction from suffering for some. There are times in all our lives when we need relief of the facts of our lives."

At that, Padre Cisco stood, indicating we were through, reached out to shake my hand, and said, "It was good to see you, Peter, stop by anytime if you want to talk again."

The abruptness of the ending startled me, but I told him I would like to talk again and I would call. With that, I left, looking back over my shoulder and waving. Heading down the lane, I looked in the mirror and saw him standing at the end of the path, watching until I reached the bend in the road and drove out of sight.

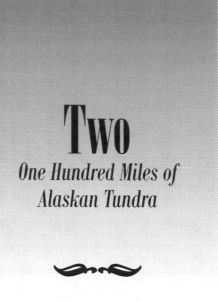

Two

One Hundred Miles of Alaskan Tundra

"Abba, I feel so lost."
"What do you seek, my son?"
"My path, Abba."
"Are you not on it?

Driving home, my head was a swirl of confusion. *Presence...a ministry...Distraction...*I had never thought of what I do as a ministry. *I don't even go to church.* I had difficulty concentrating on my driving. I wanted to get home to Gen. I needed to talk, to process aloud. Gen is my sounding board, and the compass in my life. I drove without awareness of the world around me. How I made it home without mishap was a miracle.

Gen works from home; she is a database computer geek. I've read her résumé; I can sound out the words, but I don't know what they mean. "Hi, Rocky," I heard as I walked in, "I'm in the office. I saw you arrive. Let me finish this string, and I'll be right with you."

Sure, finish the string. Techie terms are curious. Next, she will be telling me about some ball of wax she is developing. I was out of sorts, flummoxed, or as my friend, Melinda calls it, *kerfuffled*. I went to the kitchen to brew a cup of coffee and wait for Gen to finish.

We met in graduate school at ASU when I was working on an MFA and she was finishing her PhD in the field of variable data and large numbers. Again, nothing I understand. I was a couple of years beyond a failed marriage, which at least bore no offspring as it bore no joy. Gen had been in a couple of fledgling relationships that ended when her companions could not adjust to her intellectual drive and surfer girl independence. A boating accident took her parents when she was in college. I think that and being an only child added to her sense of independence.

Her parents were avid surfers, and following in their wake, she grew up on the beaches of southern California. Her parents' love for surfing led them to name her Genevieve, Celtic for "white wave." When she came of job-seeking age, she saw the advantage of a non-gender-specific name. She began writing Gen on her applications, a practice she later expanded.

She is tall for a surfer, wears her brown hair cropped. She is shapely, which is testament to her diligence in the gym. She wears large, plastic-rimmed glasses that she claims make her geekier and win her maturity points with her colleagues. She studies yoga and practices daily meditation.

We met in a crossover class on art and society taught by Dr. O'Shaughnessy and an unmemorable art prof. We each took the class for a divergence from our professional studies. I was smitten from the first time I saw her.

Growing up in Akron, Ohio, the closest I ever got to surfing was skateboarding. It was a slim point of common ground, so I pitched my experience with the wave pool at Big Surf in Tempe. She was unimpressed. Nevertheless, we gravitated to each other. We hung out after class at coffee houses and wine bars.

We took a trip to San Diego, meeting up with my friend Smitty to surf real waves. In spite of my demonstrating a distinct lack of skill on the long board, we hung out together any chance we had. The shared joy of watching the 6'7", 280-pound Smitty crash the waves likely sealed the deal. He floated in on his board grinning ear to ear, giving the phrase "tail end over tin cup" new meaning.

Gen and I thought we were too old to be dating, and *hanging out* seemed to be a more acceptable label. Funny now, we were barely thirty, and we thought we were too old to date. Hanging out led to living together, living together led to marriage, and marriage to Alex and Morgan. Twenty-five years later, it led to this, whatever this is that I am now experiencing.

Gen and I live a quiet life, both working out of the house. We were home for the kids when they were young. Now, we just enjoy having the time to eat together and talk together during the workday. My loss of *SoCal and Knuckles* and its daily deadlines put a strain on our routines. I found myself interrupting her more than normal. I always talked about taking up painting in my retirement years, but I didn't think the advent of that would come so soon. I felt lost around the house. Actually, I felt completely lost.

Gen smiled as she emerged from the office. She hugged and kissed me. "I missed you, Rocky." She gave me her usual pinch on the butt when she greets and leaves me. "How was your visit with Dr. O'Shaughnessy, or I guess Padre Cisco as he is known now?"

"It was fine," I said. "That's dismissive. It was more than I expected." I mentioned what had transpired, how surprised I was at how I just sort of gushed all over myself about my feelings, and that I am probably more confused than ever.

"Are you glad you went?"

"Yes, I am, and we talked about my going back out there."

"I want to hear more, but I need to get back. This morning, I sent Gary in Seattle the patch we've been working on for him to verify. He is going to call me in a few minutes. We're holding a videoconference with the manager at *Fantasy Corp* this afternoon. Can we talk over lunch?"

I went to the kitchen and set about fixing soup and sandwiches. Gen joined me, as I was finishing. We set the table and sat down.

"So, tell me about it, Rocky? That is other than what you already related. You said that you gushed all over yourself. That's not like you. I usually need a pry bar to get you to open up."

"That sounds like my phone conversations with Morgan though conversation is an overstatement. I seem to do most of the talking."

"I have the same experience. It's just who she is right now."

"Right now?"

"Okay, it's just who she is. So, back to your time with the padre."

"I am surprised as you are. When I spoke about gushing I probably should have said, 'at least for a guy' to clarify it."

"Well, there is that," she said with a roll of her eyes."

I ignored her and went on. "Padre Cisco asked me what took me out there, and I couldn't say anything but that I had a lot of questions. I listed some of them, and he asked me what the deeper question was. I didn't even know what he was asking. He suggested we just sit and think about it. At least that's how I interpreted it. We sat for a few minutes, and my mind raced through forty years of stuff. When he asked again what the deeper question was I just sort of let loose with even more questions. I know what I expressed was just the extent of my confusion. You know, Gen, just saying it was cathartic."

"In itself, Rocky, that must have been a good feeling."

"It was, and it is, but I'm not sure I am any further ahead. The padre told a story about throwing pebbles into a pond. He said that after he retired he learned that he was to be the pebble, not the thrower. I have no idea what he meant by that."

"Give it time, Rocky. You've just begun."

"Well, time is something I have a lot of, maybe too much. Losing my strip has stirred up a lot. I'm questioning the worth of all the years I invested in drawing comic strips. Was that all art was to me? I have a lot to figure out."

"You will. We will, together. I'm glad you went to see the padre. After all the years knowing him as Dr. O'Shaughnessy, I'm having a hard time thinking of him as Padre Cisco; but I'm glad you are going back to see him again."

We talked over lunch, over dinner, and in between for the next two weeks. We discussed the ideas of presence and ministry. I talked about my perspective and myself more than I had in months or maybe years for that matter.

Gen and I always have had frank dialogue about our life together. We feel safe with each other, but I'd never felt the need to talk much about my feelings, concerns or aspirations. The short conversation with Padre Cisco unleashed a torrent of things I never considered.

* * *

Winter came the day I next drove out to Padre Cisco's; it was just after Thanksgiving. It was a cool, windy day. Those of us living in the Southwest deserts are wimps about cool much less cold weather. After living here, our blood thins, and we feel the cold more. It rained the night before then cleared, dropping the temperatures. The shadows were long, showing off the rugged relief of the desert floor. Even in the afternoon, I had my heater on.

My winter started last July when the syndicate dumped me for a younger artist. I rounded the bend turning toward his house. *It's like being divorced for a younger, hotter guy.* There was no gate or fence to define his property. I learned later that he owned five acres. He wanted less, but it was the smallest parcel he could buy in the sites he had chosen for the watershed and drainage, and the availability of clay in the soil. I saw him ahead on the road. He was dressed as usual in shorts, wide-brimmed hat, long-sleeved cotton shirt, and sandals. He stood there in a now-familiar pose with hands folded together at his waist. His posture was welcoming, yet more than that. He'd stood in that same way when I left. It had a sense of both welcoming and sending forth. In one instance, he was drawing me in. In the other, he was following me as though I were not leaving alone.

He reached out to shake hands, clasping mine with both of his, and again the intentional pause. He asked how I was and Gen and the kids as well. "It is a nice day, let's sit on the veranda. Coffee?"

"Absolutely! It's what I come here for." His eyes darted at me in response to my weak attempt at humor. We walked around the house, and he motioned me to sit in one of two Adirondack chairs. They sat at a slight angle toward each other and rested on paver bricks. I was again amazed at Padre Cisco's industry when said he had fired them in his homemade kiln. He had stationed the bucket between them and a small chiminea fireplace stood behind. It had the glow and aroma of mesquite charcoal that I learned he also baked in his kiln.

He went for the coffee, and I sat down. *Nice day? It's freezing out here.* I had on long pants and a sweatshirt. Returning, he handed me the mug, sat down, and said, "Let's rest a spell." We sat there looking southeast at the desert. The hues of cayenne, ochre, and umber captured me. I soon felt warmed by the fire. *It* is *a nice day.* I took off my sweatshirt.

Without changing his gaze, Padre Cisco broke the silence. "How is it with you?"

I virtually blurted out, "Weird, just weird. I don't know who I am anymore." I ignored the rehearsing about what I would say in response to such a question. This in itself diverged from my usual practice of pausing and thinking before I respond. Gen has always said she appreciates that about me. *Maybe she's right when she says that I am not myself lately.*

Padre Cisco sat, listening, waiting for me to continue. I didn't know what to say next so I too sat listening and waiting. *Maybe he knows I need time to pause and think. There seem to be many maybes in my life right now.* I sat for a while longer, my mind wandering from subject to subject. Breaking the silence, I said the safest thing on my mind. "I seem to be full of maybes right now. I don't seem to be able to settle on anything. I feel lost. I used to be so sure of who I was, what I was doing, where I am heading. I just don't know anymore."

Padre Cisco sat, focusing on the coffee cup resting on his lap. He held it the way Gen holds her cup. His hand wrapped around it with his second finger through the handle pointed away from him. Raising his head, he said, "So you feel lost." He returned to his cup, and after a few moments looked up and began again. "When I was a young teacher, before I went to the university, I worked with a science teacher named Tom Kreuser. Tom is a hiker, outdoorsman, and climber. Climbers named a dome on the McDowell Mountains northeast of Phoenix Tom's Thumb for him. He was the first person to climb it.

"He once hiked solo across a hundred miles of Alaskan tundra. I asked him, 'Didn't you get lost?' and he replied, 'Oh,

I was lost the entire time. Lost is just not being where you thought you would be when you thought you would be there.'"

My brain stopped to focus on that statement, and I missed the ensuing things he said. It checked back in, and I heard Padre Cisco saying, "Compasses are not accurate that far north, so I asked Tom how he found his way. He told me how you walk out the estimated number of days to cover the distance based on the knowledge of your pace in the type of terrain, and you set up camp. The next day, you continue out for a half-day, seeking your destination. If you don't find it, you return to your camp spot and try another direction the next day, repeating the process until you ultimately find your destination. Years later, having been on many journeys with alternate paths, I began to understand his words. They are true not only for the physical treks in life, but for many journeys on which we embark. Wherever you thought you were heading, Peter, you simply have not arrived there when you thought you would."

"But that's the thing, Padre. I no longer know what my destination is."

"Well, assuredly it begins with death, Peter."

"That's not a destination I want to contemplate yet."

"I did not say your destination ends with death; I said it begins with death. Perhaps death is not a destination but rather an embarkation."

"What do you mean?"

"Death in the spiritual sense does not refer to physical death. It is more about giving up or letting go of old ways, out with the old, in with the new. The Apostle Paul writes to members of the church of Ephesus to put off their old self and to put on the new self. Spiritual death is as much about spiritual renewal as it is about death."

"This is not something I've considered before. I feel out of my element."

"I have a colleague, Chris, who begins virtually every new thought with the word *perhaps*. It is not unlike your word *maybe*, but perhaps coveys a connotation of conjecture or 'possibly' and thus 'possibilities.' Perhaps the maybes in your life signal an opening to new possibilities, new paths, or new ways of viewing things. They could be an embarkation into the unknown. I am afraid you will hear a lot of *perhaps* from me. I have grown accustomed to use it as a preface for the possibilities associated with many ideas."

I knew there was something here I needed to understand, but I wasn't sure what the questions were, much less the answers. "Padre, I think I need to go, think, and come back again."

"Perhaps you might spend time *not* thinking about it."

"How would I do that, Padre?"

"Pray? Meditate? Listen?"

Three
Pygmies to Bicycles

"Abba, give me a word."
"Anticipation, my son."
"What about anticipation, Abba?"
"I can hardly wait to learn, my son."

My head was swimming, my thoughts caught in eddies of deep water. I didn't know what I was thinking or what to think. *Death…old, new…embarkation…lost…the entire time…not being where…when. Well, I am lost, and I don't even know where I thought I would be.* I drove home. *I hope I can find it.*

Gen was in the living room reading when I walked in. She looked up, and her eyes widened. She sat up straight, and put down her book, and immediately asked, "How'd it go?"

"I have no idea. I know less now than when I went out there. I don't know what I expected. I'm not sure going out there is such a great idea." *You'll return, Rocky.* Padre Cisco had stirred something in me; I just didn't know what it was. "That man is confounding. He speaks in ways I know nothing about. We talked about getting lost as a good thing and death as an embarkation. I think we were talking about religion, but I'm not sure. He suggested I pray. Well…it was more a question than a suggestion. Maybe he wanted to know if I am religious."

I'm not a religious man. I hear people saying they are spiritual but not religious. I don't know what that means, so I can't even say I'm spiritual. I gave up going to church when I went to college, and when I got divorced I gave up on the church altogether. It didn't seem to be very relevant to my life. I believe there is a god, or at least something *like* a god, but I don't do church stuff, and I don't get off on walks in the woods.

I asked Gen if she wanted coffee. I was buying time. I wasn't sure what I had to say. I went to the kitchen, brewed a Sumatra for her and a French roast for myself. I returned with the coffee and sat down next to her on the couch. She curled one leg up under her, and I handed her the coffee. She cupped both hands around it and drew it near her nose, savoring the aroma before she took a tentative sip. She leaned back against the pillow in the corner of the couch and said, "So?"

"So. So, I wish I knew. This all started out as a simple opportunity to gain some perspective and get some advice. I lost my job. I'm not ready to retire. I'm past middle age, but hardly ready for retirement. For the first time in my life, I have no purpose. Maybe, or as Padre Cisco would say, 'Perhaps,' that's what it's all about, purpose. It seems to be more than that. I can't seem to put my finger on it. Maybe I am embarking on something new."

"Well, Rocky, this kind of conversation is in itself something new. What else did he say that rattled you?"

"The first time I went to see him, he talked about ministry, my strip as a ministry of diversion or something like that."

"Distraction, I think you told me."

"Yes, that's it, and he spoke of presence as in, 'All ministry is a ministry of presence.' You know me, Gen; I certainly have never been a minister. I'm there for you and the kids when they will accept it, but not always for other people. Is ministering what I am supposed to be doing?"

"Maybe that's a question you should explore."

I fidgeted with my cup and squirmed in my seat. "I haven't seen the inside of a church in nearly thirty years, much less be a minister."

"Maybe it isn't about church inside or outside."

"Now you are sounding like Padre Cisco, minus the perhaps. I need to check my mail." With that, I got up and went to my study. Gen returned to work.

A few days after bailing from the conversation with Gen, I called Padre Cisco and made an appointment. The next couple of weeks were filled with misgivings and busy-ness. I caught up on chores I had let slide. I painted the utility shed and brought my study back to order. I found scads of things to do to keep me from thinking about what I was or wasn't doing. I was lost, of that I was sure. My world had changed. I wasn't prepared for it, and I had to figure it out. I started walking. Years of sitting at my drawing table had diminished my fitness and increased my waistline. The French, Italian, and Oriental cooking classes Gen and I took and the resulting dinners we prepared made their contribution. I learned to avoid mirrors. *I am pudgy*, I admitted. *Maybe some good would come out of this mess after all.*

"Peter!" came the greeting as Padre Cisco rose from a chair on the front porch. The house has wraparound, roofed porches except for the veranda where we sat earlier. It faces south and has a high trellis that provides shade in the summer and allows for slanting sunshine in the winter. It was a beautiful low desert, winter afternoon. Padre Cisco was in his standard garb, and even I wore only a long-sleeved shirt, though long jeans.

He stood in his classic pose, his eyes marking my approach, and then walked casually toward me, opening his arms wide in greeting. He took my hand, wrapped the other around my shoulder, and turned, guiding me around the house.

"You are well, Peter?"

"I am, and you?"

"Best day of my life," he replied with a grin. "Sit. Coffee?"

"Of course."

He seemed to be in great spirits, and this lifted mine. He went for the coffee, and I sat in one of the Adirondacks. He returned, sat next to me, and said; "Drink, refresh, listen, and then we will speak." We sat, hardly settled in, listened to I am not sure what, and waited to speak. Within moments he said, "There now, that was good. So, speak." He grinned again.

"Wow! That was not what I expected. I was prepared for the lengthy, quiet listening and reflection time. You've taken me by surprise. Give me a moment more."

"For what, Peter?"

"To collect my thoughts, Padre."

"Have you strewn them about?" He laughed.

"What?"

"I can see you squeezing and pulling thoughts from your head and tossing them about like Frisbees, some in the corners, some behind the chairs, others onto pot shelves, into the desert, and who knows where? Then you go hippity hopping about trying to gather them up and stuff them back into your head. They keep slipping out and fluttering away, the wind gathers them up, and you chase after them with even more frenzy. What an image; what great fun."

At first, I wondered if he was making fun *of* me, but that wasn't his nature. I realized it was fun *with* me, and I laughed with him. I became aware that the tension I had carted out there was leaving, and the settling in was arriving. I sat back ready to speak of my hitherto-uncollected thoughts, but before I uttered a word he said, "So what do you think now of the idea of a ministry of distraction?"

"How so?

"Did I not just engage in a ministry of distraction? Perhaps such a ministry is to not only to distract a person from his ideas or problems, but also to distract those thoughts from the person. Perhaps it is not only a distraction from something, but maybe it can be a distraction to prepare for something. You are prepared to speak, hold conversation, be here now, are you not?"

"Absolutely. Much more so than when I arrived."

"Well then, that must have been pretty good ministry. I must be a pretty good minister." He laughed again. "Yes and no. Yes, that was pretty good ministry. I knew you left in a quandary. You were all a dither about some things I said and ideas we discussed. I surmised from your drooped shoulders when you arrived that you had brooded about these things. As to being a good minister, that is not so. All I did was create the conditions for you to minister to yourself. It was a ministry of distraction, or maybe a ministry of the farcical. You moved yourself out of confusion into the farce. I was simply a servant of ministry to you. If you remember your Bible stories, this was the lesson Jesus taught through washing his disciples' feet. That is, I should say, lest ye misquote me, Jesus' lesson was on being a servant, not on the ministry of the farcical.

"That's a description of ministry that I didn't learn growing up in Akron."

"Ministry is not just about church; it is about service to others and how we see ourselves in that role. When we are about being of service to others, we are engaging in ministry.

"Wow, didn't we get off on that? I certainly have been waxing on. But that isn't what we are here to talk about, is it?"

"It is part of it. I have been questioning what the idea of being a minister means, though that is not what I thought I was bringing today."

"What is?"

"I do want to talk about death as embarkation, death to the old, life in the new, and being lost; but what it all comes down to for me is that I don't know what to expect anymore. I'm not where I expected to be, and there is no map. That place doesn't exist anymore. Consequently, I don't know what to expect."

"An interesting word, expectation." Padre Cisco sat for a moment, seeming to muse on it. "Let me examine it for a moment. It carries with it a sense of surety or predictability. It seems to relate to outcomes. There is a win-lose quality to expectations. Given certain conditions, we expect a given outcome. That surety helps us navigate life. This is a good thing; otherwise, we would live in a terribly frightful situation. When parents set expectations, boundaries, they establish security for children. Children may not like boundaries, but deep down they want them. They know they need them.

"At the same time, if we don't allow for the unexpected to be as true as the expected, expectations can get in the way of our growth and development. As people mature, they need to learn to stretch the boundaries and question the expectations. In his work with faltering corporations, Michael Francis used to tell a story about Colin Turnbull. May I?"

"Surely…please."

The crux of the story was that Turnbull was an anthropologist working with pygmies in the Belgian Congo in the early 1950s. He took some tribal elders from the density of the African jungle on a trek to the edge of the savanna. Looking across the savanna,

Turnbull pointed to a herd of water buffalo. The pygmies fell down laughing, thinking he was daft. Inquiring as to the joke, the pygmies answered, "Those are not water buffalo; they are ants." Wanting to show them the buffalo were such, he walked with the elders nearer. When they were quite close, Turnbull pointed out that the animals were in fact buffalo. The elders didn't believe their eyes and vindicate him. They said, "What great magic has turned our ants into water buffalo?"

Padre Cisco said, "Isn't that just the way of it?"

"I don't understand, Padre. What is the way of it? Why did they assume it was magic?"

"The pygmies' entire life experiences to that point had been in the jungle. If they saw something as small, it was small. They had never seen beyond the immediate into the distance. They had no depth perception to accommodate what they were seeing. Water buffalo at a distance were outside their realm of expectation. They used the assumption of magic as their recourse to validate their inability to perceive. In the pygmies' case, their perceptual limitation was physical. For most of us, our limitation is psychological. Richard Rohr would say that we are addicted to our own thinking. Our ego wants to hold on to our expectations. As with the children, our expectations create surety, security, and comfort. We like our comfort, don't we?"

"Well, Padre, I definitely have been outside my comfort zone. I don't feel insecure, but I certainly have had my sense of surety questioned."

"You said the map you had to your expected future no longer applies. The landscape has changed, and you have no map. Perhaps the map is there, but you cannot see it. You might need to change your perspective to see the map. Perhaps, the difference is about the place of expectations in your life.

"Michael Francis is writing a book called *Dance Partners*. It pairs and compares words. I know he sees anticipation and expectation as dance partners. He has written about living in anticipation but without expectation. He says that expectations place us in a win-lose relationship with outcomes. The focus on outcomes associated with expectations steals our opportunity to experience new perspectives and shackles our freedom to grow."

"It is an interesting consideration: the ability to change perspective outside of our expectations. Isn't that often what we need to learn and grow? If we only learn what supports our previous perception, our expectation, then have we actually grown? Have we even learned, or have we simply reinforced what we already knew?"

"Well, Padre, I am not sure of what I know anymore."

"That unknowing can be a good thing, a precursor to change. You will change. Life's circumstances have laid that upon you."

"Of that piece I am well aware, and obviously I'm not happy about it."

"Consider Michael Francis' idea of living in anticipation rather than expectation. He told me that he was in college when he first noticed that his father watched him leaving to return to school. His father would watch him drive down the road until he turned the corner out of sight. His father didn't call out or wave. He simply stood there cleaving to Michael Francis until his last glimpse expired. After many visits, he realized that his father held on to a piece of Michael Francis until he returned. He came to believe that piece was his father's image of Michael Francis driving toward his home. His father held no expectation for his son's return but did live in anticipation of it.

"In a similar experience, my sister and brothers and I went to visit our grandfather at his farm shortly after his wife died."

Illustrating his sister's words, he said, "My sister remembers seeing him standing at the gate in his hat and coveralls, pipe in one hand, and waving with the other as we drove off. I know that in watching us leave, he was already anticipating our return."

"I can see that picture. Gen and I have experienced that with our kids."

"There are cultural implications to this idea beyond the mindset of an individual. It is the idea of the collective unconscious."

Okay, this is getting heady now.

"A classic cultural example of living in anticipation without expectations is the phrase 'Wait till next year' annually uttered by Chicago Cubs fans."

Heady? Boy, was I mistaken on that one.

Padre Cisco waited. I think he was letting his curve sink in. He continued. "We are told absence makes the heart grow fonder. That may be true, but what if it is not the only truth? What if anticipation also warms our heart and hastens our return? A comfortable three-day drive to visit two of my children's families I complete in two days because the nearer I get the sooner I want to arrive."

"Gen loves the movie *Out of Africa*. She talks about a scene depicting Baroness von Blixen pecking a kiss on the Baron's cheek as he is leaving on safari. When he remarks, 'That is not much of a goodbye kiss,' she replies, 'I am better at hello.' Gen has always been better at hello than goodbye. Maybe Gen is more about anticipation than expectation."

Padre Cisco said, "I think anticipation is one of the undervalued emotions in our lives. You hear people say don't anticipate, just take it as it comes. I think they actually mean don't expect. By not anticipating, an opportunity to experience a certain kind of joy is lost. Anticipation is expectation without the judgment that comes with 'failed' outcomes. If we anticipate something and it does not happen, we may be disappointed, but there is no feeling of failure. If we expect something and it does not happen, our feelings reach beyond disappointment. Resentment, anger, loss, or a similar suffering response may result. By the subtle altering of our perception from expectation to anticipation, we take ourselves out of the win-lose, success-failure relationship with life."

"I certainly experienced all of those emotions when the syndicate cut me loose. I didn't expect it. I did resent how it happened. I put my heart and soul into that strip for a lot of years. I was angry. And loss? It was more than loss of a job. They took something from me, my reason for being. If I were religious, I might say it was my soul."

"Do you feel they took your soul, Peter?"

"I don't want to go there, Padre. I don't know why I said that. I am probably overstating the case. I do know it was about how I see myself."

"Let me ponder that for a moment."

We sat for a couple of minutes then the padre began again. "I do think we should talk at some point about your sense of loss. We can wait if you prefer."

"I would, Padre."

"Okay. Then perhaps we can return to the *how* of how you see yourself. You are the artist, Peter. You know that art is in the eye of the beholder. You have a practiced eye. You see differently than some other people. I am suggesting that we can practice learning to see things differently, alter our perception, and break the boundaries of our expectations. This does not imply that we must always abandon our expectations. What I am suggesting is: we have a choice."

"The difference between expectation and anticipation is, as you say, subtle. I understand you in principle. Practicing seeing the world differently might be another matter."

"Here is one more piece of this. Michael Francis told me about a bicycle shop in Japan that is certainly curious by Western standards. I don't know if I can remember all the details. I am not a cyclist, but I know the gist of it. It is a high-tech shop connected to a high-tech factory. Customers go there to be fitted for a bike."

"People get fitted for bikes…really?"

"They must. The shop has a bike-like contraption to measure the customer. They relay the information with the customer's choices to the factory. The factory builds the bike within hours. All this is well within the realm of computerized production in any advanced country in the world. However, unlike most places in the world the Japanese store owners and manufacturer have you wait three to four weeks for delivery."

After a pause I said, "And?"

"What do you say?"

"Something about anticipation over expectation."

"Exactly, the Japanese, or at least that particular business, places value on the attitude of anticipation. It creates opportunities for the anticipatory experience. I think they practice the art of anticipation. Perhaps the world would be better off if we were to focus on creating anticipation for others rather than setting expectations. If you can let go of your expectations of where you 'knew' you were headed and embrace the anticipation of new beginnings, perhaps you can change your perception about the future and see a new map."

"You have my head swimming again."

"Well then let me add Eric's story."

"Okay."

"Eric's son was visiting him in the hospital for the first time after Eric had his leg amputated because of cancer. In a childlike plaintive voice his son Jack asked, 'Will you be able to go swimming with me next summer, Dad?' 'Sure,' Eric said, 'but you know I'll be swimming in circles.' Grinning, Padre Cisco said, "You didn't expect that one, did you?""

"I think you have moved from the ministry of the farcical to the ministry of the ridiculous."

Padre Cisco laughed and said, "I would certainly relish that."

"Let me see if I can capture what you have said, Padre. Ministry is about how I see myself as a servant. A ministry of distraction can be distracting from, distracting to, or distracting in preparation for. Living with expectation is necessary, but living inside expectations can be limiting. Living with anticipation in lieu of expectations is simply a subtle difference in perception. By altering our perceptions to live outside our expectations we can learn, maybe even change. Creating anticipation is an art form. If I'm swimming, I'm swimming in circles; and if I'm going to buy a bicycle in Japan, I am going have to wait for it. Is that about it?"

Padre Cisco grinned and said, "I think that sums it up."

"I am swimming in circles; I need to think. Can we meet again in a couple of weeks, possibly an hour earlier? I might need more time. I have some work to do, but I will be ready for you next time."

"Terrific! I will be here," he replied with a broad smile.

With that, he saw me out, down the road, and around the bend.

When I got home, I went into the den to catch up on things, though I didn't know what things I actually had to do. Remembering Padre's references to Michael Francis set me to wondering. *Maybe that is where the padre got the notion of his greetings and farewells? Maybe it is the other way around. Could he be the college boy in Michael Francis's story? Holy Moses, he has me calling the guy Michael Francis as though I know him. No maybes about it, I need to pay more attention to our comings and goings. If I didn't learn anything else today, I know I need to pay more attention to creating anticipation in many aspects of my life. Maybe I need to examine my expectations. Blast, there I go again. It's time to practice not thinking about it.* I closed the door behind me.

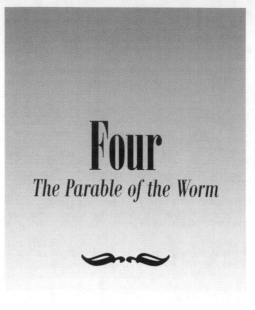

Four
The Parable of the Worm

"Abba, give me a word."
"Loss, my son. Consider the word loss."
"What is important about loss, Abba?"
"That it is loss, my son."

"So, Peter, would you like to talk about loss? That is our primary topic, isn't it? Perhaps I should ask are you ready to talk about loss? That likely is the deeper question, isn't it?"

During the previous visit, I had again brought up my loss of syndication. I knew that was driving my thoughts much more than getting older. "Yes, Padre, I would." I sensed he had something to share. More to the point, that's why I went out there in the first place. I had successfully sidestepped the topic up to that point.

We were starting to develop a "your turn my turn" pattern that seemed to work. I knew Padre Cisco experienced the death of friends in the previous year, and he lost his wife years earlier. It was part of his place in the cycle of life and mine as well. We had postponed our meeting an additional week because of the Christmas season, and then another when he had a funeral to attend. The two thousand seventeen New Year was a rough start for both of us. I arrived a few days after his return. I imagined it was still weighing on his mind. We sat in our usual spots, I in the tablechair and he in the wicker. We had fresh coffee and sat quietly.

I waited for him to begin, listening for his movement. That day he seemed more than saddened, almost apologetic in attitude. The afternoon sunlight cast shadows, drawing attention to heavy eyelids and slackened cheeks. Even when I closed my eyes, I found myself focused more on him than on my own contemplation. I heard the chair creaking as he roused. I opened my eyes. He leaned forward and took a long gulp of now-tepid coffee. I knew he was ready to begin. "Peter, do you remember *The Parable of the Worm* story? I have delivered it a number of times."

"Yes, I do. I've heard it twice. You told it down in Green Valley, last year. I can't remember the other occasion. It was before that."

The story was about an experience with a granddaughter. Mo-ma, who is the Padre's sister, her daughter, and three granddaughters, had gone to his house for a sleepover. He described it, as less a sleepover than a bivouac given all the provisions young girls seem to need.

Bailey, his middle grandchild, arrived with a worm, the lone survivor from a school project. Her mother convinced her the worm would die if she left it in the plastic Burying it with the myriad companions in Papa Cisco's garden was a better idea. A ritual of interment was the first order of business when they arrived.

Along with the honored guest, they gathered at the edge of the chosen site. The padre turned over soil to demonstrate that there were little worm friends waiting to befriend Wormie. Bailey decided the garden was a suitable place where her charge could grow to adulthood.

All went well. Bailey placed the worm adjacent to some potential new acquaintances, and he covered them with soil. All went well, but they missed the cultural requisite of capturing the image. I remember him saying, "I did not realize Wormie had any expectations for a selfie." In tears, Bailey exited Eden to the veranda.

He thought that she was fussing because she had missed getting the pictures for her school project. Mo-ma's grandmotherly wisdom intervened. He said, "Mo-ma instinctively knew that the girl was experiencing loss. Loss isn't only about death." Bailey wanted the pictures for her album. She wanted to hold on to the memory. They re-enacted the ritual and she took the pictures. He said, "A later conversation with Mo-ma reminded me all loss is loss and is an experience to be grieved."

That was a confession from a man who recently has had a number of deaths around him, and who just finished reading a book about grief. Yet, when the moment came he did not recognize it and was not attentive to a little girl who was suffering and needed compassion.

He told the audience that he arrived there a few minutes later when he realized Bailey was not amid the hubbub of activity with the other girls. He saw Mo-ma go back out to the garden where grief consumed Bailey. I remember him joking, "Her realization that her reenactment pictures were of one of Wormie's stand-ins will come later." He said something to the effect that the feeling of loss she had would the memory, and more than that Bailey will remember the compassion shown through the wisdom of a grandmother.

"Do you remember how that story ends?"

"Not exactly, but I remember that usually your audiences applaud your stories, but in Green Valley they just sat silent."

"That was certainly different. I think it was because Green Valley is a retirement community, and the audience was mostly grandparents. Most of them are acquainted with loss. I ended with, "I learned all loss is significant, and may need to be grieved. My lesson came from a worm, a being as simple as imaginable.""

Padre Cisco closed his eyes momentarily as though reflecting. He took a drink, set his cup down, folded his arms with one hand to his chin, and sat. It certainly didn't take me long to respond. I had myriad questions, but I opened with a statement. "So you are saying that I need to be grieving a lost job." It was more of a challenge than a statement.

"I am not saying you need to do anything."

"Then why the story?'

"What do you think?"

"I think you are messing with me." My tone had an edge on it.

"Peter, that is the last thing I would want to do. It was simply on my mind. I thought it might create some context to our conversation. Did the story resonate with you?"

"It certainly did."

"How so?"

"I am not sure yet, but I just heard myself getting defensive. I think the last line challenged me. I've always thought of grief and grieving as associated with death. It never occurred to me that I might need to grieve the loss of a job, much less giving away a worm."

"Perhaps you have lost not only a job but what the job represents to you as well; and there may be loss associated with that."

"That's the thing, Padre. I do realize how tied to my work I am. When people ask me who I am, I tell them I am an artist, a cartoonist. I answer with what I do, not who I am."

"You are not alone here, Peter; it is a major guy thing, particularly a your-age-range guy thing. Men have a constellation of attitudes and feelings related to their work. You might be surprised how many things will emerge related to this event in your life."

"That is beginning to become evident. I didn't realize how much of my self-concept relates to my productivity, sense of accomplishment, providing income, security, etc. Isn't that how we measure our manhood? We can't go out and slay the saber-toothed tiger anymore. How do you define manhood, Padre?"

"I would have to think about how I define my manhood, but I know that I measure it by how few of my foibles embarrass me." He chuckled to himself. "I didn't always. In the first half of my life, the measure certainly was about accomplishment and influence."

"First half of your life?"

"It is not a fraction but more an approach to life. It is the part of our lives in which we establish our identity, develop our ego, build our place in society, secure our family, our future, and ourselves. Richard Rohr calls it 'building our container.' I spent nearly sixty years in the first half of my life. If only that *were* a fraction, I can hardly imagine what the next sixty would be like. I would be as old as Moses would though hardly as wise. You might want to read some Richard Rohr. He writes about the halves of life in *Falling Upward*. Good stuff. It might turn some ants into water buffalo for you. It is a place to start, but it is not for the faint of heart. I have not heard you speak much of what you read so I take a risk in recommending a book to you. Perhaps books might be a future topic for us."

We ended with handshake, set a time to meet again in three weeks, and I made my leave.

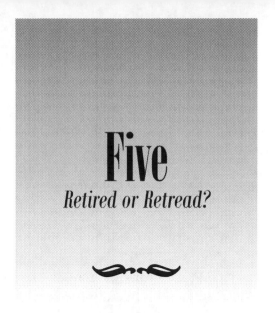

Five
Retired or Retread?

"Abba, why do you live in the desert?"
"For its blessing, my son."
"But Abba, it is so stark, so empty."
"That is the blessing, my son."

A few days before meeting with Padre Cisco again, I had a bout with the flu. It sent me to bed for a couple of days. I called to tell him I couldn't meet. I rambled my apologies, and we postponed for a week. He suggested we might take a walk if I felt up to it and asked if I had good shoes. I said that I did and that a walk would be a welcome activity.

I arrived geared up in hat, long-sleeved shirt, hiking shoes, water bottles, and sunscreen. The dawn sky was cloudless, and the air was crisp. The full bloom of the desert spring was yet to come, but there were signs of an early awakening. Valentine's Day is the average last day of frost in the Southwest low desert. We were more than a week past that. The winter months brought the intermittent, long, quiet rains that make for a flurry of spring color. I looked forward to what might be a preview of coming attractions. I was glad to be there in the hope of finding some answers. The padre was not the source of the answers. He was the guide to the questions.

"Ready for a little walk?" Padre Cisco said as he met me in front of his house.

I nodded.

"Perhaps it will slow us down a bit, and let the world go around without us. My walking demands a gentler pace. More than that, I just enjoy the greater communion with the land when I am not in such a rush." Padre asked if I had water, sunblock, and a stick. I had water and sun block, but I hadn't brought a walking stick. He went into the house, returned with an adjustable stick, and I set it to my height. We set off to the southeast at an earnest clip for someone who spoke of the demands of a gentler pace. I was glad I had been doing some walking. I would have felt like a wussy not keeping up. Even so, after a couple miles I was breathing heavily. Occasionally, the padre would stop and poke his stick on the other side of a boulder. "Just checking. It is generally too early for rattlers to be out, but it is prudent to check."

We crested a ridge, and a narrow valley awash in bright sunshine lay before us. Padre Cisco suggested we stop and sit for a bit. I was grateful. We sat up against a rock outcropping in the shade, drinking in water and the view. I re-laced my shoes for the third time. Even in the coolness, I felt a soft breeze wipe the sweat from my forehead. The land below was green as desert landscape goes. The rains had brought forth the winter grasses. The filaree with its tiny red blooms was always the first to return. The mariposa lilies were blooming, as were the cotton top grasses

"Remember the first time you came to visit, Peter? You were full of questions: who am I, what am I, what am I doing or supposed to be doing, where am I going, is it all worth it, etc."

The yipping of coyotes surrounding their prey interrupted the silence. I was prey to my own questions. "I haven't found a whole lot of answers, at least answers that seem satisfying."

"Perhaps it is enough just to rest in the questions or seek the deeper questions."

"But I need to get on with it, to start something, *do* something."

"Are you in a hurry? Is there a timeline in front of you?"

"Well, I'm not getting any younger."

"Hopefully not. There is a Native People's saying, 'No wise person ever wants to be younger.' When you were a younger man a couple of months ago and we talked, you spoke of disliking the idea of retirement. You said it was not in your vision of your future. Have you thought about that since?"

"Somewhat, Padre, though not exactly about retiring, but more about the question why I am so averse to the idea."

"Did you reach a conclusion?"

"I'm not done I haven't been in the studio, but I know I will be. I haven't stopped thinking creatively. I don't know what I am going to be doing, but I know it will be in the art world. Retirement connotes you're finished. I don't want to be finished. I have thought about what you said that losing my job might be about greater loss. I know it's more than just losing my syndication, but my work defines who I am."

"Ah, identity. Is it not all about identity?"

"Maybe so."

"Remember me asking you what is the deeper question?"

"Oh yes, and I had no idea what you were talking about."

"Perhaps that is what you are doing, asking the deeper questions."

"How so?"

"Identity questions are not just about a single thing such as work in your case. They are about life. They are the questions man has asked for eons. Who am I? Why am I here? What am I doing? What is it all about? What is my purpose? Is this all there is? The first time you came out here you asked those questions."

"I remember."

"Do you know the movie *Saving Private Ryan*?"

"I've seen it."

"Among other things, it is an *have I led a good life* movie."

The movie opens in modern day with a World War II veteran and his family walking a cemetery in Normandy. He finds a particular grave and falls to his knees. The movie flashes back to the Normandy invasion. Private Ryan's has lost his four brothers. The army sends a squad of soldiers led by Captain Miller, played by Tom Hanks, to save Ryan. They save Ryan, Matt Damon, but most of the rescue team lose their lives in the process. In the throws of death, Miller says to Ryan, "James... earn this. Earn it."

The final scene returns to present day and reveals that the distraught veteran is Ryan at Miller's grave. As Ryan rises, his wife approaches. He asks her to confirm that he has led a good life. He says, "Tell me I am a good man." She responds, "You are." He stands at attention and salutes Miller's grave. The movie ends.

Have I led a good life? "That line is a major question as we age, regardless of which half of life we are in. It is perhaps the primary question that leads many of us into the second half of life journey."

"How so, Padre? I'm not sure that's what I'm asking."

"As men get to be about your age, and certainly those who have experienced loss, the questions morph into the am

I worthy questions. What have I accomplished? Do I matter? Has my life had meaning? These are more than just emotional or psychological questions; they are spiritual questions. They are fundamental questions of life, particularly second-half life.

"Life threw you a curve. All of a sudden, it did not turn out the way you expected. I remember once saying to my father on such an occasion that more life had happened to me than I ever expected. Let me speculate: you feel betrayed, confused, and at loose ends. You experienced denial and disillusionment. You do not know what to do with yourself; you are worried, possibly angry or resentful. Then one day you woke up and told yourself to snap out of it, do something, anything. You did not know what to do, so you set out on a journey to find out. Is this a fairly accurate accounting?"

I shifted in my seat. Whether it was from the chair or the topic I was feeling uncomfortable. I said, "Certainly the betrayed, confused, and loose ends. I'm not sure about the journey part."

"When you were younger you were told that you would have to find your path, your passion. Your elders told you that had to find yourself, and you did. You built your container. You lived the next twenty or thirty years comfortably inside that container, complete with its assumptions, perceptions, and expectations. Then wham, life as you knew it is gone! Life as you knew it. You as you knew yourself. It is not that you are lost. It is that you lost you, the self you knew yourself to be. You did not lose all of yourself, but you did lose a defining piece of your personal puzzle, a corner piece so to speak. You set out to find that piece. It was a corner stone of your container, perhaps, even the keystone.

"And so, your journey began. It started before you came to see me. I am just a way station. Having gotten this far, you know you cannot go back, but you do not know how to go forward. You have more questions than answers. This is a good thing. It might not seem so right now, but it is. Does this sound familiar to your experiences in the last few months?"

"Mostly so. I am definitely in the I can't go back but don't know how to go forward part."

"Peter, this *is* the journey of the second half of life. If you think you are on it, you are. If you are having the conversations we are having, you are."

Padre Cisco stopped, took a drink, and just sat looking as though he were trying to see something in the distance. He closed his eyes and tilted his head back against the rock face. I waited; I knew there was more.

He continued, "Ranier Maria Rilke, the Bohemian poet, wrote about living the questions into the answers. He said that some questions are just too big to answer. I do not remember all of it, but I can get the gist. He wrote, '... love the questions themselves...Do not now seek the answers, which cannot be given you because you would not be able to live them...Live the questions now. Perhaps you will, without noticing it, live along some distant day into the answer.' That is what you are doing. Living the questions into the answers. As I said, this is a good thing. You may be swimming in circles, but you are still swimming. Let's head down the hill." He stood and strode down what was not much more than a deer path.

I followed him though I wished that I had two walking sticks. He was more surefooted than I was. He had pegged me. *He's made this hike before. He knows the route. Does he know my journey as well?*

We reached the bottom and turned to follow a small stream that led into a copse of cottonwood and palo verde trees. I heard rustling and grunting, but Padre Cisco moved ahead undaunted.

As we came around a bend in the stream, a javelina band scurried off into the underbrush. The path widened. We were able to walk side by side.

He resumed the conversation telling me about the first time he retired. He said he wasn't sure what he was. Retired? Partially retired? Retired and embarking on a new career? Retread? The retirement thing was confusing. The retread thing was equally so.

We paused by the creek, resting from the mid-morning sun under the shade of a cottonwood. In the quiet, I could hear the faintest melody of shallow water over stones.

He quoted Yogi Berra, "'The future ain't what it used to be," and Tennessee Williams, "'Security is a kind of death." He said he concluded that security in the future ain't what it used to be and will be a kind of death. He laughed saying, "No wonder I was ambivalent." Turning to me, he asked, "You up to going a bit further?" I said that I was, and we headed downstream along the creek.

"Can you imagine, Rocky? After forty plus years working, supporting my family, I would be relying on the government to support me. It sounded a lot like going on the dole. I knew that applying for benefits meant gaining access to my own money. I would be a recipient of government services rather than a contributor. It had a sense of capitulation. It said you're old; you're on Social Security. When I was young everyone on Social Security was old, real old."

We spooked a mule deer, and it interrupted his train of thought. "Imagine that. I am usually quite alone out here. From its size, it looked like a buck. He must be thirsty to come into the open this late in the morning. Perhaps the critters have come down to check out you." On the gender of the deer, I agreed, but I wasn't so sure if he was serious about the second comment.

"The old part did not bother me; I knew better. Jack Benny said, 'Age is strictly a case of mind over matter. If you don't mind, it doesn't matter.' What did matter was the idea of someone thinking I am done. What others think shouldn't matter, but I did not like having the bar lowered for me. My feelings were not about retirement. They were about my self-image, my identity. Why don't we take that trail to the left and head back? I want finish before the sun gets high."

We made the turn. The sun was over my left shoulder, and I realized we had been yawing to the left for some time. I thought a nautical term in the desert seemed out of place. With mule deer around, I probably should say, "hawing," and it hit me. "Padre, I recognize that I have been hemming and hawing a lot. I think it has been about the perspective piece you mentioned. You've dealt with the same questions. How did you cross those trails?" As usual, his response came from an unexpected direction.

"A few years back, two thoughts came upon me. Reading Lawrence Peter's *The Peter Principle* in the early 1970s was the first." He told me Peter's book essentially stated that people, managers in his study, rise in an organization to their level of incompetence. From that point the best they can accomplish is to move to a position of comparable authority, which he called a *lateral arabesque*. The padre said, "Is that not a quaint label? I would have loved at some point been able to respond to a colleague that it was not a promotion. I was a lateral arabesque. I would have chortled over that bit of buffoonery."

He told me when he read Peter's book he was a neophyte adjunct professor without a full-time position. He saw the grand opportunity ahead of him, and could not imagine rising above his level of competence. He questioned neither his abilities nor his potential. He had come of age. He said, "My colleagues were but Ponchos to my Cisco Kid."

The padre usually told stories of a friend or from another time or culture. That day he spoke of his own journey more candidly than he had before.

By the time he was in his sixties, he was a full professor with no aspirations for chairmanships or administration roles. He said that institutionally, there was no room for him to grow. He wondered if he would need to look outside the university to advance professionally or personally. I was familiar with that condition.

We moved slowly even though we were walking over level ground. The desert is never as flat as it appears from a distance or from the air. Violent forces of nature shaped the Sonoran Desert. It was once ablaze with volcanoes, and currents at the bottom of an ocean carved and molded it for eons. The metaphor did not elude me, but I let it pass, focusing on the padre's story instead.

"You said there were two things, Padre."

"Ah, yes. I read a magazine interview held with the Dalai Lama. The interviewer asked him for an opinion regarding an international political issue. His response was that he no longer had opinions on such issues. 'I have withdrawn from international politics and leave it to others.' He may have said, '...to others more qualified.' Padre Cisco went on to say he realized that if the Dalai Lama could withdraw from international politics, he could withdraw from institutional life.

He said he was spending more time and energy working for the institution than with the students. He thought he was getting too old to affect circumstances through institutions. Institutions are too slow to change, and he simply could not live long enough. That was when he knew he would become a private person. With a laugh he said, "The Dalai Lama and I were going private."

"Padre, I appreciate you sharing your story. What strikes me is how intentional you were about your decisions."

"Peter, that is the story as I tell it now. You got the *Reader's Digest* version. It was not as easy as I portray it now. It took time. There was a lot of angst that went into it."

"I'm trying to see the parallels to my own dilemma. Leaving my job was not my choice, and I was not in a position associated with an institution."

"Leaving your job may not have been your choice, but leaving the circumstances of that event behind is your choice."

"Maybe. Or should I say, perhaps?"

"Now you are messing with me…perhaps."

"It's a fact. You get to have your turn in the barrel, Padre."

"True, Peter. It is well deserved. He flashed a grin at me. He took his hat off and wiped his head and face with a bandana. Perhaps only your circumstances are different. Are not the questions and the choices the same? I was a teacher. I am and will be a teacher. You are still an artist. Perhaps you are now a freelancer."

"There certainly are freelancers who have clients for whom they produce work. Freelancer, also, can be a euphemism for unemployed artist, Padre. I knew I was an artist before I became a comic strip artist. Even as a kid when I was drawing caricatures I was a working artist. I've always viewed myself as a working artist."

"Do you mean working artist as in being paid for your art?

"In the literal sense, yes; but it is more than that. When I think of *working artist,* I think of being productive or being able to support myself through my work. It is also who I am.

Maybe the term should be professional artist. There are artistic people who don't consider themselves artists. There are artists who describe themselves as amateurs, or who refer to the art as a hobby, pastime of maybe avocation. They don't define themselves by their art."

"Peter, did you lose your art or your job? It sounds as though you are saying when you lost your job you lost your identity as an artist. Is this so?"

"That's what I am trying to figure out, Padre. Intellectually, I can say obviously no, but emotionally it seems I've lost more than a job."

He stopped and looked directly at me. "Many Sundays, I get to listen to a priest, Father Jim, who is not afraid to challenge his congregation. During one of his homilies he asked us, 'Can you give up what you know to discover what you don't know?' That is what life is asking you to decide. That is the entry question to the second half of life."

We walked along in silence for a while. I could sense that we were nearing his house. There was a familiarity to the terrain. I was tired, though we had walked only five or six miles, but I didn't want our hike to end. I realized that I didn't want the conversation to end. I felt I was beginning to formulate something. I didn't know what it was, but something that was new to me arose. We rounded a final butte, and I could see the house not far ahead. *What a metaphor for the place I am. Can I give up what I know to discover what I don't?*

INTERLUDE

Coffee

If this is coffee, please bring me some tea;
but if this is tea, please bring me some coffee.
~ Abraham Lincoln

Gen and I sat at our favorite coffee roaster on Tanque Verde Road after our morning workout. I had increased my walking in frequency, pace, and distance. I graduated to jogging and something that approximated running. I was going with Gen to the gym, lifting, and doing stuff, she called "core activities." It wasn't fun, but the briefest glance in the mirror reminded me how much coring I needed. Gen's amusement at my agony drove me harder. I didn't know where I was heading, but I didn't want to remain where was. I certainly did not want to return to where I had been. I was losing weight, not so much that I needed new clothes, but enough that I was able to wear the clothes I owned.

My physical progress gave me courage to glance at the mirrors of my emotional, psychological, and even spiritual selves. I stopped in my tracks when I first used the word *spiritual*. I thought about my parents, Dad in particular, my brother's death, and my younger sister Mary, who was still at home. I reminisced about growing up in Akron, the hurt of leaving home to go to ASU, my early struggles to be recognized, and Morgan's illness. That was the second time she had popped into my head. I made lists and wrote notes about a jumble of memories. I knew I had to get back in the studio. That's where I could make sense of life.

The coffee house isn't exactly a quiet place. We took a table by the window that provided a view of the mountains. Gen had a caramel mocha latte. I ordered an Americano, forgoing the added fat and sugar of the designer drinks. It hardly would make big difference in my waistline, but I did feel nobler for it. I dislike the machinations of ordering specialty drinks: double this, low fat that, and words like vente, grande, and macchiato. They seem pretentious to me. I'm not party to the insider language of drink ordering, only because I resist the protocol. It's my small railing against artifice in life.

We were enjoying the leisure of Saturday morning without the press of getting on with the day. Gen and I strive to live on the same calendar and schedule. It helps us remain connected. Though I had no deadlines, she did. Her schedule still governed our routine. I relished the uninterrupted time with her.

"So?"

Gen has more ways to say *so* than I can count. There is the emphatic *so*, indicating that I am to continue, the common *so what*, and the drop of the voice *so* that asks for summation. Her affectionate *so* sounds as though it has two syllables with the second fading into a smile. She has a disbelieving *so* combined with squinting her eyes and tilting her head. This *so* was her inquisitive rendition of the word.

"So," I replied in my head-bobbing, eye-rolling, and acquiescent variation. I didn't need to ask what her question was. "So, I'm okay. I'm probably more than okay. I'm starting to feel better physically, and I feel as though things are beginning to come into perspective."

"Wow, Rocky, can you be any more generic?"

"I know. I know." I put up my hands in mock surrender. "But I do feel better, and things are starting to perk, no pun intended. I don't know how I let myself get so out of shape; I like feeling fit. I do know how I got so out of sorts, and it wasn't just the loss of the syndication. SoCal and Knuckles represented many things to me, most of them related to work, but it is more than that. I've had a lot of time to think."

"Really? Shall we add time to think to generic? Oh, Rocky, I'm sorry; that was unkind. I really am listening. I'm a doodle. I'll stop; please, go on."

I grimaced saying, "As though this isn't already hard enough for me. I have been thinking, wondering, reminiscing, and even a bit of meditating. It's funny how our minds work. I latched onto a memory when Mary and I were teenagers. We would introduce ourselves as Peter Paul and Mary. We thought we were so clever. Sorry, I got off topic.

"I started with trying to think my way out of my dilemma. I just got angry. That's where I was when I first went to see Padre Cisco. I've shared with you the things we've discussed. I've thought a lot about being lost. I have been lost for the last few months, but in a certain sense I've been lost since I left home."

My leaving to go to ASU wasn't acrimonious, but it definitely was contentious. Dad and I were never quite the same after that. He changed after John Jr. died in Nam, and he changed even more when I left. We didn't lose touch, but we certainly weren't *in* touch. I'd call home and talk with Mom, but the conversations with Dad were terse at best and punctuated with silence. The time between calls increased.

I didn't go back to help Mary when Dad and Mom moved to the senior center. Mom has Parkinson's. That was, also, when Morgan was sick. I think having to carry that burden on her own still bothers Mary. I had to choose. I had my responsibility, and she had hers.

"Lost, Rocky? How so?"

"Aimless. Out of touch. Disconnected."

"You have been in better touch with your parents."

"The last time I talked with them, Dad said, 'I told you that cartoon thing wouldn't work out. If you had joined the union and come into the plant, you would have a pension to fall back on.' Forty years. He just never lets go."

"Maybe he was just telling you what he thought you expected to hear. Maybe he was trying to get your goat. Maybe you have some things to let go of. Have you thought about going back there? You have time. Whoops, that was probably inappropriate," grinning and shrugging her shoulders.

"That's twice." I wagged a finger at her, and Gen assumed her most contrite pose. "Yes, I have, and I say that knowing I am opening myself to your amusement."

"It might be a good idea, a chance to resolve some things."

"So who's being generic now?"

"You know what I mean. Your parents are getting up there. I don't imagine you want to look back at a lost opportunity. You have the freedom, the kids are gone, this project has me buried, and you have fixed just about everything that needs fixing. Think about it."

"I will." I turned to look out the window, or more precisely to *be* looking out the window. I sat staring at nothing. Gen waited, and I stared. I wondered how many times we had replicated this scene. I turned back, looking straight at Gen. "Morgan."

She slowly nodded her head. "Ah, Morgan," as though waiting for me to say her name.

"Morgan. I need to talk about her."

"Yes, you do," and after a pause, "So?"

"Actually, it isn't Morgan per se; it's me...and Morgan. Gad, I hate that; 'me and Morgan,' I sound like a teenager."

Silence. Gen waited, no snappy response, no quip. She would wait until I could get it out. Finally, after another stint with the window I said, "I let Morgan down. I let you down. I let Mary down, and I let myself down. I didn't listen to her, Morgan, not Mary. More than not listening, I was not present. My work and the deadlines controlled me. I've been a deadline fanatic for thirty years. How many times did I not show up for us because of the blasted deadlines? I didn't pay attention when she needed me. That she didn't die was a miracle, or at least was of no credit to me. No wonder there's a gulf between us."

Gen sat.

"I'd like another coffee; you?"

"Black, please."

Gen's latte limit is one. Three people stood waiting to order. How people can stand in long lines waiting for coffee is beyond me. Don't they have some place else to be? The maximum length I'm typically willing to endure is two, but I was thankful for the time to gather myself. *Why is this so hard? It's been ten years. What am I afraid of?* I ordered the coffees and stood to the side for the interminable wait. *Why do I make such a big deal about waiting? Is there some place I'm supposed to be? Yes, there is, the present,* came the answer. I forced myself to refocus. *Morgan…meningitis…listening…presence,* I had to deal with it. My deadline had arrived. I handed Gen her coffee and sat down.

"So, what about Morgan and you?"

"The short answer?"

"If you want."

"Morgan never yelled at me. She never said anything directly. She just sulked. I don't think she ever forgave me."

"You're right on that, Rocky."

"I knew it."

"No, you don't. You've never gotten it. She never forgave you because she had nothing to forgive. She didn't blame you. If anything, she blamed herself. She was sulking, yes, but not about you as in you exclusively. She was sulking about everything. She was a teenager; worse than that, she was a bona fide, akimbo-standing, eye-rolling, hair-tossing, petulant-with-a-capital-*P* teenager. Teenage girls are a universal conundrum. They may be the one problem that will bring the world to the peace table." She got a laugh out of me with that. "Her actions were not about you or anything you did or didn't do. She was into herself, discovering herself. That was her job. Our job was to endure it and pray for patience."

"But I thought, I felt…"

"Yes, you did, and your feelings are real. They are just misplaced. They are not her feelings. They are yours. Morgan is not the source."

"You are saying I am the source?"

"Your feelings are your feelings. No one can create feelings in another person. You didn't cause Morgan to feel or act the way she did. She didn't cause you to feel the way you do. She may have suffered disappointment; that's normal. Teenagers are constantly disappointed in their parents; it's their calling.

It is part of breaking away, but there was no blame attached. You are powerful, Rocky, but not that powerful. If you were, we would be elevating your name, and the world needs only one Saint Peter."

"What about now and the tension between us? That's real."

"Yes, it is, and I have my thoughts; but they are just that. I don't have any confidence about them. She just may be still trying to find her independence."

"Padre Cisco talked about being in the first or second half of life. The first half is about building our container. Maybe that's what she's doing. Alex seems to have a better handle on it. The padre mentioned a book about first and second halves of life called *Falling Upward* by a guy named Richard Rohr. I guess he's some kind of self-help guru or the like. Padre Cisco was talking about loss when he brought the book up. Maybe I should read it. I know I am dealing with loss and obviously guilt. Maybe…perhaps…I'll give Padre Cisco a call, and see when he's available." I thanked her for listening. We finished the dregs and headed to our respective errands with plans to meet at home for lunch.

Spring

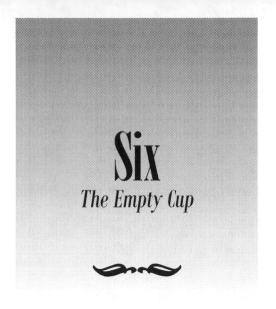

Six
The Empty Cup

"Abba, you always have a cup of coffee."
"Yes, my son."
"You must really like coffee, Abba."
"It is not the coffee, my son; it is the cup."

I looked forward to the conversation and the coffee as I drove out to Padre Cisco's place. It is an oasis. It's set apart and quiet, much the same as my studio. I go to both places to work out my ideas, but both can be the scenes of vexing experiences. I like the drive, and getting out of the hubbub of the city. It gives me time to settle mentally and emotionally. The colors of the desert flowers and bushes showed the renewal of life that comes with spring. I wondered if that was what I was feeling about my art. I had a sense of anticipation and renewal about my life.

I thought about the serious discussions Gen and I have held over coffee. We've made many decisions with a cup of coffee in our hands. We started our relationship in coffee houses and still hang out there in lieu of date night. I was fifteen when I began drinking coffee. It has been integral to my day for a long time.

The thought took me to college and Dr. O'Shaughnessy constantly carrying a cup. He once spoke of his time as a junior high teacher. He referred to it as his dapper years when he dressed formally, wore ties appropriate to the subject of his lessons, and carried matching cups. He related that one day he stood with a cup of coffee monitoring the playground. A young girl came up to him and said, "Mr. O'Shaughnessy, you must really like coffee." "No my child," he replied, "I like the cups."

We all knew better. Even then, he roasted beans, let them rest for a couple of days, and ground them immediately before brewing. He said he wasn't a coffee aficionado, but he was a coffee snob. The only things that seemed to have changed in that practice were the simplicity of his dress and cups. Both represented a change in his life. One thing that hadn't changed was that he never seemed to say or do anything that was entirely random. He would have been a great chess player.

Padre Cisco sat down and put his cup on the bucket. I mentioned my trip down memory lane and how much I look forward to his coffee. He began to tell me one of his stories, and he had his cup back curled in his hand before he finished a sentence. "When I was in the school biz, I knew a principal who was seldom without a giant cup of coffee. Each day, he walked about the school through every classroom greeting staff and students. He asked what they needed and how he could help. He seemed to have enough time for everyone during what I know was a busy schedule. He never hurried; he couldn't hurry, or he would have been constantly spilling coffee.

"What for many is a necessary stimulant to starting their day was to him a calming mediator of a frenetic life of school. I don't blame my coffee habit on him. I do think he was the role model for moving about with a cup in my hand. I learned to slow down and to be more patient. Occasionally, I pick up a partially full cup and carry it just for its effect on me."

"Coffee has been such an integral part of my life, Padre. Gen and I grew to know each other over many cups of coffee."

"I read a poet named Joyce Rupp. One of her books, *The Cup of Our Life*, uses the cup as a metaphor for our relationship with God. In a section on readiness to receive, she writes that you must empty the cup before you are ready to fill it. Each of us has experienced emptiness in our lives. At times, that experience is so tragic that we cannot imagine our fulfilled lives again. She writes, 'When we cannot stand on our own strength…we are being readied to receive. The near-empty cup is a symbol of my readiness to listen…'

"A newly poured cup of coffee is never completely full, and it is only nearly full for the briefest moments. Joyce Rupp writes, 'Emptiness is a gift that opens us further to the transforming power of God.' Our lives and our love runneth over with cups, sometimes empty cups. You seem to be at that place, Peter."

"That is a curious twist on an old adage. My cup has been emptying, Padre. When I left here last time, something was bothering me. I'd call it a stirring."

"Sometimes, those are the "teachers" we need. The stirrings that feel negative are ones that we particularly need to pay attention to."

"Teachers, Padre?"

"There is always something to be learned from our feelings."

I told him about my conversation with Gen, working out in the gym, and my readiness to get back in the studio. I told him I had begun *Falling Upward* and about my mischaracterization of Richard Rohr. He got a good laugh out of that. "Rohr says that we can't move fully into the second half of life until we have resolved the issues in our first half. I'm nearly sixty, and I am not sure I've done that."

"How far have you gotten into *Falling Upward*, Peter?"

"I've read the Invitation, Introduction, and Chapter One."

"Did you read the front matter: praise, copyright, etc.?"

"No, I skipped that."

"Many do. There are quotes in the dedication from Carl Jung and Lady Julian of Norwich. The quote from Jung, I believe, is a key to understanding the process of falling upward. Jung writes, 'The greatest and most important problems of life are fundamentally unsolvable. They can never be solved, but only outgrown.' Rilke says we grow into them.

"Peter, if you are to continue on this journey into the second half of life, I think you have to acknowledge that statement. There is no surety to be determined. The questions outnumber the answers. There is no destination and no map. It is a journey of many paths, or the pathless journey, as some call it. This is what Rilke referred to as living into the question. If you thought you were lost before, traveling on this journey may be your ultimate experience in being lost. That is quite inviting, isn't it?"

"Well, I wouldn't recommend you for an adman's position. Truly, though, I do have an excitement; maybe it's anticipation."

"A good place to start." Padre Cisco sat for a while looking at me. I didn't feel he was staring. His look was benign; it seemed to be one of appreciation. It warmed me. "So tell me, Peter, what do you think is unfinished?"

I didn't respond. I knew what I wanted to say, and I knew that to say it was to make a commitment. It was that single step in the longest journey moment. I clung to a multitude of images, delaying my response. It meant the hawing and yawing would end. Sheer terror of being honest with myself replaced the expressed excitement a moment earlier. To be honest with Padre Cisco demanded honesty with myself. I had to choose. I realized I had no choice. I couldn't go back. I had made my choice by showing up. I was eighty percent there. I had only to summon the real me to complete the final twenty percent.

"Dad," I almost whispered. I paused, and let it sink in. In a single word, I had taken the proverbial flying leap. "My Dad, my parents, my sister, my daughter. My relationships stink," came oozing out of me. My head slumped, and my eyes closed. I breathed deeply.

Padre Cisco waited until I looked up. "Can you tell me about your relationship with your father?"

"I told you I was nicknamed for Rocky Colavito. Dad loved baseball; he loved the Cleveland Indians. He grew up in Youngstown before moving to Akron. Both cities are hotbeds of Indians fans. He was tough. You had to be tough growing up in Youngstown. We played a lot of catch. I was always the pitcher. I was 'Bullet Bob' Feller."

I closed my eyes trying to recall what would describe my relationship with my father. *It all centered on JJ. What? Where did that come from?*

My dad is a large man, or I should say *was*. He has lost height and girth as he has aged. He played baseball as a kid. He was a catcher and pretty good judging from the clippings he kept. He played some semi-pro when he returned from Korea. Swing shifts at Firestone ended that.

By the time I was old enough to play, he had enough seniority and was back on days. I would wait in the living room for him to come home from work. He would come through the door and say, "Ready for some catch," then greet Mom, John Jr., and Mary. Playing catch was the first thing we would do before dinner. In the winter, we would play in the basement. I missed our game the days he worked for the overtime pay. He always said he was sorry, but we needed the money. JJ seldom played with us. He was big like Dad, but his passion was football. He was the all-state fullback and middle linebacker. He was my hero.

I read the sports pages in the paper so I could pretend I knew what was going on with the Indians. One day, Dad chided me that I was just parroting the sports writers. I learned to read the box scores. We talked a lot of baseball. It is probably the one thing we still have in common.

Dad graduated from high school in 1951 and a week later enlisted in the Army. He served in Korea, returning in 1953. He married his high school sweetheart. Ten months later, JJ was born. Three years later, I came along, and Mary two years after me. I have no memory of Dad ever mentioning Korea. When anyone would ask him about it, he would just turn his head or walk away.

JJ turned eighteen in 1972. The army was using the lottery in the draft. Dad wanted him to go into the plant, secure a job, and wait for his number to be drawn. He told JJ if he were drafted, his job would be there. JJ enlisted. He spent two days in Nam before he was killed. He never fired his weapon. That day was the last time Dad and I ever played catch. *That's where it came from.* When I responded I condensed my memories to the crux.

"JJ's thing was football. Mine was baseball. Playing catch was the only thing with my father that was exclusive. When JJ died, I lost more than him. I lost my relationship with my father."

Padre Cisco leaned forward and quietly asked, "Can you describe how you felt?"

Words jammed themselves into my throat. I sat mute trying to untangle my emotions. After a half-dozen deep breaths, I began. I could barely whisper. "It was after dinner, just getting dark. We were watching the news reports from Nam. Mary and I were sitting on the bottom step of the stairway."

I related the scene of the taxi pulling up in front of the house and wondering who was coming to see us. People in Akron don't travel by taxi. The scene played in my memory like a slide show. JJ wasn't the first on our street. The driver got out. He came up the sidewalk. The doorbell rang. Dad went to the door. The driver's head hung down. There was hushed conversation. Mom stood. The driver left. Dad screamed, "Damn! Damn him, damn you, God. Damn it all." Mom gasped and slumped to her knees. Mary and I rushed to her. Dad turned, walked past us and out the back door.

"It was the only time I ever heard him curse. You asked how I felt. How do you think I felt?" The padre straightened at the rancor in my voice. He covered his mouth.

I didn't need a response. I didn't want a response. I closed my eyes and sat reliving a day chiseled in my memory. I was in the uncharted territory of Tom Kreuser's artic trek. Only I didn't know my pace, much less the terrain. I sat in silence thinking back to those days. Padre Cisco sat back, folded his hands in his lap, and waited.

I told him how Mom doted on Mary after that, not that she didn't before if you were to have asked JJ or me. Mary worshipped JJ. She understood his loss even less than I did. The two us of banded together. We vowed to take care of each other. I didn't hold up my end of the bargain.

As soon as I graduated from high school, I left. Dad wanted me to go into the plant. That was the last thing I wanted. I had found cartooning and already experienced some success. The high school paper included my cartoons, and I had a couple published in the *Akron Beacon Journal*. I did the artwork for the yearbook my senior year. I wanted to be an artist. Even as a kid, I had a sense for social and political commentary. I learned that expressing it through cartoons was not only socially acceptable; people solicited it.

My best friend Smitty was recruited by Sun Devil coach Frank Kush as an offensive lineman, and he accepted a scholarship to ASU. I was as tall then, but a lot thinner. I was a decent basketball player, but not of college caliber. I was, however, a good student. I applied to ASU and was accepted. They had an art department, but I had no idea of its quality. It didn't matter; I just wanted to get out of the house and out of Akron. Dad disapproved of my career hopes and my choice of schools.

Smitty had a car, and we drove to Arizona. I had little money until I was able to find a job. I slept on an army cot in Smitty's dorm room for the first four months I was there. That was one of those "turn about is fair play" times. Many nights, Smitty had slept on the couch at our house. He would come home from school with me. We would sit in the kitchen doing our homework while Mom fixed dinner, and he would just stay the evening. It was strange, now that I think of it. I never asked him why. I guess things weren't so good for him at home.

Life at ASU was tough at first, but I hung in. I couldn't go home. My pride wouldn't let me. Smitty blew out his knee his senior year, ending his football career. He finished his degree in finance, moved to San Diego, took up surfing, and we have remained friends all these years. I think Gen may like him more than me. We have great fun together.

Padre Cisco motioned toward my cup. I shook my head, "No." Following an almost a predictable pause, Padre Cisco said, "Peter, I imagine you know of C.S. Lewis."

"I read *The Chronicles of Narnia* when I was young."

"Lewis as much nonfiction than fiction. He was an observer of his own life and of the human condition. Lewis wrote about his mother's death in his childhood memoir *Surprised by Joy*. Bear in mind, Lewis wrote about his experience in the context of living with a father who he described as having 'uncontrolled emotions.' I would have used the less flattering word *tyrant* to describe his father. Lewis wrote that two things happened. The first, which he called a good thing, was how he and his brother drew closer together – 'two frightened urchins huddled for warmth in a bleak world.' The second he labeled *evil*. Out of their fear and having confidence only in each other, their father lost his sons as well as his wife. He added that their withdrawal actually occurred during his mother's illness. It was then that he and his brother learned to lie to their father. He corrected himself to say it was at least he who learned to lie. I think that is why he termed the event evil."

That gave me pause. I had never considered that my father lost Mary and me as much as we lost him. I had compounded the loss for my parents and Mary when I left home. I said, "Maybe I should be sharing the blame as well as the guilt."

"Maybe neither." The padre's eyes darted up at me then down again. He paused as though gathering himself. He slid his chair forward, leaned in toward me, and took my hands in his. He fixed his gaze into my eyes and spoke with a certainty in his voice I had not heard before. "This is not your fault. This is not your fault. This is not your fault."

Tears welled up in me. We sat there for the longest time bound to each. Finally, I sat back, and he released my hands but held me in his eyes. I wiped my eyes and smiled shyly. He nodded and smiled in return.

I closed my eyes, and we sat in silence. The echo of *this is not your fault* resonated in my mind. Finally, I had to move. I stood and took my cup motioning at his. He nodded. I went to kitchen and refilled them.

When I settled back in, he began again. "Peter, this may be about your feelings of guilt, but it is not about blame. There is no blame to share. You were children. Children have an idealized view of their future. They have an idealized view of who their parents should be. People talk a lot about child rearing. From an alternate point of view I would say children work hard thinking they can raise their parents. They have high expectations, and when their parents don't turn out as they hoped, they leave home wondering where they went wrong.

"Children often bear an unrealistic understanding of their power to affect their world. As children, their parents are the world. Children do not pray to God; they pray to their parents. Unfulfilled, they often do as you did – leave, seeking greener pastures. In the truest sense, this is, as it needs to be. It is the first journey. There is no blame to share. There is no blame to share. There is no blame to share."

"If this is in fact what happened, what can I do to fix it at this point in my life?"

"Peter, you can't fix it. You can only learn from it. Fixing it assumes that it is broken. Nothing is broken; *it* is simply the life you have and the lives your family have. It is your story that will continue on pages not yet turned. You get to decide. That is the free will part of life. You get to choose to learn or not. You get to allow the learning to change you or not.

This is what Luke's classic story of the prodigal son was about when he wrote, 'And he came to himself.' The lost son, the prodigal, learned and changed while his older brother stayed home and remained the same. I have read a Rabbi Lawrence Kushner's commentary that questions the degree to which the lost son changed, but that is a discussion for another day. The heart of the story is that each day, each new learning is an opportunity to come closer to yourself, the person you are meant to be."

I said, "Maybe we should stop here. I want to talk to you about Morgan and her illness, but I am not ready for that. I'm a bit overwhelmed right now."

Gen was gone. I thought Morgan just had the flu or something. I didn't take care of her. When I finally got her to a doctor, he diagnosed her with a combination of a bacterial infection and meningitis stemming from valley fever. She became gravely ill and went into a coma.

Padre Cisco replied, "I understand. Would you like to just sit together for a while, and then we will quit?"

"I would like that."

We sat for five or ten minutes; I'm not sure. I let the conversation sink in. I had a lot to consider. I remember thinking that I have a lot to pray about. It was the first time in thirty years I'd thought about praying. I didn't even know how to pray, anymore. *Maybe I had never known how to pray. Maybe there is a teacher here.*

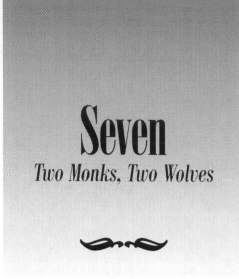

Seven
Two Monks, Two Wolves

"Abba, give me a word."
"We have a special today, my son."
"A special?"
"Yes, two for one."
"The two words, Abba?"
"Pain and suffering."
"What about them, Abba?"
"We acquire one but invite the other."

I arrived home in twilight. I love driving up to our home in the soft light. The house sits on the top of a hill, providing a panorama of Tucson and an eagle's-nest view of crimson skies. I knew at first sight that we had found our dream home. It mirrored meeting Gen. We moved to Tucson after the twins entered college. They were less excited about the house than we were. They said they wouldn't have their home to come back to. After their first time back from school, we realized they were right. It was a home to us, but only a house to them. I could identify with that.

The second stall was empty when I pulled into the garage, and I remembered Gen had a yoga class. I was glad because

I wanted the down time. That bothered me. I wondered why guilt all of a sudden was rising in me. It wasn't my nature. At least I didn't think it was my nature. I wondered if I had suppressed guilt. *Oh crap, I'm parked in the garage, but I'm driving myself crazy. Lighten up, Rocky.*

Of the many things we liked about the house, in addition to its curved lines, viga ceilings, and ample use of stone, were the five bedrooms. It gave us each office space and still left rooms for guests. The detached building that would become my studio was the tipping point.

I went to my study and opened Kindle on my iPad to *Falling Upward.* I wanted to reread what I had already covered, but the phrase "he came to himself" kept ringing in my head. When was I going to come to myself? I didn't even know what I had to do to come to myself. I wasn't even sure what it meant. I brought up my highlights: *The further journey usually appears like a seductive invitation and a kind of promise or hope.* I didn't feel seduced, but I knew planning had not gotten me to that point in my life. I admitted I was "drawn," and I had made a conscious choice to continue. *We do not "create" our souls; we just "grow" them…Transformation is often more about unlearning than learning…*I had no idea what that meant. *The first half of life is discovering the script, and the second half is actually writing it and owning it.* That awareness was coming. *Leaving home, seeking home and arriving back home…The Mystery…growing much more by doing it wrong than by doing it right…the stages of the hero's journey…*I awakened the next morning in the chair. I had a vague memory of Gen telling me to go to bed.

She was still sleeping when I got up. I made coffee and went out to the studio, opening the door for the first time in six months. I smelled the stale air. *Well, aren't we the pair.* My sketchbook lay on the drawing table open to a blank page. I sat down and stared. I wish I could say I gazed, but I simply stared. *Is this what I'm all about now? Tabula rasa. Am I a blank page in my own sketchbook? Am I starting over?*

Gen brought coffee, rousing me from my inertia. We sat and talked. I filled her in on my visit with Padre Cisco, and she told me about her day. I struggled to make small talk. I think she interpreted that as my desire to get to work, and she left to be about her own tasks. I picked up a pencil. I didn't do much more than idly draw for the next couple of hours and the next couple of weeks. I missed being on a schedule with specific tasks to accomplish each day. I would sketch characters, block out strips, and complete a draft in the mornings. By afternoon, I was ready to complete a final draft, copy it, and send it off. I struggled to find a sense of purpose, that sense of renewal I experienced driving out to Padre Cisco's just a month before.

I divided my time between drawing, reading *Falling Upward*, working out, and conversations with Gen. I should say my time *was divided*. I had little sense of direction. My sleep cycle went crazy. I have always been an early riser, but I was awakening at two or three in the morning. I'd lie about for a while and finally get up and go to the studio. My mind ran amok. I struggled to concentrate, but I kept drawing.

Toward the end of that period, my work began to change. I found myself creating portrait sketches. I am not sure who the subjects were, but they began to morph. They were not cartoons, and they certainly were not the caricatures of my college summer days at Legend City where I made two-fifty a drawing.

Other drawings were abstract, incomplete, and almost vague. They represented places and objects, but were not exactly so. I drew rocks, trees, chairs, stairways, and lamps, anything and everything, all monochromatic. Adding color did not occur to me. If I had told people the subjects simply appeared to me, that they just were visions, I'm sure they would consider me daft. I can't say where they came from. The drawings were rooted in some emotion, anger maybe, not to memories or photographs. I didn't like what I was producing. I was just glad to be back drawing anything.

Gen and I talked about it, but she saw no more sense to it than I did. I produced dozens of sketches, large and small. Some of the subjects would reappear. My imagination ran rampant. I was content with its haphazard foray into consciousness. I was curious about what Padre Cisco may make of my experience.

* * *

We sat on the veranda looking out at the garden. Padre Cisco's hoe stood against the wheelbarrow. He had been tilling the soil before my arrival. Plants were showing evidence of future bounty. We sat for a while enjoying the warm air, clear skies, and gentle breeze of April.

"How is it with you, my friend?" Padre Cisco asked in his standard opening.

"I am back in the studio."

"This is good?"

"Yes, this is good," I admitted with a sense of joy. "I began drawing about three weeks ago. It is strange, though. I have no idea what I am drawing or where it is coming from." I told him about the faces, the bold lines, the naming, the frenetic pace of the work, and the oddity of it all. He sat for a couple of minutes with his head down and his eyes closed.

"Can you think of a time when you experienced this before?"

My senses went on alert. Alarms went off; red DANGER signs flashed. My memory raced into the ominous territory of my childhood. I felt my past welling up as though it were another being constricting my lungs. "Yes, I can. Wow! I didn't know that was there." I paused, concentrated on breathing, and barged on. "I was thirteen. It was right after JJ was killed. I remember sitting in my room, day after day, and drawing for hours. I drew with a felt-tip pen. That wasn't my style. I typically drew with pencil and maybe highlighted with pen. I drew ugly faces, contorted, frightening, and angry. I was angry. JJ was gone. Mom spent all her time with Mary. Dad sat and brooded. He wouldn't even talk about baseball. He seemed to resent my presence. I resented *him*. I was alone."

I stopped and just sat there, my head back against the chair, caught in my past. Padre Cisco followed suit, mirroring my posture, and waited. We sat there as I pulled back the curtains shrouding a childhood's measure of memories.

I said, "That was unexpected." I thought Padre Cisco might say something about learning from the unexpected, but he held silent. "I had no idea that was bottled up in me."

"Few of us do. Psychiatrist Carl Jung called them our shadow selves, parts of ourselves we do not like. They follow us around like our shadows. The shadow selves are in the recesses of our memories. They covertly affect us until we recognize them and call them into the light."

He sat; I think to allow that to sink in. Then he told a story of two monks. My rendition is abbreviated. Two monks, Aba and Bab were walking down a road. They came to a river, and on the shoreline sat a beautiful young woman. She asked the monks to carry her across the river because the water was fast, and she was afraid she would sweep her away. "Oh no," said Bab, 'I humbly beseech you, please, do not ask this of us. We have taken vows of poverty and chastity. We are not to consort with the world." The young woman's eyes turned to Aba, and without hesitation he said, "Here, climb on my back, and I will carry you across." She got on his back, and Aba carried her across the river and put her down on the opposite shore. The crossing was not without difficulty because she was of ample girth, and Aba was a small man. She thanked him and offered him alms, but he deferred. The two monks went on their way.

They walked some distance with Bab muttering to himself. Aba stopped, stretched backward and rubbed the small of his back. He turned to look at Bab who said, "How could you do that?" Aba replied, "I put her down next to the river. Are you still carrying her?"

When he finished the story, Padre Cisco sat back and waited.

"Yes?"

"Yes, what?"

"Are you saying I just need to put all this behind me?"

"Oh no, Peter. It is not as simple as that. If it were, the memory would not have risen in you as it did."

"What then?"

"Good question. What does the story tell you?"

"It's about choices. If I think of it as a universal story, then we always have a choice."

"Yes. What else?"

"Bab was angry. Am I Bab in this story?"

"Are you?"

"Perhaps," I laughed. "I'm the one grousing about my situation."

"By your situation do you mean your life? Grousing about one's situation recognizes the temporary nature of pain. Grousing about life is defining your life as one of enduring suffering."

"I don't think I've graduated to complaining about my life, Padre. I am blessed. I am blessed with Gen, great kids, a fun, creative career, and the trappings that go with it. Are there things I wish I had done differently? Absolutely! Only in hindsight, the twenty-twenty of the rearview mirror. I wouldn't have the blessings I do if I had not done what I did."

We refreshed our coffee and sat for a while. As he so often did, Padre Cisco came from a different angle.

"Peter, back in my art and lit days at the university, I taught from the presumption that all art and all writing were metaphoric. You might examine the monks' story from that proposition, what each element of the story represents to you. Beyond that, I always think to look at what the wisdom teachers have to say about any given thing. There is the anonymous quote, often, though incorrectly, attributed to Buddha: 'Pain is inevitable; suffering is optional.' There is some truth in that, as in most adages. 'The longest journey begins with a single step.' As trite as that may be, it is true. 'God doesn't give you more than you can handle.' I am not so sure about that one. By the way, it is not in the Christian Bible, though Christians sure quote it as it were. I think it may be from Confucius.

"The statement I prefer is 'Without pain, there would be no suffering; without suffering, we would never learn from our mistakes.'"

"Is that from a Buddha?"

"No, it is from Angelina Jolie. Not all wisdom teachers have to be ancient, bearded, or Asian monks." He smiled at himself for that one. "In the Western world, we equate wisdom with truth and truth with veracity. That is not always the case. The person in my day who understood this as well as anyone was Art Linkletter. He knew kids were not only funny, but they were at times also wise."

"I saw many of those shows. My parents wouldn't miss it. Was that *Kids Say the Darndest Things?*"

"That was the name of the segment. The show was *House Party*."

"Yes, that was it."

"To return to Angelina Jolie, she goes on to say, 'To make it right, pain and suffering is the key to all windows, without it there is no way of life.'"

"That's what Richard Rohr is saying when he writes about necessary suffering, isn't it?"

"Yes, it is the suffering people experience when they leave everything behind. He says that in order to enter into the second half of life suffering is essential. The person I think who totally understood this was Elwood P. Dowd."

"Elwood P. Dowd?"

"Have you seen the movie *Harvey*, Peter?"

"Oh, yes, the Jimmy Stewart character. Harvey was the giant rabbit."

"Pooka, and he was six foot three and a half inches as Elwood would specify. In a scene at the asylum, Dr. Chumley, played by Cecil Kellaway, asks Elwood how he came to be the way he is. Elwood said in that thick-tongued speech pattern Jimmy Stewart had, 'Years ago my mother used to say to me, she'd say, *In this world, Elwood, you must be - she always called me Elwood - In this world, Elwood, you must be oh so smart or oh so pleasant*. Well, for years I was smart. I recommend pleasant. You may quote me.'"

"If I my memory is right, Padre, Elwood spent quite a bit of his second half of life in Charlie's pub."

"That he did. Do you think that is significant?"

"Oh, I don't know, Padre. Isn't everything significant in a movie?"

"Perhaps. I heard a related occurrence that sheds some light. Johnny Carson asked Jimmy Stewart a similar question one night on *The Tonight Show*. Carson asked Stewart how he came to talk the way he does. Jimmy Stewart said that he learned to talk from the old men sitting around the stove in his father's hardware store in Indiana, Pennsylvania. He said that the men had lost their teeth and wore Roebuckers."

"Roebuckers?"

He told me that before the Internet, people got many things, false teeth among them, from Sears and Roebuck through mail order. It was the Amazon of its day. False teeth were known as Roebuckers. To make sure the teeth fit, men would order them a bit large; and then to keep them in their mouths, they apparently held their tongue up against them when they talked. Jimmy Stewart claims to have learned to talk from the men sitting around his father's hardware store. He said he takes the story with a grain of salt.

"The point is, Peter, Jimmy Stewart did not take himself too seriously. He was able to laugh at himself. I think Jimmy Stewart was able to play the role of Elwood's indubitable understanding of the nature of life because he found the second half of life early. I conjecture he learned much from listening to those elders' stories. Excuse me; I was sidetracked on Jimmy Stewart. Where was I?"

"You're still there, Padre, Elwood P. Dowd and the two halves of life."

"Oh, yes. Elwood had transitioned from an old way of being and acting to a new way. It is what Christians call transformation or even resurrection."

He referred to the story of Jacob in the book of Genesis. As Jacob, he was a conniver and trickster in his early life, tricking his twin brother out of his birthright. Later in life, after suffering years of guilt and a giant bout with his conscience, he changed his ways to that of an upstanding guy. He was renamed Israel. That is the *Reader's Digest* version with a lot of the middle left out. Padre Cisco said read a rabbi who wrote that there are nuances in the Hebrew language that ascribe the idea of crooked to the name Jacob and straight to the name Israel. I thought that is just so cool and so appropriate. There is such sophistication in the Hebrew writings. It is no wonder today we read their stories so naively today.

"I don't know if I'm entering the second half of life or not, but I guess I have been suffering. Don't get me wrong, Padre, I'm not into self-pity. There are certainly millions of people who experience suffering in ways that I can only imagine."

"Perhaps suffering is not relative. You hear people say, 'She suffered terribly.' Who is to say one person's suffering is greater than another's is? 'He suffered a sudden heart attack.' Are there heart attacks that are not sudden? People minimize another's pain or even their own by such statements. Newscasters speak of 'terrible tragedies.' Ridiculous! All tragedy by definition is terrible. Tragedy is just that, tragedy. Pain is pain. Suffering is suffering. If the phrase 'It is what it is' were not used so dismissively, it could not be more apt here. The question rests not in the existence or degree of pain and suffering, but in what, why, and how long you hang onto it."

I was full of mixed emotions. I imagined it showed on my face. I said, "I'm obviously hanging on to some anger and guilt; and I'm not quite sure what to do about that." I am not an angry guy, but I have my moments. Morgan's attitudes drive me up the wall. I get angry with my dad. His comments never seem to sit with me.

I was angry that my brother was born before I was. How stupid is that?"

I related a story of leaving a bare ace in my hand that my father trumped. It was my own fault, and I knew it, but I flew into a rage at my father for playing a dirty trick on me. He was supposed to be kinder. How could he do such a thing? I saw my loss as his fault.

"I was angry with God when JJ was killed and I was left alone. I'm angry when I read the paper and become a third-party witness of man's inhumanity. Anger rises in me, but it doesn't drive me the way it does for some people. It just dissipates my desire. I'm learning that anger is one of my shadows."

"Peter, anger is a response to the denial of grace. The ego works diligently to deny grace because when the self recognizes the existence of grace and accepts it, the ego loses. The ego does not like to lose. It knows ultimately it will lose to the death of the self in this life. So it works to prolong its own existence by obstructing the self's recognition of its own vulnerability. You take a great leap forward each time you identify and label your shadows. It is the eighty percent factor, showing up to your own life. Then the hard work begins. That is the other twenty percent of remaining present to your true self."

"You aren't overstating the hard work part, Padre. I'm finding that out."

"Do you know about the two wolves, Peter?"

"Two wolves? No, Padre."

"This story is found throughout literature. It has many variations, though all carry the same truth." He folded his hands and closed his eyes for a moment as though reminiscing. Opening his eyes and told this story.

One evening, an old Cherokee told his grandson about a battle that goes on inside people. The battle is between two wolves inside us all. One is Evil. It is anger, envy, jealousy, sorrow, regret, greed, arrogance, self-pity, guilt, resentment, inferiority, lies, false pride, un-forgiveness, superiority, and ego. The other is Good. It is joy, peace, love, forgiveness, hope, serenity, humility, kindness, benevolence, empathy, generosity, truth, compassion and faith. The grandson thought about it for a while then asked his grandfather, 'Which wolf wins?' The old Cherokee replied, "The one you feed."

When the padre finished, he asked me, "Which wolf are you feeding?"

We sat for a bit, and finally Padre Cisco said, "Why don't we stop here and pick up when we meet again." We stood and talked for another few minutes. I have no memory of that conversation. I was engrossed with shadows, monks, and wolves, but I remember wondering if they were to be my teachers. *Perhaps when James Finley said find your teaching and follow it, one of the places I will find it is among the monks and wolves.*

At some point, Padre Cisco walked me to the car and I headed home.

Eight
The Three Rs

"Abba, give me a word."
"We have another special, a three-for."
"Yes, Abba?"
"Resolution, release, and reconciliation."
"How do I learn this, Abba?"
"By living, my son."

"He did it to me again. Padre Cisco tells these cryptic stories, and then just when I think I am getting somewhere, he says it's time to quit. What is that all about? Do you think it's by design?" Gen and I sat in the kitchen and caught up. I told her about the two monks and the two wolves. I shared the childhood memories I had and the feelings of anger that rose in me. "Then he quoted Angelina Jolie as a wisdom teacher about pain and suffering. Really? Angelina Jolie?"

"Oh yes, Rocky. Angelina Jolie knows pain and suffering."

"How can any woman that beautiful and that famous experience pain and suffering?"

"That's part of her pain. Trust me on this, Rocky."

"Okay, I'll back off on that. You know, Gen, I had a sense of relief talking to the padre. I was bothered. At the same time, verbalizing something that I didn't recognize was good. Maybe that's the beginning of the healing process. If I were Catholic, I would say I felt like I'd been to confession. Then again, if I were a Catholic, I would say that Protestants use the word healing for what they do in a tent."

"Speaking of healing, have you thought any more about going to Akron?"

"I have, and I haven't. I know this is something I need to do. I haven't done anything about it."

"What do you want to do, Rocky?"

"I'm not sure of the specifics, but I know I want to resolve the issues with my father and sister. I can't do that on the phone. I have to go back there."

"When do you think you will go?"

"Probably before Memorial Day. That allows time to organize. I need to check flights and call Mary to find out what might work for them."

We talked for a while longer. Gen went to her computer, and I went to the studio. I thought about how much Gen and I talked, the richness of our conversation, and how I gained a sense of direction through talking with her. I realized the impact similar conversations with Padre Cisco were having. I looked forward to the next one.

The morning I was to meet with Padre Cisco, I awakened to rain. Even a shower alters our days as snow does in the north. Children wade in the gutters the way their northern counterparts play in new snow. The hunt for umbrellas rivals a search for the rainbow's pot of gold. Wrinkled raingear emerges from closets to be ironed by the elements. Flooded roads, akin to midwestern snowdrifts, strand motorists. Auto body shops prepare for the bonanza of repairs resulting from fender-benders. Commuters discover that their windshield wipers squeak from dryness and disuse. I was one of those and had to leave early to stop at a garage for replacements.

We met indoors. The latticed roof of the veranda serves to mediate sun but does not accommodate rain. While Padre Cisco went about his coffee ritual, I sat looking and thinking about how differently we live. The disparity in the sizes of our homes is an obvious testament. He drives a Jeep; I drive a Lexus SUV. I thought how painstakingly he roasts beans and then drips coffee through a glass Melitta. Gen and I can barely wait for the K-cup pod to brew. He seems to have time for everything. He gives everything his full attention whether it is making coffee, chores, cooking, gardening, or people. He has a way of sitting that embodies a listening presence. Whether we are inside or siting in the Adirondack chairs, he leans to the side, tilts his head, and props it in his hand with his elbow on the arm of the chair. Even while walking side-by-side or standing, he seems to lean in to the conversation.

He sat down, and I said, "Tell me, Padre. How did you come to live in such a small house?" I had that question since the first time I visited. I wondered why I had never asked it before. Maybe I didn't think I knew him well enough.

"Odd you should ask. I was just thinking of a Robyn I know. She lives in the desert in an even smaller house. I once asked her how she could live in a house with just two rooms. Her answer was not one you would expect. She replied, 'I feel my life will be complete when I can live in one room.'"

I closed my eyes and tried to visualize my life in just one room. It didn't work for me living in our home with spaces for everything.

"If you think about it, she has great foresight. We all end our lives living in one room. It might be at home or away. It might be your bedroom or a room at one of your children's homes, a hospital room or a room in a care center. Some people die in a hospital bed in their living room. Think about it, Peter, dying in your living room. Isn't that a hoot? These are the places many of us end our lives. Ultimately, we are what we used to call 'laid out' somewhere. Historically, it was the parlor. It became the living room when people started taking their family members to funeral parlors; hence the modern parlance. You had better start downsizing now, Peter. There will not be space for all your stuff in that one room."

I sat up straight. My mind ran off on a tangent. I stood, walked around the tablechair, and sat again. "There may be a market there, Padre." I waved my hands like a used car salesman. "I can visualize a future with combo car lots, cemeteries, and storage lockers. One-stop service: park your car, body, and stuff all in one spot. Perhaps there are high-end plots with adjoining holes for storage sheds and garages so you *can* take it with you. That could make a terrific strip, Padre. I can see the billboard: *St. Pete's Long Term Storage. You Can Take It With You.*"

"It's good to hear you drop into your artistic mode. Maybe your time in the studio is paying dividends."

"Many of my ideas of develop while I'm standing or moving. I sit on a high stool at a drafting table, but I stand there as well. I have an eight foot white board behind me. I make notes and sketch out preliminary ideas on it, usually pacing."

"Perhaps we should take an occasional stroll around the room."

"From what you are saying, Padre, that might be a practice in the future."

"Could be. Life is about practicing. Moving into one room can be a metaphor for moving from the first to the second half of life. We have to leave things behind. There simply is not space in our lives for it all. We have to downsize our ego."

I wanted to ask about pain, but I needed a break. I suggested we refresh our coffee. When we return to our chairs, I said, "So, Padre, is that what we do with pain, leave it behind? Gen and I were talking after we last met. I said verbalizing the existence of pain or suffering might be the beginning of the healing process."

"I believe that to be very much the case. Brené Brown, a researcher at the University of Houston, has spent years studying shame. She has had success with a program, particularly for women, called *The Daring Way*, based on her book, *Daring Greatly*. She said her original goal was to start a conversation about shame. I suspect it may be initiating conversation about any wound that begins the healing process"

"Why is that? I guess I mean how does that work. How does just holding conversation start the healing process?"

"Perhaps we have to lay claim to pain. In claiming the pain or the source of the suffering, we begin to put it into our past. Not doing so allows it to remain as part of our present, whether we want it to be or not. Jim Clarke, in his book *Creating Rituals: A New Way of Healing of Everyday Life*, says, 'The soulful work of reclaiming the shadow and bringing its treasure to consciousness is courageous work.' The roots of many of our emotions are nefarious, Peter. They only work in the shadows. If they can hide in the shadows of our lives, we don't see them and hence do not deal with them. They will rise in us again."

I glanced about the room looking at the shadows in corners and under shelves. I wondered if I had laid claim to the emotions hiding in my own shadows.

"I feel like I am preaching, Peter, and you know my opinions on preaching. There are exceptions. Nadia Bolz-Webber is one of them. She writes about this in her book *Accidental Saints*. When asked to talk on preaching at a preacher's conference, she did not know what to say, so she asked her congregation. They gave none of the expected replies. She writes, 'Almost all of them said they love that their preacher is so obviously preaching to herself and just allowing them to overhear it.' Now there is preaching I can accept. My priest, Father Jim, shares that approach in his homilies. I always feel honored to be privy to what seems like a private conversation.

"I have been talking at some length. Please note that I am preaching to more to myself as much as to you. I hope I am not just deluding myself, but I think you are aware that I know I do not have *the* answers. I have answers, but they are only opinions. With that disclaimer, I will prattle on if that is copasetic."

"Oh yes, Padre, what you are saying is what I know I am dealing with. I know that there are long-standing issues involving my dad and family. I am aware that I need to find resolution, or they are going to just keep pestering me. I've scheduled a trip back to Akron to visit my parents and sister. I hope to work through some things though I worry that it will turn out to be contentious like so many of my conversations with Dad. There's a chance that I will just make things worse."

"There is always that chance. We all face trials sometime in our life." Padre Cisco told me about when his wife died. He was about my age. It was the first time I heard him talk about it. "Like you, Peter, my life turned on a dime." He said was angry with God, with doctors, therapists, and with himself. The future he knew no longer existed. Time did not exist anymore. He said that when he returned to teaching and the students were there, he was relatively sane. He was as normal as one might expect, but when they left the class, he did not know what to do. Weeks went by without looking at a calendar. Michael Francis, whose wife's death preceded his by a couple of years, would ask him, "How far out are you?" meaning are you looking to the future. He laughed and said he would glance at his watch. About five months into it, Michael Francis asked the same question, and he said, "October." It was three months away, and he had bought tickets to an Eric Clapton concert. "Life moves at variable speeds, and as much as you might want to you cannot rush it."

"I've been at this for six months now. Shouldn't these issues be sorting themselves out by now, or *I* should be sorting them out? My days and nights are still topsy-turvy, I get edgy with Gen, and I get tired and listless. I'm a smart guy. I should be able to figure this out."

"While your issues, as you described them, are long standing, your awareness is new. Practice Wu wei, Peter."

"Wu wei?"

"The art of non-doing."

"I'll pass on that one, Padre."

"Read up on Wu wei, Peter. There are things there to learn. Talk with Gen about her meditation."

"Perhaps."

"Peter."

"Okay, Padre, I'll check it out."

"Do you remember a couple of months back I talked about the Peter Principle and the lateral arabesque?"

"I do."

"That certainly was part of my decision to retire from teaching, but I think the larger part was the spiritual questions I had to face. I had to choose who I wanted to be in light of my changed circumstances. I had to decide what my new normal was going to be. It was not just about leaving the university. It was about going *to* something, an unknown something that I had to choose. In hindsight, I can say I received the opportunity of choosing. I not only had to decide who I wanted to be, but, also, *how* I wanted to be."

"I still have difficulty seeing my circumstances as an opportunity."

"It is a gift, Peter."

"Really, Padre, I hardly see it as a gift."

"Do you remember Richard Bach of *Jonathan Livingston Seagull* fame?"

"Absolutely, I remember reading it as a teenager and liking it. Though I don't think I realized the significance of it at the time."

"He wrote another book, *Illusions*, a few years later. I think it was equally poignant. Remember it?"

"No, I didn't read that one."

"It is sub-titled *The Adventures of a Reluctant Messiah*. I loved that thought. There were two characters, Donald Shimoda, who was the messiah, and Richard. One day, Richard asked Donald, 'How do you learn to be a messiah?' Donald answered, 'They give you a handbook' and handed it to Richard. Throughout the rest of the book, at appropriately trying occasions, Richard would turn to an apt page in the handbook. The only passage I remember was something to this effect: Every problem has a gift for you in its hands. You seek problems because you need their gifts. I know that is not exact. I probably should look it up, but the gist of it has served me over the years as much as the exact quote might have. Richard Bach understood death as an embarkation that we talked about earlier. He knew life is about thousands of little moments in which we have a chance to see things differently and start again anew."

"Well, Padre, it still is hard for me to see my circumstances as a gift."

"I will not take that as a challenge, but I will bear it in mind. On a related note, choosing is becoming more difficult.

I just learned this. According to Barry Schwartz, a psychologist at Swarthmore College, the more choices we have, the more difficult is the choice. That might be expected, but there is an unintended consequence. The more choices we have, the lower our satisfaction level is. The level of satisfaction with our choice decreases because of expectations for being able to make the perfect choice. Is that not just great news for your thrust into your new normal? I need to quit watching TED Talks. It is my cure for a short sleep cycle, but it is addictive. I learn more things than I want to know."

"Like every problem has a gift for you in its hands, Padre?" I said with a bit of payback in my tone.

"Touché, Peter. So where were we?"

"Choosing your future when you left the university."

"Oh yes. As I believe you do, I felt that I was a victim of my circumstances. We do not have to be victims to think and act like victims. We all are the victims of our own making. Some of us in our anger use victim status to justify our thoughts, feelings, and actions. Some people use this to seek vengeance. Most of us probably just think about it, and we do not call it that. Vengeance is much too harsh a word and much too accurate. We have euphemisms for it: just deserts, poetic justice, righteous indignation, eye for an eye, retribution, or satisfaction, to name a few. They serve the ego well in the first half of life. They assuage the feelings of guilt and anger and sometimes lead us to remorse, which is a step forward."

"I really haven't had those feelings. I don't want to get back at anyone. Well, maybe my agent. Then there's the agency, the syndicator. I could add...no, I'm just putting on. I don't have any need for retribution. I just want to get settled with my family and on with my life."

"I do not have any illusions about that, Peter. I have sensed that your challenges, the source of your anger and suffering, are internal not external."

"I think that's true."

"Let me, if you will, diverge for a moment and talk about the idea of framework."

"I'm all ears, Padre."

"A friend of mine, Enrique, tells me I have a model for everything. My response is always of course I do. I am a social scientist. We develop models to describe society. However, Peter, models are just models unless we apply them. As much as being a scientist, I am a teacher. Teaching was the venue where I applied the models. The models became my framework for viewing the act of teaching. Are you with me?"

I said, "I'm there, Padre," surprised that he even asked. I had grown used to the patience needed to listen to the padre's roundabout thinking.

He told me that while teachers work to serve each student individually, most contact is by class. Like each student, each class has its own personality. He used two frameworks to identify and manage classes. The first was from psychologists, Jordan and Margaret Paul, who identified two paths that people in conflict take: learner or protector. The second was from VAK researchers who identified students' primary learning style as visual, auditory, or kinesthetic.

"As an artist, you are obviously a visual learner, Peter. These two rudimentary tools gave me a simplified understanding of each class and helped me decide my approach."

"That makes sense to me. I know I see the world differently than other people."

"In a similar fashion, early on I found an organizing framework for my understanding of my faith. It was in the *Cursillo* movement."

Cursillo means short course. In this case, it is a short course in Christianity, *Cursillo de Cristos*. It is a lay movement begun among Catholics. It spread to other denominations. Protestant groups call it *Walk to Emmaus* or *Tres Dios*. It is a three-day retreat divided into three themes: piety, study, and service.

"This experience gave me a framework to begin to learn about the faith in which I grew up. The Cursillo experience is an application of the term fundamentalism at its best. It is three days of love and grace. I began to learn the fundamentals of Christianity. This was many years ago, but I remain connected to it and the people in the Cursillo community.

"Once I had a grasp of the fundamentals, I began looking beyond faith itself into the realm of spirituality. I read everything I could get my hands on. Each book led me to another and another. I expressed to Mo-ma that I was reading backward, and I wished someone would give me the list. She replied that I was just reading backward in time, but I was reading forward for me. She is a wise woman. I realized that I needed a new framework. I found it at a retreat with James Finley."

Finley is a psychotherapist by profession and a modern-day mystic by countenance. He was a Trappist monk early in life, and had as a mentor Thomas Merton, the American 'big dog' in the world of Western mysticism. Finley said there are three things we need to do. Find your teaching and follow it; find your practice and practice it; and find your community and enter it.

"Finley's thought was so simple, yet extraordinarily complex. I knew it was what I was seeking. I had to define my faith, understanding of God, and relationship to God. I had to translate that into daily life and develop practices that support it. In the way that the Cursillo community supported me at an earlier time, I had to find a community of support and enter it. Christianity is a team sport."

"I have some sense for that, Padre. I hadn't identified it until just now. I am one of those who call themselves spiritual but not religious. But I can't say I really know what it means to be spiritual or how I go about being spiritual."

"You are spiritual, Peter. It is something you are, not something you do; but there are things you *can* do. One is an awareness of your place in the scheme of things."

"That's certainly crystal clear, Padre."

"I am sorry for that. What I mean is that spirituality is simply an awareness of your desire to be in the presence of the Holy. It is not something you are other than in the sense we are all spiritual beings. It is not something you do. There are things you can do to develop and enhance your awareness, knowledge, and understanding. We refer to them as practices. That is what James Finley means when he says to find your practice and practice it."

I drained the dregs of my coffee and said, "I'm with you."

"So, Peter, way back when, before I went off on that byway, we were talking about healing. When it comes to healing, I must consider the act of reconciliation because the God I know is a reconciling God. You mentioned resolution with your family. Perhaps healing is not solely a matter of finding resolution. Resolution is a step along the way, but it is often an inner development, not an interpersonal action. Finding resolution is to resolve one's thoughts, feelings, emotions, and beliefs within one's own self."

"We can partially heal ourselves through resolution, but total healing comes through the process of reconciliation. Resolution can give us release, but it is release from our own suffering. Release can be the platform from which to seek reconciliation. We find release in reconciliation with others. Ultimate release is in reconciliation with God, or whatever each of us calls his higher power.

We were getting to the nut of it now. I shook my head as though that would make things clearer. My brain was a mishmash of thoughts, feelings, emotions, and beliefs. The padre's ideas and my own thoughts challenged me. He suggested we take a break and refresh our coffee. I concurred. We stood in the kitchen and share the last cup in the pot. We stood looking out at the rain, making small talk: the rain, garden, cleaner air, and such. It was a welcome break.

We returned to our seats, and the padre said, "I needed that. Are you ready to go at it again?"

"I was, knowing the break was for me."

"In the first half of life, we tend toward simply finding resolution. In a recent poll, researchers asked the question, 'Would you rather be right or kind?' The vast majority responded right. I see this as an indictment of our society. It tells us that in general people are willing to settle for resolution, often a resolution that affirms their position. They are not seeking reconciliation. Reconciliation requires kindness, thinking about others. Healing is not about resolution. It is about reconciliation. Seeking reconciliation is the path to healing."

"That is an interesting distinction, Padre."

"These are ideas I have been working with for some time now. It is good to have someone to share them with because I am still trying to put it all together for myself."

"Let me recap my own situation. I started with seeing my father as angry and aloof. He became taciturn when JJ was killed. I moved to recognizing my own anger and the part my departure had in his feelings. As my awareness of my, anger developed, I recognized the need to figure that out. I began to see the anger as mine, but as part of my relationship with Dad. What I hear you saying about reconciliation versus resolution is that the problem is ours, not just mine. That helps."

"And therein lies the gift."

"Ah, the gift, Padre; you did it to me again."

"It is a developed skill. I am a practiced creator of cognitive dissonance."

"Cognitive dissonance?"

"It is the anxiety people experience when what they see, hear, or feel does not match their expectations, their reality. It is the concept of intellectual conflict."

I closed my eyes trying to cement that idea into my brain. I certainly was full of cognitive dissonance. The padre waited. When I said, "Okay," he continued.

"I began working with the idea after I read Jordan and Margaret Paul's book. Their work was with interpersonal conflict and how people respond as learners or protectors. My experience is that most people are protectors. The task of a teacher is to bring down the walls of protection so people can become learners. I applied it to interior conflict. Part of the art of storytelling is to create a different story or to help the listener hear an old story in a new way. To hear differently, the listener must move off the expected or what she or he already knows. That is cognitive dissonance. Most of us want to be comfortable. We are homeostatic beings. It takes some work to get us out of our comfort zone. Someone said that there is no comfort in change and no change in comfort."

"I can attest to that, Padre. I've been very uncomfortable for months, and at times you do a good job of adding to it."

"That is my gift to you."

"I'm not sure I want to thank you for that."

"No need, Peter, it is simply a necessary step. It creates the conditions for you to hear the teachers. I counted my successes as a teacher based on the times someone had reason to think differently about an idea. Now, as an *un-teacher-storyteller*, creating cognitive dissonance has become my calling." He laughed heartily at the idea.

"I understand."

"Why don't we pause, and I will make a fresh pot of coffee?"

"Good idea."

Padre Cisco went to kitchen to grind beans, and I headed to the bathroom. My mind was racing. I was needed the pause, but I didn't want to stop. I was on edge, but for the first time I saw some light. We returned to our respective chairs. Padre Cisco picked up where he left off.

"So, let me give you what I think is the next part."

"Okay."

"Just as reconciliation may grow out of resolution, forgiving is a beginning; but reconciliation is about more than forgiveness. Forgiving is about excusing, exonerating, or overlooking a wrong or an assumed wrong. It says you wronged me, but I forgive you. Reconciling another to *one's self* is to move beyond the idea that a wrong was committed in the first place."

"That's what happened to my friend Smitty."

"How so, Peter?"

Smitty was out of the country and did not get back for his nephew's wedding. When he was finally able to return, Smitty visited his brother and shared how saddened he was by not being able to attend. His brother responded, "That's okay; I forgive you." Smitty didn't want his brother's forgiveness. He wanted his empathy. Smitty felt he did nothing wrong. He didn't need forgiveness. He told me he knew what his brother meant, but it still left a hole in his heart.

"That is a classic story. If only Smitty's brother had read about Jesus and the adulteress, he might have responded differently. If you remember, it is the *He who is without sin cast the first stone* story. In that story, Jesus told the adulteress, after those who would stone her had left the scene, to go and sin no more. He did not say I forgive you, or even you are forgiven. He had compassion for her and merely indicated that she was reconciled to the community. She was to accept that and move on in the grace she received. Reconciliation is built upon an attitude of compassion."

"That is not something I was taught in Sunday school, Padre."

"There is one other piece of this, Peter. Nadia Bolz-Weber writes about the demonized death of Judas after Jesus' crucifixion."

Nadia Bolz-Weber wrote that Judas isolated himself. He did not experience God's grace because of his disconnection from the community in which he could hear it. She said that when Jesus healed someone, the healing was not complete until restoration to the community occurred. She wrote, "In the Jesus business, community is always a part of healing." The padre said that reconciliation, as healing is not an individual endeavor but one of community. He said, "I think that is one of the reasons James Finley said find your community and enter it. It is in community that we find reconciliation. When we are lost, it is to the community we are restored."

"So you are saying, Padre, that I have to do this healing piece as part of a community, but I am not part of a community."

"You are part of a family. A family is a microcosm of community."

"So I have to do it with my family."

"Is it not why you are going home?"

"Do I have a choice?"

"You have made your choice. You have come to yourself. You are the prodigal son. You get to live out one of the classic stories in the Bible. Be of good heart. It turned out really well for the lost son in the Bible story. Check out the fifteenth chapter in the book of Luke. What a trip to take. You are going to have a great time."

"I'm glad you're so enthused about it. The whole thing scares the dickens out of me."

"That's a good thing. The dickens reference comes from a contraction of devilkin in Middle English. It is a good thing to have the devilkin scared out of you."

Padre Cisco was more amused at all this than I was.

"Peter, you notice that many of my examples derive from the Christian Bible. I do not mean to Bible pound you, but Jesus' teaching is the teaching I follow. Jesus said, 'Follow me.' That is what I try to do. Christianity is the context in which I understand the world. We find wisdom in many places. I seek it in many of those places, but the place I ground myself in is the metaphoric understanding of Christianity. The Hebrew writers of the Old Testament stories and the Hebrew writers and one Gentile writer of the New Testament were wise guys. They expressed truths that have held through the ages. They are truths that can re-understand in each age and apply to daily living. That is what find your teaching and follow it means to me."

"How do I apply what you are saying to my situation, Padre? I am not a practicing Christian. For that matter, I am not a practicing anything. I am not even sure what I believe."

"Is that not what you came out here to talk about in the first place, Peter?"

"Well…uh."

"I know you were distressed, you lost your employment, you felt lost, and you wanted to regain some sense of direction. However, even as we began, did you not have a sense that there were larger questions? Is that not what keeps you driving back out here?"

"Probably."

"The first time you were here, you asked if your name is the only thing stellar about you. At one point, you said you don't know who you are anymore. While walking in the desert, we talked about identity questions. Who am I? What is it all about? Is this all there is? I said that these are among the age-old questions of mankind. Are not the questions about what you believe the fundamental questions you want to answer?"

"I guess they are."

"It is okay, Peter. We all have them. This is the true gift you received when you lost your syndication. It is a bit more complex than taking up golf and cruises; but it is a gift, the gift of adulthood. You get to choose what you believe. The challenge as an adult is to translate your beliefs into your daily living. This is apart of the second half of life. Some would say it is a double-edged sword. I do not think so. That implies a cost-benefit relationship of believing and acting. We get to, I say again, *get to* act upon our beliefs. We get to try to live our life wholly. Everything is a benefit. There is no cost. It is all a gift. Our beliefs become our motivators and our map, referring back to the map you said you no longer had."

"Give me an example, Padre."

"Sure. I believe God is not a noun. God is not a person, place, thing, or even an idea. God is greater than that. For God to be a noun, God would be containable. God is too vast for that. God is a verb. God is even more than *godness*. God is not only a god of love, creation, and reconciliation. God is action. God is *goding*. That is, God is creating, loving, and reconciling. God is a god of relationships, but to be so God must be in relationship. God exists in relationship. God is a condition of *existing* in relationship with all, and we get to be a player in that existing. We exist in God. Therefore, I am to be a loving, creating, reconciling person in relationship with all. Pretty simple."

"Hardly." I looked askance at him emphasizing my point."

"There is a bit more to my personal belief system, but that gives you an example. Life in its wholeness is about reconciliation, reconciliation to one's self and to God. It is about reconciliation, reconciliation to our family, our neighbors, and to the 'least of these.' We are restored through reconciliation. We find release and wholeness through resolution and reconciliation. Those are the three Rs of my belief system, well actually four. Now it takes a lot of reflection and reconstruction, but through release, we find redemption, even resurrection. I guess that is eight Rs."

I sat back in reflection and let out a deep sigh. "This has been a lot to take in, Padre."

"Like Mary, you can ponder all things in your heart. Is there anything else you want to add or ask?"

"There is, Padre. I would like to talk more about this, or maybe I should say listen because you have much more to share than I. Is it possible to meet in two weeks before I go back east? I can use all the guidance I can get."

"Absolutely, Peter. I enjoy our sessions. I learn so much I do not know I know. I might be even more prepared to eloquently pontificate next time. You should beware what you ask for. You might get more than you want."

"I'll risk it, Padre."

We said goodbye, and I drove home with a lot to ponder.

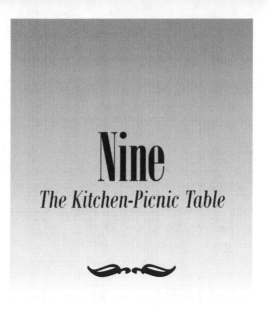

Nine

The Kitchen-Picnic Table

"Abba, give me a word."
"Compassion, my son."
"How do I learn compassion, Abba?"
"Open your heart, my son."

The two weeks passed quickly. I busied myself with trip preparations. I hadn't traveled in a while so I gave myself plenty of time. I was trying to approach the trip as routinely as possible, but it weighed on me. Gen and I talked about gifts to take, and even went shopping; but I couldn't settle on anything. I had given each of them original SoCal and Knuckles art along the way. That was always my backup gift, but it wouldn't serve this time. I wasn't sure why I thought I should take gifts. Maybe they were peace offerings.

I thought about the visits we had made. When Dad and I would have time alone, he always seemed to bring up the plant and why hadn't I been willing to work there. Why did I have to move so far away? He never understood that those very questions were the reason I left. Fortunately, we had baseball. Talk about baseball was always the saving grace.

I finished *Falling Upward*. I wanted to talk with Padre Cisco about it, but the onus of the trip captured me. I didn't feel prepared. I needed guidance. I wanted a crutch, a solution, or maybe it was resolution. Reconciliation versus resolution kept coming back to me.

Padre Cisco stood in the driveway as I approached. Hola, Pedro. Bienvenidos came the greeting. "¿Cómo es contigo? How is it with you?"

"Muy bien, gracias, y usted?"

"Muy bien, tambien."

"You are into your Spanish this morning, Padre."

"I have been reminiscing. You respond like a native."

"I know Cómo está and dónde está el baño? Those two get me by. I can greet someone, and I can ask for a bathroom." I got the darting eyes of disbelief.

Padre Cisco said, "Let's sit on the veranda. It will not be long before the mornings are too warm to sit out."

"Good idea."

We walked around the house. I went to look at the garden, and Padre Cisco went to the kitchen for coffee. The garden was flourishing. He had been harvesting. It was nearing its endpoint when the lettuce would bolt and the summer heat would begin to burn up the plants. For the first time, I noticed a pipe connected to a valve next to the windmill running to the garden. He had attached lengths of punctured hose that wound along the furrows. The irrigation would delay the eventual demise of the plants. Padre Cisco had turned over one end, beginning the preparation for the next planting.

"You've been busy, Padre."

"A farmer's work is never finished." He chuckled to himself.

We sat in the Adirondacks for a while, and I savored the coffee.

"What would you like to talk about, Peter?"

"How about my trip?"

"Your trip home? Are you ready to go?"

"Pretty much so, Padre, though I don't have the feeling of going home. I left home a long time ago. Home is where Gen and I are. Maybe I think of the house in Akron as the *homestead*. My parents aren't there anymore. Mary and her husband live there now. One positive outcome is that I am more in touch with how our kids feel now. They talk about coming to visit rather than coming home."

"You can imagine my kids trying to identify with this place. That would be a stretch."

He got up, went to the garden, and moved the hose. He watched it for a moment, turned, and fell into his story telling voice. He became animated leaving his usual quiet, measured pace behind. He switched into to his brogue.

"Andrea and I bought our only house when she became pregnant. Our meager savings went to the down payment. We had a bed and dresser, a couch, and a couple of old chairs for the living room. We had no furniture for the baby, the other bedroom, or the kitchen. We wondered aloud if we would be moving into a half-empty house." He returned to veranda and leaned against the post as though reminiscing. I saw the image of the stage manager in Thornton Wilder's play *Our Town*.

"Our folks helped us with a crib and necessities for the baby. Guests could sleep on air mattresses, but we needed a kitchen table. We had a twenty-five dollar budget and found a redwood picnic table with two benches for less than twenty dollars. It was perfect. We knew it would work for a year or so, or until we could find something more permanent.

He clutched his heart and rolled his head back. "Ah, the best laid plans. That table was still in our kitchen eighteen years later." Mimicking a painting motion, he said, "I varnished it, painted it green, later white, and eventually glued a top on it. Before that, drinks too numerous to count dripped through the slats to the floor below," fluttering his fingers in a downward motion.

With arms in wide open welcome he said, "Friends gathered there for meals, drinks, dessert, or just conversation." He reached behind himself with his face in mock agony. "They sat first on those butt-breaking benches and later on equally demanding folding chairs. The benches went to the patio. The chairs wore out, but the table endured. I did school work there. It became a picnic-kitchen-table-desk. Eventually, it, too, was exiled to the patio."

He continued in a hushed voice with the tone of nostalgia. "It was the family gathering place. Our dog, Lobo, served as a furry foot-warmer as he lay beneath it." After a pause, "That table was the altar where grace was shared and the scene for nightly discussions of a decade of school days."

"I imagine that many of us have similar kitchen table memories." I nodded in affirmation with him. "We watch TV, play games, assemble puzzles, and sit and chat. As parents, we pay our bills there or agonize over 1040s. We sit over cold coffee waiting for our children to return from first dates or first nights of driving. If our kitchen tables could talk, they could relate the joys and pains of our common memories etched into their grain." His hand caressed an imaginary table.

He folded his hands at his chest and finished in a whisper. "Nevertheless, they remain silent, and in its silence our picnic-kitchen-table-desk finally found its way to the humility of the garage sale. I miss it and all of what it reminds me."

"What a nice memory, Padre. That was fun watching you in your dramatic mode."

"It is a great memory. I am reminded of that every time I tell the story. I have read and heard some very good stories about furniture in people's lives. While I am not one to collect stuff, I do value and collect the memories of stuff. I tell that story to encourage others to do the same. Things like furniture remind us that all things can be significant."

"Thank you."

Lowering himself into his chair, he said, "Beyond that, Peter, old men just get nostalgic. I received a reminder of my age in the mail, today."

"How so?"

"I got a post card from my college fraternity titled 'Verification of Member Data.' That is just so courteous."

"I don't get it," I said scrunching up my face.

"Well, Peter, Verification of Member Data is a kind euphemism for *if you are still alive, please respond.* It was just so positive. I got a good laugh out of it."

"Did you respond?"

"Not yet. I am not sure I want them to know I am still alive. Death has its advantages. Michael Francis and I talked about this once. It reduces the solicitations for donations. You die, but no one knows it. Your social security checks continued to arrive. Your utility bills and food costs go down. You get a great backlog of magazines and catalogs to peruse. Your feelings of expectation to meet others' demands reduce. There are obviously uncounted perks in an unaccounted death. However, we decided the downside ultimately outweighed the perks." He chuckled at the very notion of it, as did I.

Once again, Padre Cisco's uncanny ability to change my frame of mind amazed me. I could arrive at his place in a state of vexation and within minutes feel lighter about my life and the world. He seemed to know how to take life seriously without taking himself seriously.

He interrupted my mental walkabout. "Tell me about growing up around your kitchen table, Peter."

"I suspect it was much as you describe it, Padre."

Our kitchen was large with a butcher-block trestle table in the center. I don't ever remember a cloth on it. I loved to run my hand over it, following the grain except for the burn marks where Dad's cigarettes had fallen from the ashtray. Whenever it happened he always told Mom, he would refinish the top some day. That day never came.

We ate in the kitchen except for holidays or if we had guests. Then we would eat in the dining room. We each had our spot, Mom and Dad at the ends, JJ on one side, and Mary and I on the other. Except for the evenings, it was always set. Dishes migrated from the sink back to the table as though life was an ongoing meal.

In the winter, we spent more time at the table playing canasta or pinochle. Mom or Dad would take turns as the fourth in pinochle. Dad liked playing cards. I told you about my episode with pinochle and my dad. JJ and I played checkers. We talked about learning chess, but we never did beyond knowing how to move the pieces.

We did our homework there. JJ never asked for help. He would help me, and we both helped Mary. We talked about school, but conversation was mostly between us kids. Mom listened in more than participated. She kept her back to us most of the time. Dad was usually out in the living room with his paper or the TV. We were under our mother's supervision more than any sort of tutelage.

Dad and Mom were quiet. There never was much between them. He was not what you would call the affectionate type.

I think he felt it was not manly. I think many men were like that back then, at least the factory workers around us. To say they were not prone to displays of endearment would be a huge understatement. They were hard men. We would hear our parents talking at night and wonder what they were saying. Mary's room was next to theirs, and we tried the glass-to-the-wall trick one time, but it didn't work.

Mom was always busying herself in the kitchen. She was rather stymied. She wasn't Edith Bunker, but I always wondered if she felt she had missed out on something by being married so young. She got teary a lot. I don't ever remember anyone asking her why. We all just took it as though that's how she was. Something would happen; she'd get teary and go to the kitchen or her room. She would return later as though nothing had happened.

"Do you remember conversation?"

"I guess there was some conversation, Padre. Mostly, it was talk about our day. There was always talk of the Indians at dinnertime. Of course during football season JJ's play and the high school football team was the primary subject. I was gangly, and my exploits on the basketball court were marginal. Basketball got some airtime. My contribution was less of note during baseball season, and the conversation veered to the majors and the Indians."

"What is your best memory from your kitchen table?"

"It was from the kitchen itself more than the table. The aroma."

Our house always smelled of cooking and baking. My mother must have cooked and baked constantly. She was a good cook and terrific baker. I loved coming in the door to the aroma of the day, and later I loved returning to it on our visits. I wondered if Mary sustains that.

"Do you anticipate anything in particular on your trip? More to the point, are you aware of expectations?"

"Now that you ask, probably because of your story, one expectation jumps out at me. It hadn't occurred to me until this moment that Mary might have replaced the table. I can hardly imagine that, though; upgrading at today's prices would be very expensive. Your question makes me realize I have pictured the house as it was, not as it might be. Mary surely has replaced the old furnishings with her own things. I remember being there, and Mom and Dad still had a TV with dials on it. Replacing that might start the ball rolling. Mary's a traditionalist, but she is of her own mind."

"Does she have a career?"

"She is a tax accountant."

My parents were in their early seventies when they moved. Dad couldn't care for Mom anymore. When that happened, Mary went back to work. She keeps books and prepares taxes. She's suited to it; she is very thorough. That's when Mary and her husband, George, moved from their apartment into the house. George was never a go-getter, and they lived very simply for many years. They never had children. They talked about adopting but didn't. She adores Alex and Morgan and laments that they are so far away. For that matter, so do Gen and I.

"When do you leave?"

"Two days."

"How much baggage are you taking?"

"Just a carry-on, though I've been trying to figure out some gifts I could take."

"That is not quite what I was asking."

I bowed my head and shaded my eyes. I laughed, smiled at the padre, and said, "Oh, that kind of baggage. I suspect I am though I'm trying not to set expectations."

Padre Cisco said, "When the lost son in the prodigal son story was returning home, I imagine he was full of all kinds of expectations about his reception. Boy was he surprised. Luke wrote in his account, "But while he was still a long way off, his father saw him and was filled with compassion for him; he ran to his son, threw his arms around him, and kissed him." His father defied all expectations; he ran to him. Men of his father's station did not run. Moreover, his father clothed him, gave him jewels, killed the fatted calf, and threw a big party."

"I am not expecting a party, or should I say I don't *anticipate* a party. My father is rather irascible."

"When was the last time you were there?"

"Six years.

Mom and Dad would visit most years. It gave them a break from the winter. Mary came a few times, and George once. The three of them came for the kids' sixteenth birthdays and graduation. They stopped coming when Mom's condition wouldn't allow it anymore. That was five years ago. They've never been to our new house. We should have made more effort to get back there, but we always seemed to be so busy.

"Six years is a long time. Perhaps things have changed."

"Not my father."

"So you do have expectations, Peter."

"I guess I do. I don't envision him as having turned over a new forest. Don't most of us become more entrenched as we age?"

"Possibly. Sometimes. Some people. However, you have changed have you not, Peter? Might not that make a difference?"

"Possibly."

"Perhaps that possibility hinges on whether you are seeking resolution or reconciliation."

"That could be, Padre."

"We must reconcile to ourselves those things that are unsettled within us. We may seek resolution, but we need to find reconciliation. In an earlier time in my life, I was driven. I worked, I pushed, I drove myself, and I drove those around me. I came up the hard way. I had to fight for what I got. I earned my stripes, and I was not about to give them up.

"I haven't ever thought of academic types as fighting for what they earned."

"I had hardline ethical stances. I was full of righteous indignation. I could be uncompromising and not very collegial. I thought that if I had to choose, it was better to do the wrong thing for the right reason than the right thing for the wrong reason. I could have been one of the respondents in that poll on right versus kind. Too many times, I chose to be right. It was the wrong choice."

"And now?"

"I only ask if it is the right thing to do. The reason is not a consideration.

"Padre, I don't even recognize that person as you when I was in school."

"I worked in an ego-driven, power-laden mix master of the lunatic center. It was not the fringe. These were the stalwarts, the Pharisees of university academia.

"My memory is that you expected a lot of us. You were demanding, but I saw it as demanding of excellence and demanding we be all we could be. Ha, I sound like an army ad. Maybe, you were the drill sergeant, but you are talking about more than that, aren't you? What changed?"

"The turning on the dime. Life changed, and I had to come to myself."

"I remember that. Your wife died."

"Yes. My life stopped, and I had to find a way to start it again. It was the first time in my life I was powerless. I could do nothing to save her. Guilt consumed me. I said that I earned my stripes. I did. I believed in the American dream. My sister, brothers, and I were poster children for the American dream."

"Excuse me, Padre. Are your brothers and sister's faith similar to yours?"

"In varying degrees, Peter. We each grew up with a strong faith. We were Catholic because our parents were, but we all have chosen to remain Catholic. My understanding of religion and faith is different from theirs, but it is rooted in the traditions of Catholicism. My faith is what got me through those times."

"Explain that, Padre."

"My acceptance of my faith is what emerged when my up-from-the-bootstraps, I'm-in-charge-of-my-own-life mentality no longer served me. Wilkie Au and Noreen Cannon write in *Urgings of the Heart,* 'Pharisaic self-righteousness not only blocks our path to God, it also robs us of compassion and solidarity with others who suffer.' I had lived a life that robbed me of compassion. I needed some basis to forgive myself."

"I don't mean to render judgment, but you seem to have done that."

"I hate to sound academic, Peter, but I read a lot. I am still the academic. Marianna Cacciatore wrote that forgiving ourselves is a way we learn compassion. She says, 'We practice on ourselves and learn to share it with others.' I had to learn to forgive myself. It was through my understanding of my faith that I found that ability. And then a miraculous thing occurred."

"A miracle?"

"Yes, a miracle. When I began to forgive myself, I began to become more forgiving of others. And behold, a second miracle occurred."

"Which was?"

"Others began to see me differently. My relationships changed. It took time. I had a lot of healing to do. I was not an overnight success. Few, if any of us, are. Like your friend Smitty, who did not need his brother's forgiveness, I did not need others' forgiveness. I needed to forgive myself, but I needed others' compassion. This hard-nosed, pile-driving Pharisee experienced others living out their faith in their understanding of my need for compassion. I began to look to my own faith in those moments. I am not speaking of my religion. I am talking about the faith I have inside my religious tradition.

"How long did that take?"

"Ten years and counting. You see, Peter, as I experienced the compassion others showed toward me, I began to experience the gifts of compassion. It is what the Apostle Paul called the fruit of the Spirit: love, joy, peace, patience, kindness, goodness, faithfulness, gentleness, and self-control. I began to develop compassion toward myself and a compassionate heart toward others. It did not come overnight. Compassion is not necessarily in our hearts in the first half of our lives. Father Jim says it has to be 'grafted onto our hearts.' Grafts need a while to take before they can begin to mature on their own. It takes time. I am learning. It is what Rilke was saying when he wrote that we live the questions into the answers."

"Okay, Padre, let's say I follow you, and I can even subscribe to what you are saying. How does it apply what I am facing?"

"Good question. I have no clue. Perhaps, you will have to decide that."

"Padre, don't do that to me."

"I am just kidding, Peter. Let me take a stab at it."

"Please. I am drowning here, Padre."

"You are not drowning, Peter. You are in the desert."

I rolled my eyes.

"I do tickle myself every other now and then. That was funny though at your expense. I apologize. Peter, I am still developing some of those fruit of the Spirit. Sometimes, six hundred years of genetic programming as a Druid just takes over. The Leprechauns in my DNA emerge to play their tricks." Padre Cisco had fallen into his brogue and paused to gather himself. He took a drink of cold coffee and resumed. "To use your metaphor, Peter, you are not drowning. Even if you were in the largest ocean, you know how to float. You are in what the mystics call a liminal space. You are between places. You are moving out of the life you have lived into the life you are living. You have experienced movement, but have not made the shift. This is normal. Movement takes time and repetitions. Shift needs the repetitions of movement.

"For such a long time, your focus has been on resolution, finding balance in your life. You have only just begun to seek reconciliation, the place where you find harmony. Give it time. Take the time to allow compassion to emerge in you. Compassion is the source of reconciliation. Maintain your focus on how you can reconcile your own life. As that develops you will see the path to reconciling relationships with those you love. That is the place to begin. That is the place you have begun, yourself and your loved ones."

"It is a challenge, Padre. We've built forty years of history on contention. I'm not sure where to start."

"You have already started. You are not trying to love your enemies. That demands an entirely different dimension of understanding. This is your family; you already love them.

Peter, you have shown yourself to be a compassionate person. Allow compassion to take over your life. Au and Cannon write, 'Personal struggles and weakness expand our capacity for compassion.' Look at others from the point of view of how they are suffering. That is what compassion is. We are compassionate when we see others from the perspective of their suffering. You are suffering in relationship to your father, you know that, but your father is also suffering in relationship to you. You likely know that as well. Focus on your father's suffering, and you will find the way."

"That is good advice, Padre. I have much to consider before I get to Akron."

"It is at most that, advice. It is barely knowledge. These are just notions I have from having too much time to think. I am not generally one to give advice, but I thought you might profit by the musings of my experiences. I hope that is true."

"I certainly hope so, too. To learn to live out of compassion is a lot to ask of a has-been professional cynic."

"Perhaps you are just a used-to-be-professional cynic. It used to bother me when people would introduce me as 'he-used-to-be.' Now, I accept it, as the context for the person they know me to be. It is not their fault. They do not know me as the person I am now. It gives me an opportunity to grow on them, perhaps grow *with* them. I much prefer it to has-been."

"I like the idea of growing with them. I think that is what I need to do."

"Peter, you are blessed by your current consciousness as an adult to be able to experience and observe your experiences. This is an act of the second half of life. I wish you well on your journeys, the one coming up and the one to come after that."

"Okay Padre, let me see if I have it here—you know, the *Reader's Digest* version?"

"Give it a go."

"Restoration has three Rs but there are other Rs as well. That makes spiritual seekers 'R-gonauts' and my story *Rocky and the R-gonauts*. I just threw that one in, Padre. Thanks for the eye rolling. I, too, will behave myself.

"Let's see, God is a god of restoration. Restoration occurs in community. God is a god of reconciliation. Man in the first half of life, that is man's ego, is a seeker of resolution. Resolution can lead to release, which may lead to seeking reconciliation. Reconciliation is a second-half-of-life endeavor. Reconciliation occurs in community, or at least jointly. Forgiveness is a first-half-of-life act. Compassion can exist in the first half of life, but it develops more often in the second half of life. In compassion, we move from resolution and forgiveness to reconciliation. In reconciliation with others, we find release, but ultimate release is in reconciliation with God. Swimming, even in circles, might not be swimming at all, but just floating in what you called liminal space. There might be a party waiting for me in Akron. Finally, I anticipate that if I search dutifully enough, *perhaps* I will meet some leprechauns and Japanese pigmies riding well-fitted bicycles. Is that it, Padre?"

"It is. You passed the test: 'A' plus. Pigmies riding bicycles, you have a good memory, Peter. Too much."

"Thank you, Padre. It's been instructional, and at times confusing or frustrating, but also fun. I *anticipate* we will have much to discuss the next time we meet."

Padre Cisco walked me to the car. As I drove toward the highway, I glanced in the mirror to see him standing there, I think watching for pigmies on bicycles riding down the lane.

INTERLUDE

Tea

*Come, let us have some tea and
continue to talk about happy things.*
~ Chaim Potok

Gen and I spent the evening after my visit to Padre Cisco talking about the trip. We talked about reconciliation, compassion, Dad and Mary. I realized I didn't need to take presents; I needed to take memories. I rummaged through boxes of old pictures, albums, and memorabilia. I found baseball cards, newspaper clippings, school programs, ribbons, and the like. I picked out some pictures I thought Mary or my parents might not have. I printed recent photos of the kids. Passing my phone around wouldn't cut it with Dad. I thought about taking a connection for their TV but decided it likely wouldn't be new enough. I found enough to create that second piece of baggage, albeit a positive one.

We talked at length about what Mom, Dad, and Mary experienced after JJ's death, the effect of my leaving home, and how my parents' lives had changed with Mom's illness. We hashed out shouldas, wouldas, and couldas. We discussed our long absence from them and my part in our tension.

I called Mary one more time to tell her I was on my way. She said she would pick me up, but I'd rented a car. I told Mary I didn't want to impose on her, but what I really wanted was the ability to escape my circumstances. Overall, I was more ready when Gen drove me to the airport. Perhaps I was coming to myself, though I had little doubt of the angst I would face during the flight there. I remembered one of my oil studio profs at ASU repeatedly saying, "Argue your limitations, and they are yours." I had disregarded that admonition in this case.

I arrived in Akron early in the afternoon. I stepped out of the terminal surprised by how warm it was. I sent a text to Gen, letting her know I'd made it and I loved her. I received a heart emoticon in response. She was obviously busy. I made a mental note to call her later. When I drove up to Mary's house, I had an odd feeling I was in the wrong place. I discarded the thought, drew a deep breath, walked up the steps onto the front porch, and rang the bell tolling my moment of truth.

"Rocky's here," I heard Mary call as the door opened. She stepped onto the porch, pulled me to her with my shoulder bag dangling from my elbow, and wrapped me up in a warm hug. She had lost weight and cut her hair, but not died it allowing gray strands to peak out among the brown. Fortunately, Mary inherited Mom's genes, and she is of average height. She was dressed stylishly in beige slacks and a light blue blouse. The color complemented her eyes. In recent years when I had seen her, she had taken on the countenance of our mother. Now, she showed the effects of having returned to professional life. "Oh Rocky, how good to see you. Look at you; you're fit. You're tan. You look like a movie star. Welcome, welcome. George, Rocky's here."

George came to the doorway, stepped across the threshold, said, "Welcome, Rocky," and retreated to the entry. George is a man of soft features. His round face shows none of the ravages of life for his age. His stomach is round, and his handshake is loose.

Mary said, "Come in, please, come in." My fears for the first leg of my journey melted through the cracks in the floor.

I stepped into the living room. I would have thought I was in the wrong house except for the aroma of apple pie. Mary had transformed the place. Not only had she changed the furniture, but the colors, the wallpaper, and the door were as well. Mary had swapped the door and a window to get the door out of the middle of the room. It no longer cut the room in half. *She certainly knows how to work with what she has and obviously can stretch a dollar.*

"Have you eaten? They never feed you on planes, anymore."

I knew better than to eat on the way. Feeding guests was mandatory in the culture there. The city probably had it written into the code. *"Come in, sit down, eat, and we'll talk in that order, or the fine shall be…"* "No, I haven't, Mary. I came straight here."

"Good, come, sit; we'll have a bite to eat. You must be famished."

I love the predictability of it all. We went into the kitchen, and I realized I wasn't a guest. The kitchen had a new floor, cabinet tops, appliances, and fixtures. It was beautiful and more functional. Best of all, the table was the centerpiece. It was unchanged except the cigarette burns were gone.

"What's wrong, Rocky?" Mary asked.

"Not a single thing, Mary. It's beautiful. You have done an extraordinary job redoing the house. I am impressed. I didn't know this was one of your talents. The kitchen is fantastic with the granite tops and hardwood floor. I love the commercial stove look with the hood. And, Sis, I'm so glad you kept the table."

"As to my talent, there's a lot on the web now, and I couldn't part with the table. It has too many memories in it. You can have it someday to give to Alex or Morgan. I don't have anyone else to give it to, and I couldn't sell it."

I wanted to tell her that they might not want it. I wanted to say that they were struggling enough with us having moved and replaced some of our furniture. Somehow, I knew better. That was a first.

We sat down to eat. There were three places set, two on one side and one on the other. Mary told me that she couldn't sit at the ends. The end seats were for Mom and Dad. I appreciated the tenderness in her decision.

"The soup okay, Rocky?"

"It's wonderful, Mary, and I haven't had bread like this since I left home."

"I don't bake every day the way Mom did, but I knew you were coming. It gave me an excuse. Don't you be expecting this every day now, George." She darted a glance at George. Returning to me, she said, "I have to be careful not to spoil him too much," with an emphasis on the too. "We'll have some pie, and then you can take a rest. I made up your old room. Afterward, we can go out to Creekside and see Mom and Dad. They will have had their nap. Then we can go to the dining room for dinner. They will want to show you off to the residents. You can ride with us and save the miles on the rental. It's not far. You'll know the way, if you want to drive out on your own tomorrow. You can decide then. As Sarah Young says, we don't need to rehearse tomorrow's problems."

I had no idea who Sarah Young was, but I should have known Mary would have everything organized. The pie was terrific. Had I not known Mary had baked it, I would have thought it was Mom's pie. It was an unexpected treat and a thoughtful gift. She had killed the fatted calf. I headed up to my room to unpack and lay down wondering if it was the same as it was when I was a kid. I was relieved to find she had refurnished it along with the rest of the house. I think I was asleep before my head hit the pillow. I awakened to Mary's call from the bottom of the stairs that it was time to leave. My mind hit on a memory of visiting my grandmother in a convalescent home, and a foreboding rose in me. I was seven or eight. I remember opening the door and the combined odors of Lysol and urine overwhelmed me. I didn't want to go in. I hoped Mary had found something better for Mom and Dad.

* * *

We approached Creekside Retirement Community through a winding, tree-lined lane. The Tudor-style buildings were set behind a sprawling lawn reaching to an amphitheater of maples, oaks, and pines. I could hear the creek when we got out of the car. Mom and Dad couldn't have asked to have a more beautiful place to retire.

We entered a large lobby to the sound of classical music. I saw a high school-aged girl at a baby grand piano. The sight dispelled my fears. We registered at the front desk, passed through the lobby and into a large sunroom. Mary took me on a quick tour of the facilities. George sat in the lounge. We peeked into the dining room, passed a beauty salon, a Wells Fargo bank branch, and gift shop. She showed me the library, exercise room, and game room. The place was like a miniature town. We passed back through the sunroom, and George got up and fell in behind us. We turned down a hallway to our parents' apartment. Mary tapped lightly and opened the door announcing us as she entered. She spared me from the solitary ringing the bell, standing in the hallway awkwardness. *Eighty percent of life is just showing up.* The thought reminded me that I needed to be present to fulfill the other twenty percent.

"Rocky," I heard my mother call out. I stepped through the doorway with George trailing to see Mom sitting in her old chair. Dad was next to her in his favorite. It hadn't occurred to me that Mary had all new furniture because Mom and Dad had taken theirs with them. Mom looked frail. She was noticeably shaking. The Parkinson's was taking its toll on her. She was a lesser imitation of a once robust woman. A walker stood before her, and Mary hastened to help her get up. I went to greet her. She stood, and I hugged her as she held onto the walker. Dad stood with some effort, reached out to take my hand, and said, "Hello, Rocky, welcome to our humble abode" as though he had practiced his lines. He held onto my hand as he lowered himself into his chair. It was the most intimate moment I'd had with Dad in years. He looked smaller, also, though his middle had grown. I thought the food here must agree with him. He showed the effects of having worked a physical job for many years.

Mom said, "Sit, Rocky, Mary. You, too, George, sit please. Tea anyone? Mary, I made some iced tea. Would you get some for everyone? Rocky, you want sugar, lemon?"

"Lemon, Mom, that would be nice."

"There are cookies, too, Mary. I made Snicker doodles; I know they're your favorite, Rocky. Actually, Mary did most of the work. I'm not so handy in the kitchen anymore."

I sensed George stirring in the seat at the other end of the sofa. I couldn't remember the last time I'd had Snicker doodles.

I imagined Mom had also instructed the cook not to serve ham loaf because fifty years ago I turned up my nose to it at a neighbor's house. Mom was embarrassed. I got an earful from her, one of the few times she corrected one of us directly. She left that role to Dad.

"How are the kids?"

"They're great, Mom. Busy, living the college life, and all that living in the Bay area provides."

"I thought they were at USC. It's in Los Angeles, isn't it?"

"They were there for undergraduate studies. They are in graduate school now. Alex is studying law at Stanford, and Morgan is in med school at Cal Berkeley. They've talked about coming out before fall semester."

"I'd love to see them."

"Maybe we could all come this fall over one of the holidays."

"Oh, that's too much to expect of Gen and the kids. They're so busy. It's too expensive. They don't want to spend their holiday with old folks like us." Changing the subject, she asked, "Did you bring pictures?"

"I did, Mom. I left them at the house." I couldn't quite call it Mary's house, and certainly not Mary and George's, in front of Mom and Dad.

"Did you have a nice flight?"

"Yes, Mom. It was clear. I got a great view of Akron. It sure has grown."

"I suspect it has," Dad chimed in, his intention clear…at least to me, thinking he was referring to how long it had been since I visited. "Well, Rocky, what are you doing with yourself? Are you retired?" Dad was not one to beat around the bush. He was finished with the social pleasantries.

"I have been busy, Dad. I'm trying some new things in the studio. I've read a lot, and I'm figuring out what my next step is." I knew better than to mention Padre Cisco, and certainly not that he was Catholic. That would raise some hackles.

"You'd have your thirty in if you'd gone into the plant. Heck, more like forty. You'd have a tidy sum retiring as a foreman or shift manager."

"That's the truth, Dad. You've got that right." I hoped to take the wind out of his sails. "It certainly worked out well for *you*," I said, which was the truth.

"With a college degree and all, you might've been the plant manager. That would've been something. My son, the plant manager."

Oh my word, he had a dream. It wasn't just security he wanted for me. It wasn't just to have me follow in his footsteps. It wasn't even a small dream. He had big dreams. He had aspirations for me. I never knew. I never even imagined. "That really would've been something, Dad. Though, I'm not sure I would've been very good at it."

"You could do anything you set your mind to, Rocky. You weren't like JJ." My antennae went on alert. "Things came easy for JJ. You had to work at things, and you did. When you set your mind on something you were going to do it."

Wow, that's something else I never expected to hear. This is a different perspective. "Well, Dad, I guess that was good and bad. I wasn't too good at listening to anyone else."

"Ah, that's all in the past. So, what do you think of what Mary's done with house? She's a regular Martha Stewart, eh?"

"I am impressed. She's done wonders with the place." I was surprised Dad had embraced the changes. I thought he would've wanted to hold onto old memories of it. "How long did it take you, Mary?" Like Dad, I wanted to move the conversation off my circumstances.

Obligingly, she gave us a step-by-step account of the process of renovation. By the time she was finished clearing the glasses and plates, Mom said we should start moving to the dining room. "Start moving to" was an apt phrase because it took quite an effort for her and even Dad to get going. Mary knew the drill and helped Mom get a sweater on and "pack" her walker. Dad pulled a three-pronged, aluminum cane from behind the chair. The short walk we made from the lobby took much longer on our return.

The dining room was nearly half full when we arrived. Mom and Dad made numerous stops to introduce me to residents, who were all very pleased to meet me. Others enacted the scene in reverse as they arrived and made their way past my parents' table. It was a procession of walkers, canes, and wheel chairs in the measured movements of people who seemed to take their status in good-natured resignation. I wondered if the environment had affected Dad's attitude toward life. He seemed different from the times I'd seen him over previous years.

The dinner was nice. Except for George, we made small talk dominated by the success of the Cleveland Indians that spring. Mom and Dad executed their deliberate passage back to the apartment with Mary in the mother hen role. George and I followed. With Mom and Dad reseated, Mary said that we should go so they could rest. I told them I would be out the next day. Mom said, "Come for lunch. Saturday is hamburger day. You like hamburgers." I said I would. Dad told me the Indians would be on TV and suggested we could watch the game. I leaned over and hugged Mom, shook hands with Dad, told him the game was a great idea, and we made our leave.

When we got back to the house, I told Mary I wanted to call Gen. I went to my room and sat thinking for a few minutes. I made the call and filled her in on the day's events. She told me about her day, and we hung up. I didn't realize until I talked to her how tired I was. I never made it back downstairs to talk with Mary.

* * *

I took my small cache of pictures and mementos with me when I returned to our parents. I was glad I'd brought them. They were a crutch. The sunroom was set up for lunch. Mom and Dad were coming down the hallway when I arrived, and I turned and walked with them. They had a schedule based on their limitations, but I wondered if Dad wanted to demonstrate that they retained a measure of independence.

We sat down at tables of eight. The folks at our table greeted me warmly, and I received smiles, nods, and waves from residents at other tables. I felt like that special toy my parents brought to school for show and tell. The sense of community was evident even though it suffered regular attrition. The waiter took drink orders. Mom and Dad ordered hot tea, and I followed suit. This trip was turning out to be full of "firsts." The hamburgers were thin but tasty; the fries appeared baked. I was not among a group of hearty eaters. They may not have made a big dent in the main course, but they devoured the apple cobbler.

Mom asked if I had brought the pictures, and the kids were passed around the circle to exclamations of "She's so beautiful," "Isn't he handsome?" "They must be twins," and "You must be a proud father." I was, and I am. Mom asked, "Did you say Alex is in law school and Morgan med school?" obviously leading the witness. I gave my dutiful, embellished affirmative describing their achievements. Dad in his typical fashion added, "Well, they must be smarter than their dad" to my mother's chagrin and appropriate groans from the others. Slowly, the residents, some with assistance but most on their own, began their trek back to their rooms. We were the last to leave the table.

"The game will be on soon, Rocky. You staying for that?"

"Of course, Dad. I don't want to miss a chance to watch a game with you. It's been a long time. Too bad we can't be at the park. It's a beautiful day for a game. A couple of beers and a dog, it would be like old times."

"The doctors don't let me drink beer anymore. It's one of the prices of high blood sugar. They don't let me have a lot of things. I get one cup of coffee a day. Try to keep fresh coffee around at that pace. I'm stuck with instant. In a whisper he said, "Don't tell your mother, but every now and then I get a chance to sneak an adult beverage. Some of the men have connections on the outside."

"I could work that out for you before I go, Dad. I could slip a couple of cans into the back of the fridge."

"That's a picture isn't it, connections on the outside? You could draw that into one your comic strips, a bunch of old codgers in the county home bootlegging in some hooch."

"Yeah, drinking boiler makers, and placing bets with their bookies. That could be fun." He wasn't far off. An idea stirred in my head. "Never think crazy out loud to an artist, Dad. It's where we live." It was the first we laughed together in a long while.

"What are you boys gabbing about?"

"Oh, nothing, Mother. We're just making small talk."

We arrived at their apartment. I asked for the key and learned they didn't lock their door. Dad said, "The place is secure. We don't have anything left to steal except for photos, your drawings, and the TV, and it's too old for the thieves to sell."

I hadn't noticed, but above the sofa next to the family photos were two framed originals of my strips.

We looked at the pictures I'd brought. I got out the clippings from Dad's ball-playing days. They enjoyed perusing the past. After about thirty minutes, Mom said she was tired and was going to lie down. I asked her if she wanted my help. She declined, saying she could manage. *Manage without me since I'm not there most of the time, anyway.* The shadows were knocking at the door. *Get hold of yourself, Rocky. There's no reason to think she implied that. It's not her nature. She probably just wants to give you some time with Dad.* I told her to enjoy her rest and I would be there when she awakened. I sat down in her chair next to Dad, and he turned the TV on to the pregame show.

"Rocky, there's some iced tea in the kitchen. Would you pour some?"

Dad said, "No sugar," as he motioned with his index finger and thumb close together.

I brought the drinks with the sugar and sat back down. Al Pawlowski, announcer for "Indians Live," was talking about the day's matchup with the Orioles. The Indians were in second place in the division. Dad was optimistic.

"They lost last night, but Danny Salazar is starting today. He's been pitching well. It should be a good game."

"Yeah, Dad, I've been watching the standings. They're playing some ball. The D-backs are off to a tough start and already have been hit with injuries."

"I don't follow the western teams much, too late."

"I'm with you on that. Even in Arizona, it's too late for me sometimes." The game was about to start, and Matt Underwood and Rick Manning had taken over the broadcast. "Those two have been calling Indians' games for a while. Who was the announcer when I was a kid?"

"The were a bunch of them, Herb Score, Ken Coleman, Bob Neal, and Harry Jones among them. Rocky Colavito took some turns in the booth. Ken Coleman was good. Herb Score understood the game, and he sure could tell what was going on with the pitchers. That's when guys knew how to call a game. These guys, today, think they have to talk all the time. Mostly, they just tell what we are watching. They must think we spend all our time in the bathroom and don't know what's going on. Well, now that has some truth to it." He laughed at himself. "Vin Scully is the only one who still calls a game right."

"I heard this is his last year."

"That's too bad. He's called the Dodgers games more than half a century. Clear back to Brooklyn. We all get old, too old, I guess." The national anthem finished, and the Indians took the field. "At least they still sing The Star-Spangled Banner. I thought they might even replace it. We all get replaced sometime, Rocky."

"What are your favorite baseball memories, Dad?"

"I remember Colavito's slam, though that was radio. You know, Rocky, he was born the same year I was. He's still alive. There's sure a bunch of them that aren't."

We sat for a while, and I turned to ask something else, but he had fallen asleep. We weren't out of the first inning. *What now?* This wasn't going quite like I expected, but then again I really didn't have any idea what to expect. From conversations with Padre Cisco, I wasn't sure I should be expecting anything. Dad was talking, but everything had a ring of despondency to it. *Maybe that just comes with age.* It wasn't long before I fell asleep.

I awakened to Mom's rustling in the kitchen. It was the bottom of the fourth, and the Indians were ahead six to nothing. Ubaldo Jiminez, the Orioles' starter had been replaced. I didn't recognize the reliever. I'd slept for over an hour. Dad was still dozing. I muted the TV, stood, and called out to Mom so I wouldn't startle her. I went to the kitchen, put my arm around her shoulder, and gave her a kiss. I sensed the tears welling in her. She just stood there for a moment. Then she said, "Come sit down. Would you like your tea freshened?"

"Yes, Mom, I'll get it. You want some?"

"Please, plain."

I hovered as she moved to her chair. I got the tea and returned. I sat on the sofa across from her. I thought about times in the kitchen we had our backs to each other. Here she was right in front of me, and there was barely anything left of her.

"Did you and your dad have a nice chat, Rocky?"

"Yes, Mom. It was good to talk baseball again."

"He still likes his baseball."

"He seems sad, Mom."

"That may just be age, but I think he worries about me. My illness has been hard on him, maybe harder than on me. I think if he could trade places with me, he would. Then again, he'd just worry about being a burden on me."

Dad began to rouse. "I must have fallen asleep. Is Rocky still here, Mother?"

"I'm right here, Dad."

"Good. I thought you might have left."

"The game's still going, Dad. The Indians are taking care of business. I will need to go soon, though. I told Mary I'd take her to the store. George has the car, and I have an errand to run. I'll stop back tomorrow before I leave. I have a noon flight. I can come by on my way to the airport. It would be about nine or so, if that would be alright."

"That would be nice, Rocky," Mom said.

We talked a while longer, and I left with reminders to come back tomorrow. I wanted to stay longer. I think Mom and

Dad wanted me to stay, but they seemed to have reached their endurance level. I knew it was time to leave, and I did have an errand to run. An idea had risen in my consciousness. When I got to the car, I Googled Michaels' arts and crafts stores to find one close to Cedar and Broadway near where Mary lived. There was none. The closest was in Cayahoga Falls, but that was just five or six miles away. I followed the directions to OH-59 and found the store on Howe Avenue. I made my purchases and followed the same route back to Mary's house. I picked her up, and she directed me to the supermarket.

I helped Mary unload and unpack groceries and returned to the car to get my supplies. I usually carry at least a sketchpad when I travel, but didn't think I'd need one on this trip. I set my parcel on the kitchen table opposite the place settings and asked Mary if I could set up there.

"Sure, Rocky," came the reply. "What are you going to do?"

"I have an idea for a sketch for Dad. I think he will get a kick out of it."

"What is it?"

"Give me a chance to work it out, and I'll show you."

I set about peeling cellophane and shrink-wrap from pencils and pens and got the pad, gum erasers, and such out. I set the good paper, the mat board, and frame aside. Mary busied herself preparing dinner. I sat down and began to sketch. We worked at our respective tasks in the silent comfort of each other's presence. I did concept drawings blocking out the space with basic shapes; and I drew large caricatures trying to get ideas for portraying old men. I was just settling in to an idea when Mary spoke.

"Rocky?"

"Uh huh."

"What's your take on Mom and Dad?"

"I can't say I was shocked, Sis, but I was surprised by the degree of their decline. There's barely anything left to Mom. I didn't know Dad was using a cane."

"You couldn't have."

"I know."

It was out, stated plainly and bluntly without the embellishment of judgment. She had to say it, and she had to hear my acknowledgement. Mary pulled a "Mom" and turned back to her preparations. I returned to my drawing, though my pencil had no mind of its own and sat waiting for me to move it.

"Sis?"

"Yes, Rocky?" came the reply without a change in posture.

"Dad does seem different."

Mary put down her knife, wiped her hands on her apron, turned off the stove, and came over to the table. She turned the chair to face me, sat down, and folded her hands onto her lap. "How so?"

"It's a combination of things. He's frail, yes, but it is more than that. He seems to have mellowed. He still makes those acerbic remarks, but they are different, friendlier, sort of."

"Maybe it isn't Dad that's different; maybe it is you."

"Could be, Sis, but there is a sense of resignation about him. Mom says that he's just worried about her."

"Sure, he's worried about her, Rocky. He's worried about himself, as well. I'm not sure he tells us all that is going on with him."

"His comment to everything we talked about was about being replaced. He said it about ball players, announcers, even the National Anthem—everything but himself, but I think that was the implication. His voice had sadness in it. Do you think he worries about dying?"

"I think he worries about you."

"Me? Why would he worry about me?"

"You know the answer to that. Come on, Rocky. Why did you finally make this trip?"

That was a question I didn't want to answer. "You seem to have the answer. You tell me." I was sure Mary could hear the defensiveness in my voice. I could.

"It isn't important whether or not I know the answer, only that you do."

"You're not letting me off the hook here, are you, Sis?"

"Nope."

I sat. She waited. It was like a game of emotional chicken. Who was going to flinch first? I knew the answer to that question, as well. "I felt the need to square things with Dad."

"Well, God bless you, Rocky. Now you know how Dad feels. Now you know what's bothering him. He worries about you. He wanted to protect you the way you wanted to protect your children. Your eyes widen? Rocky, Gen and I talk. Haven't you ever figured that out? Women talk. We've talked on and off for years."

"Well, I know there's no statute of limitation on a woman's memory."

Mary laughed but said, "There's no statute of limitation on your Dad's memory, either. He knows who he was. He knows he can't go back and change it. He needs to know he didn't fail as a father. Maybe more so he needs to know he hasn't failed *you* as a father. Remember Harry Chapin's 'Cat's in the Cradle' lyrics? 'I'm gonna be like you, Dad.' I don't want to sound harsh, Rocky, but the two of you have lived that song. That's your reality. I think Dad's biggest worry is that he's running out of time to, as you said, square things with you."

"What can I do, Sis?"

"You're doing it, Rocky. Just keep doing it."

"Wow!

"I better finish dinner or we won't have anything to eat. George never misses a meal."

I stood, took Mary in my arms, and hugged her for as long as I could. I whispered in her ear, "Thank you, Sis. Thank you for your honesty and directness. Thank you for being the woman you are." She kissed me on the cheek and returned to the sink. I virtually slumped back into my chair. I was spent. I couldn't even think about drawing.

After dinner, I helped Mary clear the table. She went about readying for the next meal. I went back to drawing, and George went to the TV. I relished her presence. I hadn't realized how much I missed her. I enjoyed just being there in the kitchen together. Two hours later, I finished the strip. I had a sense of satisfaction, but more than that, I felt joy. It was my first completed piece in months. I had drawn in hours what usually would take days. I realized my motivation focused more on my purpose than on the precision of my drawing. At the same time, I was satisfied with the quality of the art. I wondered about the implications of what I just experienced. I mounted it on the mat board and framed it. I titled it *Geezers* and subtitled it *First and Only Edition*. At the bottom I wrote *1/1 ~ Prepared Especially for John Stellar, Sr. by Rocky Stellar*. Mary had found enough to do to remain in the kitchen. I called her over to share it.

I explained its origin and the sign Riverside Geezer's Health Club. I had men at a table drinking shots and calling out their bets to a man on the phone with a bookie. I added members explaining to a newcomer that he had "connections on the outside" to some hot senior babes. Mary was thrilled and couldn't gush enough. She said that she was proud of me and that it would make Dad very happy. We hugged, said goodnight, and I went upstairs to call Gen.

* * *

Mary made a full breakfast and a pot of coffee for my benefit. She insisted I eat, reminding me that I wouldn't get anything on the plane. She asked if she could package my art supplies. I asked if I could leave them there for my next visit. She smiled at the thought and said, "I will store them in your old room." On the porch, we hugged our goodbyes with her saying, "Just keep doing it, Rocky. You don't have to always come back. Just call. Keep contact. Be present in their lives. It won't be long." *Be present in their lives.* I thought she must be talking to Padre Cisco as well as Gen. Her last statement had an ominous sound to it. I think I read more into it than she meant.

I went by Creekside and gave Dad the strip. Mary was right; he did appreciate it. "This is a riot, Rocky." Turning to Mom, he asked, "Where can we hang it? Oh, never mind. That will have to wait until the guys see this. It'll crack 'em up. I have to tell you, Rocky; your mind does work differently. What a wonderful surprise. Thank you, son."

"You are welcome, Dad. It's the most fun I have drawing in years. It was that off-the-cuff work like years ago when I was doing caricatures."

We drank more tea and spent an hour talking about Gen and the kids, work ideas, and baseball. Dad held on to Geezers the entire time. I wasn't ready to go when I stood. I hugged Mom and told her I loved her. She returned the sentiment and reminded me not to stay away so long. I told them I would try to get back with Gen and the kids. Dad walked me to the door. We shook hands, and he put his arm on my shoulder. "Thanks,

Son. You have no idea." He started to say more, but his speech faltered. We stood there embracing each other and the moment. Finally, he added, "Travel safely. Give our best to Gen and the kids. Tell them we love them." After another pause he said, "And I love you, Son."

I leaned into him and patted his back. "I love you, too, Dad." I waved to Mom. She smiled through the tears. I called out my love and stepped into the hallway. At the end of hall, I looked back. I saw Dad standing there with his cane in one hand and the strip in the other. I waved. Fumbling with his cane, he waved back. I turned the corner. I was heading home, but I was leaving home.

Summer

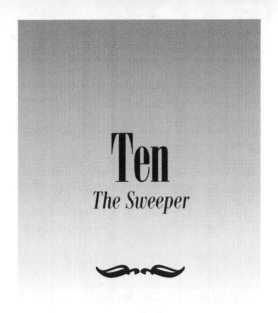

Ten

The Sweeper

"Abba, give me a word."
"Practice, my son."
"How do I learn to practice, Abba?"
"By practicing, my son."

I exited the concourse, passing the last security guard, and saw her. Gen will drop me curbside but won't wait in the cell lot to pick me up at the curb. She will abide with the "peck and fly" kiss at my departure, but like Baroness von Blixen, she says she is better at hello.

She wrapped her arms around me and kissed me as if I had been gone on the Baron's safari. I was Odysseus returning to Ithaca. I left home to come home, my arrival celebrated with hugs punctuated with a pinch.

"I'm glad you went. I'm proud of you, Rocky. You have been carrying a lot."

"I'm anxious to talk with the padre. There's a lot to discuss."

"Well, thanks a lot, Rocky! I thought you might have a lot to talk about with me. I thought we might have a lot more to do than talk."

"Gen, I'm sorry. I didn't mean it that way. I grimaced and hung my head. Yours is the much more alluring offer."

We walked arm in arm to the car where she had water rather than coffee for me. I showed her the photos of Mom and Dad and the picture I had taken of the strip. My parents' decline startled her, and she was as appreciative of the strip as Mary was. She fell silent as she navigated the exit from the airport for the twenty-minute drive home. We turned off Tucson Boulevard onto Valencia Road. Without taking her eyes from the road she said, "So, Rocky?"

"So, Gen?"

"How do you feel?"

"I'm tired. It was a long trip in a short time."

"That's nice to know. It is not what I am asking. How you feel about the trip."

"Oh! Why didn't you just ask me that? Why can't a woman be more like a man?"

"Fortunately, we are not."

"Okay. I worried much more than necessary. I have such a sense of relief. I wonder if that is the 'release' Padre Cisco talks about."

"That would be a good question to ask him."

"I don't know if what I experienced was reconciliation. As much happened in what was not said as in what was. It was curious. It was as though things that happened in the past didn't matter. It isn't part of who we are now. Mary was so gracious, so welcoming. George was George, but that was to be expected."

"Those two have an unusual relationship, or maybe it isn't that unusual. I have never understood why Mary married him. I guess it's not my place to question. People probably wonder why I married you."

"Thanks, Gen; I thought my arrival would remind you why you married me. I guess the grand homecoming is over before it got started."

"Rocky, every day is homecoming with you."

"You're redeeming yourself, Gen."

"So, tell me. Why did you marry me?"

"Is that one of those 'Does this dress make my butt look big' questions?"

"You're testing me, Rocky."

"Well?"

"Not at all, but you should know better."

"Then I'll tell you, Mrs. Stellar. I know exactly why I married you."

"Go on. I need a little more romancing."

"You know the restaurant scene in *As Good As It Gets* where Jack Nicholson tries to pay Helen Hunt a compliment, and she doesn't get it?"

"I think so. Maybe. Keep going."

"He fumbles around in his wacky way then finally says, 'You make me want to be a better man.' Well, Genevieve Stellar, you make me want to be a better man."

"Ah, Rocky, that may be the nicest thing anyone has ever said to me."

"That's what Helen Hunt said."

"Okay, you, also, are redeemed."

We arrived home, went to kitchen, and opened a lite beer and ale. We sat at the table across from each other. Gen put her elbows on the table, laced her fingers, and rested her chin on her thumbs. She said, "Go back to Mary and George."

Mimicking her pose, I said, "Just Mary; George wasn't part of this."

"That's redundant, and I'm being serious, Rocky."

"Even noting that is redundant. Okay, I'll be serious. I sat back, and took a drink. "So!" adding a parting salvo. Gen's eyes darted upward. I said, "Back to Mary."

"Thank you."

"This sounds like a little thing, but it stands out as a pivotal moment. It rather represents the whole weekend encounter. Mary had a moment when she said her piece, but it was as though that was all that she needed. It was three words. Think of that. She expressed her feelings in three words."

"And?"

"When I said I didn't know Dad was using a cane, she chided, 'You couldn't have.'"

"That could mean a lot of things, Rocky. It doesn't necessarily mean she was irked."

"It was the context, her tone, and her body language. I guess you had to be there."

"Okay."

"She said, 'You couldn't have.' I replied, 'I know.' The air was clear. It was over. I don't mean set aside, or swept under the rug. It was just over. We moved on."

"Just like that?"

"Just like that. Afterward, she came and sat down. She spoke of my relationship with Dad in such a matter-of-fact way. She understood it all. It was as though she had been taking lessons from Padre Cisco for years."

"Yes, I think he has been slipping in side trips to Akron between your meetings."

"You love to do that, don't you?"

"Just at the right moment. It's a gift."

"Thanks, Genevieve."

"You're welcome, Peter, but seriously, Rocky, Mary's honesty was a gift. She loves you and cares about you enough to be honest with you. She told you what you needed to hear, and it sounds as though she spoke in a way you could hear it."

"You're right. The little conversation I had with Dad was like that as well. We just came together in the same place at the same time. The words were almost secondary. I held onto his hand as he sat back down. He put his hand on my shoulder. We embraced. I can't remember the last time we did that. He said, 'I love you, Son,' He said, 'Son,' not Rocky. He's never called me Son before. That was huge, and I told him, 'I love you, Dad.' Those were words, huge words, but most of it was something else."

"I'm so happy for you, Rocky."

"I am, also. I think I am beginning to understand what Padre Cisco means when he speaks of 'presence.' I know I lost my presence, when I first saw you and my mind drifted to wanting to talk with the padre."

"Oh, you were just feeling the excitement of your trip."

"Perhaps."

"So, where do you go from here?"

"Good question. Where do I go from here? To see Padre Cisco of course."

"Rocky! Now *you're* doing it."

"I know. It's a gift."

"Touché."

"One thing the trip made me aware of is how out of touch I am with people. I've blamed Morgan and Alex, my Dad and even Smitty for not calling, but it has been as much me as them. I need to, or actually, I should say, I want to fix that, particularly with Morgan. I have to become more proactive."

"That's quite and admission, Rocky."

"It is. I know. Maybe good might come out of this morass I got into."

"I have no doubt about that. You are a good man, Rocky, and when good men act, good things happen."

We talked about what I might do next, and we talked about the demands of Gen's next few workweeks. We discussed the possibility of the family going back to Akron over fall break.

We talked until more pressing concerns captured our attention.

* * *

I awakened to the aroma of fresh coffee. While I appreciate others' affinity for tea, I was glad to be back on a coffee diet. Gen was already up and brought a cup. We lay on the bed and talked.

It was Memorial Day. We took the day off. I thought I would need the rest, and I was right. We drank the coffee and went out for a run. I needed to burn off the stress. Morning in the desert summer is the most hospitable time of the day. It was still in the mid-sixties. It is one of the reasons we moved to Tucson. At more than a thousand feet higher than Phoenix, the difference in temperatures is remarkable. We did an out and back run. We started and finished together, but Gen, running much faster, nearly doubled my distance. We stopped at a bakery on the return leg and got a bagel and cinnamon roll. The bagel wasn't for me. We got back, showered, and went to the patio.

I said, "That was a good run. I needed it."

"Six months ago you wouldn't have been saying that."

"True, but six months ago I wouldn't be saying many of the things I say today. I meant to tell you about Mary and how different she seems. I told you how good she looks, but she has bearing about her that is different. I don't mean pushy. It's more what Padre Cisco would refer to as presence. She seems to go about what she knows needs to be done without regard to others' opinion, and certainly not George's."

The conversation meandered for another hour; then we stopped to take care of some chores. We wanted to get them done early so we could go out to lunch and see a movie.

I waited until the next day to call Padre Cisco. I was anxious to see him, but our schedules didn't quite jibe. It would be three weeks before we could meet. I called Alex and Morgan, got their voice mails, and left messages. Later, I received text messages from both of them saying they would call. Neither did,

I spent time trying out ideas for comic strips. I was encouraged that I was at least thinking in terms of producing a new strip. I perused Amazon for books I had heard Padre Cisco mention. I felt reading would help me get up to speed. I certainly had the time. I downloaded books by Lawrence Kushner, Wilkie and Noreen Au, and Nadia Bolz-Webber. I found *Tattoos on the Heart* by Father Greg Boyle, and it cried out *buy me*. The authors represented a cross section of roles and personalities. They included a New England rabbi; a former priest and former nun who married each other; a tatted-out Lutheran pastor who could out swear the saltiest of sailors; and a priest who works with gang bangers. I thought if publishers were willing to publish these people, they must have something to say that I needed to hear. I could see the strip: "A priest, a rabbi, and pastor go in to a retirement home..." Dad would get a kick out of that.

The summer was upon us by the time I drove out to Padre Cisco's place. I was thankful air-conditioning. I remembered that the padre cooled his house with what we call a swamp cooler. It cools by evaporation. Water drips across a box of rattan filters. A fan inside blows it through the house. The method preceded modern air-conditioning, actually back to early settlement days.

It works well until the humidity climbs. The summer monsoons were not yet upon us. June is still dry enough for the cooler to be efficient.

Padre Cisco greeted me out front, and we went inside. I was surprised how cool it was. To my greater surprise, the swamp cooler wasn't running. I soon learned of the insulating qualities of the three-foot adobe walls. I asked, "Why don't more people build this way?"

He said, "Follow the money. That is the social scientist's response to many questions. Perhaps it is too easy, or too inexpensive. If something is easy to build and cheap, who would be able to make money at it? It could be the reason for regulations against using adobe. I am just conjecturing."

I thought this might be more than conjecture. Padre Cisco went for coffee, and I sat down. He returned, and we sat in silence.

In a soft voice, he broke the spell. "How is it with you, my friend?"

"It is well, Padre. I've had quite a month." I recapped the trip, my reading, and work in the studio. I shared the sense of relief I had, and how quickly life fell back into a routine.

"It sounds as thou you have experienced movement."

"I have, and it is full of its own curiosities."

"How so?"

"The feelings of relief I had when I returned dissipated so quickly. I still can't say I know who I am, but it doesn't seem to matter as much now. I know I still want to work. I choose to define myself as a worker. I'm not sure what that work is. I am an artist. I don't want to change careers. I don't feel a need to start a new career, but I'm not sure of my purpose in this one. None of this is about ambivalence. I can say that in the last thirty seconds I have been as clear about my life being unclear as I have in months. I don't know if that is progress or not, but it seems to be movement."

"That it does."

I waited for Padre Cisco to jump in. I was hoping for some insight. I thought maybe I could outwait him, but I knew better. "When I came back from Akron, Gen and I were talking about relief. I wondered if what I was experiencing was actually release. Are those ideas the same thing? I know Mary and I resolved any conflict we had, if it was that. I can say that we cleared the air. I believe it was reconciliation. I felt the same with Dad, though. It was more of an unspoken thing. That is Dad's nature. Do you have any thoughts?"

"I do." He waited for me to continue.

"Well, thanks a lot, Padre."

"It is my service to you in helping you develop patience."

"That is so kind of you, Padre. I hope I can find a way to be of equal service to you."

We paused to enjoy the moment and to refill our cups. On the way back he said, "I have given thought to the very thing you are asking." We stood in the kitchen doorway, and he said, "Just the other day I was driving home during rush hour. I was crawling along next to an older woman who was driving an older Cadillac, one of those banana boats with a landau top. I had not seen one of those for ages. I was intrigued, and probably paid more attention than I should have, given the traffic. She had her hair in a bun, and she was wearing a business suit with a scarf knotted into a bow tie. She was the epitome of the very properly attired, government issue, executive secretary. As her car ebbed passed me, I saw a small sticker on her rear window. 'Things occur.' I loved it. I loved the very refinement of it. It was so *her*. Things occur. Think about it, Peter." He grinned.

Padre Cisco sat down chuckling. I sat across from him just glad to be there. "So how long did you wait to spring that on me, Padre?"

"Just long enough, Laddie." His brogue slipped through.

We sat quietly, savoring the coffee and the moment. I was certainly savoring the relationship. It isn't often I get to learn from someone who delivers the truth in a punch line.

"Let me see if I can cast a bit more light onto your question, Peter. There is an old Buster Keaton jingle for Alka Seltzer; *Relief is just a swallow away*. I think it partially defines the difference."

"Buster Keaton? You are dating yourself, Padre."

"Yes, it was in the fifties. The phrase indicates that relief is a quick and easy fix. Do you remember the character who came next?"

"Speedy?"

Padre Cisco nodded. "Speedy conveyed the idea that Alka Seltzer worked quickly. We know there are no quick fixes in real life, though. We also know bromides provide relief to the symptoms of distress, not the distress itself. Release is release from the cause of distress. When you remove the cause of distress, the relief is enduring. For me, the measure of release is in its enduring nature. Once you are released from the cause of the distress, you hardly think about it."

"That makes sense, Padre, when we are talking about gastric distress and Alka Seltzer. I'm not so sure when we talk about emotions."

"There is one more part to this. Perhaps it is the most important part."

"And that is?"

"Physical distress and Alka Seltzer may not provide the best analogy, but Alka Seltzer does have aspirin in it. Aspirin reduces pain by somehow interrupting the message system between the source of pain and the brain. I am sure there is more to it than that, but I am a social scientist, not a biologist. Interrupting pain may bring relief, but it doesn't release a person from the suffering. Relief occurs in the head and the body. Release is in the heart and soul."

"By that definition I would say I was released, but the key word to that is 'was.' I can't say I still have the sense of reconciliation or even the feeling of relief I had a month ago."

"It takes practice, Peter. The Buddhists would say it takes mindfulness. In the West, we are more apt to say awareness. Remember James Finley's find your practice and practice it. Perhaps your next step is to find your practice."

"I am not sure what that means."

"Let me tackle that. Your suffering may have been in the lack for words. One of my favorite Churchill quotes is, 'I have never developed indigestion from eating my words.' That is likely not the case for many of us. I think many of us suffer from eating our words, and I can tell you the remedy is not in the pop-pop, fizz-fizz."

The padre went off on one of his tangents talking about one of the greatest advertising campaigns ever that nearly doubled Bayer's flagging revenue. Before that, the recommended dosage was one tablet. They doubled the recommended dosage, doubled the packaging, and doubled the price. They replaced Speedy with pop, pop, fizz, fizz, and doubled their revenue. It worked so well that they did the same thing with aspirin. It may have been the birth of modern mass media advertising success. He caught himself and said, "Please excuse my divergence, Peter. I am still an analytic social science guy at heart."

"Maybe that is your practice."

"Well, if it is, it is a practice I am trying to leave."

"Don't get indigestion over it, Padre. The serendipity is part of why I come out here. I never know what I'm going to hear."

"That makes two of us, Peter."

"Take it as part of your allure."

"Well now, that is amusing. Shall we return to practices?" I nodded.

"I can say that the Alka Seltzer example is symbolic of our society's focus on relief from pain rather than the release from the source of the pain. If we focused on the suffering, we would not have millions of hungry children every night. Enough said on that." His voice had a hint of anger in it. He sat for a few moments, and then said, "Practice." It was as though he had to say the word to focus his thoughts.

"I swept out my house today; the need was past due. My delinquency reminded me of a man I call the sweeper. When I was still driving to work, I would see a man working in his yard around the corner from the university." His voice had changed into its story telling mode. I realized he had been recalling a story.

Daily, he paused to watch the sweeper. The man was middle-aged, dressed in gabardine slacks and a white undershirt. There was nothing distinctive about him. He may have considered himself an insignificant man in an insignificant yard, but he was significant to the padre.

The yard was a small piece of hard-packed ground no larger than the free throw lane on a basketball court. A chain-link fence bordered two sides, laying before a tiny trailer on the corner of an aging trailer park in Tempe. The park with its packed-in, aluminum containers bore no resemblance to the vacation home villages of its suburban, snowbird cousins. There were no vestiges of better days gone by.

Each day, the man swept the yard clear of debris and deposited it in a nearby trashcan. He returned to sweep the dirt into a parallel pattern of brush strokes as though tending a Zen garden. There was no hurry about him. He worked slowly and methodically like an artist before his canvas. It was his yard, and he labored in it as though it were a grand estate.

The padre said that the man's caring attitude reminded him that each of us receives a small patch of this planet for which we are responsible. For some of us, it is a spacious house in the burbs. For others, it is a tiny trailer in the urban core, and for even others, it may be just a shopping cart.

He finished with "Regardless of our leases, mortgages, or deeds, we are each only renters of our property. It is ours for a while, but eventually it will pass into the care of others. The same is true for all of our possessions. The sweeper reminds me of my responsibility to be a good steward of the gifts I receive. I hope to learn to prize what I have as much as a man who daily sweeps clean a small patch of dirt."

"This man's practice was sweeping dirt?"

"Aye."

"And he was mindful of his stewardship?"

"Aye."

"How do we know this?"

"I read his mind."

"You read his mind?"

"Let us say, I read *into* his mind."

"Meaning?"

"I am a practiced observer of the human condition."

"I need more than that, Padre."

"Michael Francis told me a story. I have doubts about its veracity, but it makes the point. He told me about a doctor who had a horse property that for twenty years the doctor claimed was a business. However, he never sold any horses. The IRS sued him for back taxes, claiming the doctor had a hobby, not a business."

"Uh huh. This is becoming harder to believe."

"The doctor went to court and won his case. The judge reasoned that no self-respecting doctor in his right mind would shovel horse manure for a hobby for twenty years."

"Now, you've lost me."

"In essence the court ruled that his shoveling was intentional as a business activity. The court based its ruling on its interpretation of the doctor's intentions. The judges read into the doctor's mind."

I said, "And the sweeper."

"The sweeper's daily practice was intentional. He was not sweeping as a random act. I use the term intentional rather than mindful. When I say I read into the sweeper's mind, I am saying I sensed his intentions from his behavior. Practices are about intention."

"So you read his intention by his actions."

"Exactly. Michael Francis also told me about an undertaker who wrote off lavish parties he held on a very large yacht. When challenged by the IRS, he responded he was entertaining potential customers. He said, 'Everyone is going to die, so everyone is a potential customer,' but I will not go into that. I just threw it in, no extra charge."

"Thank you for the gratuity. Again, I hope to be able to return the favor."

"You are welcome. Look at it this way, Peter. You were a basketball player. You wanted to get better at shooting free throws so you practiced. You developed the muscle memory of successful free throw shooting. In school, you had to memorize passages like the Gettysburg Address, so you practiced. You read it more than once. You recited it line-by-line, paragraph-by-paragraph. Perhaps you wrote it down. You realized your intention to memorize the piece through practice. Spiritual practices are no different. They are those things we do to move our intentions into successful daily living in ways that respond to our big questions in life. Being intentional is about increasing our awareness about our intentions. Spiritual practices increase our awareness of being the person we want to be spiritually. The mystics called this living in the presence of God."

"Can you give me an example, Padre?"

"I can, but first let me ask you this. Did you memorize Lincoln's Gettysburg Address when you were in school?"

"I did. Miss Catt's class. She was my seventh-grade American history teacher."

"Do you remember it?"

"Some of it."

"Which part? Illinois?"

"What?"

"Two Vaudevillians: Set-up man says, 'Do you know Lincoln's Gettysburg Address?' Punch line man says, 'I didn't know he moved.'"

"You're killing me, Padre."

"You may be dying, but I am not killing you."

"Okay, Padre, then I'm dying here."

"That's Vaudeville." We both rolled our eyes. He continued. "Actually, Peter, there is message in there somewhere. It is the 'use-it-or-lose-it' codicil. Any practice to be effective must be ongoing. You did not quit practicing free throws once you became competent at shooting them. The pros practice free throws every day. They maintain competence during the game by their practice, not by the shots during the game. However, there is no substitute for game performance either. Without practice, you lose your precision not your ability.

"That is the nature of spiritual practices, also called spiritual disciplines. The Buddhist monk Thich Nhat Hanh says that discipline is about mindfulness. To me, that is an apt description because discipline connotes the use-it-or-lose-it nature of the practice. When we practice, we are being mindful. In English discipline and practice are used interchangeably, which of itself is confusing."

I raise my hands to the top of my head and said, "Lincoln, Illinois, and Vaudeville are confusing, Padre. This is confounding."

"Okay, let me say this differently. The purpose of the practice is attaining the peace that comes with being in the presence of God. You experienced a taste of that in Akron. You were present in the moment. The practice of the discipline solidifies the peace beyond all understanding. We could as easily say the discipline of the practice solidifies that peace. Thich Nhat Hanh says, 'Once we learn to touch this peace, we will be healed and transformed. It is not a matter of faith, it is a matter of practice.' He says that when we are in the present moment we will 'touch what is refreshing, healing, and wondrous.' I love the beauty in his view of practice."

"So Padre, you are saying the sweeper demonstrated his discipline by his daily attention to his yard."

"Absolutely, but the game time of life is our daily interaction with people, or being out among 'em, as the Pennsylvania Dutch say. That is where we test our practices and ourselves. It is where we find out how intentional we actually are. Good intentions are only worthwhile when we become intentional about them. There is truth in the adage 'The road to Hell is paved with good intentions.' Being intentional is putting action into our intention. It is the difference between walking the walk and talking the talk, as people say today."

"Those are good distinctions. The comparison of practice and discipline helps. You were going to give me an example, Padre."

"Breathing."

"We all breathe."

"True, but we are not all aware of our breathing. To become aware of our breathing is the first step in spiritual breathing. We should talk more about breathing sometime."

"Okay, what else?"

"Walking, sitting still, watching, listening."

"You're really bringing up the heavy hitters here, Padre."

"You want heavy? Try prayer."

"That sounds a lot more like a spiritual practice than breathing or walking."

"Peter, what you do does not make something a practice. James Finley speaks about meditation as the stance that offers the least resistance to allow God to happen in our lives. I apply that idea to other practices. Practice is a stance that you take about an ordinary activity. Your awareness of your activity, why, and how you do it makes it a spiritual practice. This is not learning rocket science. Practice is about turning the ordinary into the extraordinary. It is about being mindfully aware of even the simplest act. It is about learning to be in the moment and being aware of the moment at the same time.

"I brought up breathing and walking because they are two of the simplest things we do every day. We just do not necessarily do them well, or certainly not as a practice, much less a spiritual practice. We are seldom even aware of our breathing or walking. We should talk about these things more."

"Definitely."

"Let me make a suggestion, something you might do before we meet again."

"You aren't going to ask me to contemplate my navel, are you?"

"Oh no, Peter. You are definitely not ready for that. My thought is that you might profit by watching *Groundhog Day*. I would recommend you watch it more than once, but that would be redundant."

"*Groundhog Day*? Bill Murray? Punxsutawney Phil?"

"That is the one."

"Can you give me a hint as to the reason?"

"Oh, I would not want to spoil the ending."

"I've seen it before, Padre."

"That should make it even better."

To my chagrin, we ended. We set a date to meet again in a month to talk about breathing, walking, and such. We stood, shook hands, Padre Cisco asked me to pass along his greetings to Gen, and I left, though not without him walking me to the car and watching me depart.

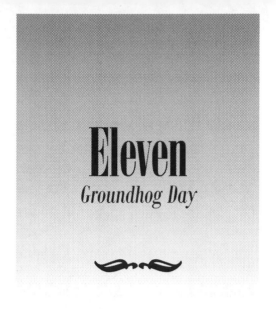

Eleven
Groundhog Day

"*Abba, give me a word.*"
"*What do you seek, my son?*
"*My place in the world.*"
"*Ah, the cosmic quest; do you hear it?*"
"*What, Abba?*"
"*The word.*"

The heart of the summer was upon us when I went to see Padre Cisco in July. We met in the morning to take advantage of the relative coolness. On the drive out there, I thought about my first trip to Arizona. Smitty and I had come of age. We imagined the whole world, or at least the West, was ours for the taking. We were young and brash. The reality was that we didn't have a clue about what we were getting into.

Smitty had this ten-year-old Ford Fairlane 500 that had been a police cruiser. It was black without air-conditioning, and it had a huge engine that sucked gas. Fortunately, gas was cheap. By the time we got to Oklahoma, the heat and noise from the open windows were getting to us. We questioned if taking the West was going to be harder than we envisioned. We stopped at a gas station on the Will Rodgers Turnpike. They were advertising window-mounted swamp coolers for rent. You paid the rental fee and a deposit. You recovered your deposit at your destination. We stuck it on the front passenger's window and cracked the window behind the driver. It worked pretty well until we got to Arizona. Somewhere in New Mexico, we added a canvas water bag because we saw them hanging on the front of other cars.

I remember coming down into the Verde Valley. I was driving. It was mid-day, and the car was blazing hot. I told Smitty to pull the cord on the cylinder in the cooler to get it wet. He said that he had just pulled it. The tank was bone dry. We hadn't faced the dry heat of Arizona. We stopped on the mountain at one of those cement water barrels set out for people with overheated engines. The Black Canyon Highway, now I17, was still a two-lane road. There was a lot of over-heating with lines of cars stuck behind trucks. We filled the water bag, filled the cooler tank, and headed out again. Smitty took over driving.

We arrived in the valley in the afternoon. It didn't occur to us to wait in the mountains and drive down in the evening. I remember approaching Phoenix and asking about when we were going to get to the desert. The desert image I learned in sixth grade was Saharan. The cooler was bone dry again, the bag was empty, and we were fried. We truly were clueless.

We found a station to take the cooler and return our deposit. We were grateful for the cash. We were already running low.

The memory captured me the entire drive to Padre Cisco's place. He greeted me in his customary manner. The monsoons were late arriving, and the padre's swamp cooler still functioned efficiently. His kitchen door and window were open. We sat in the breeze on the veranda. The pleasant conditions surprised me. In contrast, the garden parched by the sun was in retreat.

I shared my story with the padre, and he related some similar experiences.

"I never had the window cooler, but I did carry the water bags. Believe it or not, Peter, I still have a couple hanging in the shed."

"Oh, I can believe that, Padre." He was not a collector of things, but in a strange way, it made sense that he would have something as atypical as a canvas water bag.

"I drove a pickup for a long time before I could afford a car with air-conditioning. We had to get a newer car when the babies arrived, but I still have the truck."

"Really?"

"Come, take a look at it."

We walked out to the shed, which was more like a small barn. Padre Cisco pulled the cover off what, except for slightly faded paint, could be a spanking new 1951 Chevy pickup.

"Padre, it is gorgeous. Did you have it restored?"

"No, it is original. My father kept it that way, and I followed his lead. It sits covered most of the time. I only drive it after the days cool down. It looks good, but it is not any more comfortable now than it was when it was new. I prefer the Jeep."

He walked over to a cabinet and pulled out a desert water bag. "It is probably foolishness, but I keep a couple of these as part of my back-up plan. They still work, though the canvas is deteriorating from the dryness. I had some others, but a couple of years ago I gave them to a family a coyote left stranded in the desert. We don't get as many night travelers along here with the increased border patrol."

I loved his euphemism for illegals. It was so non-judgmental. He covered the truck and we returned to the house. He said, "It is warming up a bit. Shall we move indoors?" I picked up my cup, and we went to the living room.

"So, Padre, here I am forty-plus years later, not quite without a clue, but not far removed from fried, metaphorically speaking, that is."

"I had not thought of you as that self-deprecating. You underestimate yourself, Peter."

"Oh, I'm not so sure."

"I am. You have come a long way in life and a long way in the past few months. Perhaps you are entering a second coming-of-age experience."

"What do you mean?"

"I have been considering the notion that perhaps we have more than one coming of age. A few years ago when I still thought of myself as a runner, my son called me and asked me if I wanted to run the Park City, Utah, Marathon with him."

His son wanted to qualify for the Boston, and the Park City race is a fast route. It has a lot of downhill on the back half. Padre Cisco was running five and ten Ks and an occasional fifteen. He asked his son to give him time to think about it and some additional time not to think about it. A month or so later, he called his son and said that he had decided not to do it. His son thought it was because the padre didn't think he could. The padre said, "That is not the problem. The problem is I think I can. I just do not want to pay the price."

For a while, he said he called that day the day he grew old but did not like the notion. He didn't rue growing old. It was more that the thought did not represent his experience or feelings. He told Michael Francis and Mo-ma about it. They both said the same thing. Maybe it is the first day you *felt* old, not got old. Months later, he realized the experience was the realization of a second coming of age. It may be the moment or awareness of Richard Rohr's notion of the second half of life.

Padre Cisco said, "Prior to the decision not to run the marathon, I had always operated on the idea that if I could do it, I would do it. It was the first time I chose to not do something physical, not because I could not, but because I did not want to. That realization was one more portal into the second half of my life. Perhaps you are experiencing your second coming of age."

"Isn't that what *Groundhog Day* is about? Is that why you wanted me to watch it?"

"I take it you did."

"Yes, Jen and I watched it together. She said that you'd probably recommend *Mystic Pizza* next. She obviously got the mystical inference."

"That might be a stretch. What did you think, watching it through new eyes?"

"It was the first time I viewed the story as allegory of transformation. Phil, that is Phil Collins, not Punxsutawney Phil, is a modern-day Jacob become Israel."

The padre interjected, I do wonder why the common name, given that everything in a movie is considered significant."

"I wondered about that, too." It isn't like the padre to interrupt. I must have given him a quizzical look because he covered his mouth with his hand. I continued. "I realized Phil went through stages of development. The first scenes after the day began repeating depicted a narcissistic Phil. It wasn't until Phil encountered the old man who died that he began looking outside himself. That was the turning point. His lust for Rita began to change. It may have changed only to desire. That's when he began reinventing himself to win her over. Winning her heart came later."

"What did the piano playing represent to you?"

"Now you are leading the witness, Padre."

"You see through me."

"I paused the movie when it got to the piano lesson scenes. I told Gen that this is why Padre Cisco wanted me to watch the movie.' She asked me what I meant. I said learning to play the piano demonstrated Phil's willingness to practice to get what he wanted."

"This is true, Peter, but in my defense I thought you would see beyond that piece and view the movie as you did. Harold Ramis, who wrote the screenplay with Danny Rubin, speculated that the real time loop would be ten years to get good at anything. He later amended that to thirty years. That is a lot of practice."

"I wondered about how long Phil was stuck in his time warp."

"I think he was stuck in his circumstances until he changed his perception to a focus on others. He learned life was about love. He acted on love by expressing it to Rita. That is my nutshell version of the movie. It is a classic story of identity. Phil practiced learning to live into a new identity."

I sat and thought about that idea and about a second coming of age. "Padre, conceptually, what you are saying makes sense to me. It works in the physical sense, but the idea doesn't translate for emotional or spiritual development. Let me see if I can recapture my experience. We can call it *Groundhog Day II: Peter Goes to Punxsutawney.* That should bring them out to the box office."

"This sounds like an epic story. Perhaps we should refill our coffee."

"Good idea, Padre, the screenplay is pretty rough at this point."

With fresh coffee in hand, he settled back to listen. Still standing, I said, "Padre, you're the producer, and I am the pitch man."

"Got it. This is getting better by the moment," He said, flashing a broad grin.

I turned my back and drew down into myself to what I presumed was assuming the intensity of a playwright selling his story. I paced about with my head down, jaw jutted, and lips pursed. I stopped and stood to full height. In a hushed voice with my palms turned outward, I began. "The back story: A strapping young lad and his trusty sidekick forsake hearth and home. They set out on the quest for fame and fortune, the Holy Grail of modern America. As the two cross the heartland, we hear Aaron Copland's *Fanfare for the Common Man*. With minor setbacks, the lad, Peter, succeeds. It is not unbridled success, but he does well."

The padre reached for his coffee and looked to the side feigning disinterest.

"Years pass with our hero basking in the glory of his achievements. The soundtrack turns ominous. Adversity slams our now-sixty-ish protagonist. He loses his job, told he is antiquated. In the background, a tolling bell punctuates the moment."

Padre Cisco slouched, puffed out his thinnest of bellies, and splayed his legs. In the raspy voice of a hard-nosed, overweight, cigar-smoking movie producer he said, "Why in the name of Hades would I care about this guy in the first place?"

"You're getting into to this, Padre." We laughed at ourselves. I returned to character.

"Why would you care about this guy? You care about him because he is you."

"Not me; I'll never quit. I'll work until I die."

"My point exactly, Mr. B. To avoid facing the loss of your work, you'll work until you die. However, most men quit, retire, are downsized or fired. They sell their business, liquidate, or a larger company absorbs it. In some way their work life ends."

"Move on. My time and patience are getting shorter."

He's playing his role to the hilt. He's being the hard driver of his college years. I said, "You care about him because he is both of us." *Is there more than that? I wonder how many other men feel like I do. Does every man deal with this? In some way, they must. Of course they do. I just said it aloud. Why haven't I been aware of this before?* Padre Cisco moved in his chair. I realized I had stopped. I ran with my instinct. "Why would you care about him? You care about him because he is *everyman*. He is every man, who experiences failure. Not just failure, men's most common failure, losing their jobs. Even you, Mr. Big."

The padre barked, "Alright, you made your point. Let me hear the rest."

"Our now-aging hero begins to examine himself. He goes on a downward spiral into a fit of depression. His beautiful bride, played by Angelina Jolie, counsels him to seek help. He visits a trusted advisor. He learns about changing his perceptions. He begins to read and watch arcane movies like *Groundhog Day*. He asks deeper questions. He examines the meaning of life. He comes to new realizations. He comes to himself."

Padre Cisco chuckled. "*Groundhog Day, arcane, that's too funny,*" It was his turn to fall out of character.

I went on increasing my pace and volume, "Peter sets about revitalizing himself physically. He takes on reconciling past mistakes with his family, particularly his daughter. He experiments with reinventing himself. He learns about first and second halves of life, and the possibility of a second coming of age. He is primed to move, shift, transform, and become a new man. The music stops. Silence."

Blustering, the padre said, "Silence? I can't have silence in a movie. I'm paying by the minute for action, not silence. The public won't buy it. They don't want to see silence."

I interrupted. "We see him sitting there on a straight-backed chair in an empty room unable to move. He knows he cannot go back. He doesn't know how to go forward. The light through the single window grows dim. Fade to black.

"What? That's it? You want me to make a movie out of that? "Yes, I do. It's reality."

"Reality or not, I can't make a picture out of that. People don't want reality. They don't pay for reality. Hogwash!"

I took my seat. "Hogwash? That's really good, Padre, and you had me going with the *move on* comment."

"Well, Peter, that is the issue, is it not."

"It isn't high drama, but we screenwriters overstate the case for dramatic effect."

"You did that; you certainly did. Calling me Mr. Big. I loved the Holy Grail allusion and describing *Groundhog Day* as arcane. That is as funny as the movie. Seeing the humor in life's challenges can be an avenue to a change in perspective. Your perspective of work life has broadened. Are you in that liminal space? Is your status a question of facing reality?"

"Those are good questions, Padre. I could see the humor in it when I was in the role of the screenwriter. You probably noticed that I had that moment where I saw the big picture. However, the day-to-day reality is more difficult. It has been downright grim at times. That is changing, but I still face the knowledge that this is serious stuff. There seems to be nothing easy about it."

"I hear you. I would like to say it will get easier, but we can never be sure of that. There is no simple formula. There are no shortcuts to doing the work. The psychologists call it inner work. Spiritual directors call it soul work. Regardless of its name, it is work. Perhaps, it is simply your work. Let's stop here. It is a bit in the middle of things, but I think it is an apt place to stop."

"Padre, from my perspective we always seem to stop in the middle of things."

"Then we have a perfect record. Surely that is a banal enough thought on which to end."

We sat in silence for a few moments. I picked up our cups and returned them to the kitchen. He walked me out, and I left.

Twelve
Koan the Librarian

"Abba, give me a word."
"Now, my son."
"Yes, please, Abba."
"You are welcome, my son."

Gen and I spent the next month mostly indoors. We were in the throes of the monsoon season, and it was hot and muggy outside. We holed up in the way people in the northern climes hunker down during the winter snowstorms. The Southwestern desert monsoon is no more the classic Asian or African rain period than most of the desert is rolling sand dunes. We get some rain from the tropical storms off the Gulf of Mexico and the Sea of Cortez. More often, it is just giant electrical and dust storms. The definition of a monsoon has something to do with the dew point. We deal more easily with the "dry heat" of the rest of the summer. The monsoon is a season we simply endure to its conclusion.

I spent much of my time in the studio. Gen was in her office. We stopped regularly to talk and to eat. The strip I drew for Dad sparked some nascent notion that I couldn't quite capture. I thought if I just kept drawing, it would emerge, In spite of my intentions the idea eluded me. The days had an aura of earlier times. I smiled more. I was sleeping better.

My sixtieth birthday passed will little fanfare and less trauma. Gen and I went out for dinner then spent a quiet evening at home. The kids sent cards and called. That was the best present I could get. I reminded them of their intention to call seven weeks earlier. They both responded with apologies. I let them know my feelings. I'm afraid I spoiled their otherwise good intentions. My parents called, and we had a nice chat. Dad and I talked about how the Indians were on a run. Smitty called, and I had to endure his good-natured ribbing. He is a couple of months older than I am. He gave me a dose of his wisdom from experience in my new decade. Overall, but for the kid's call I was pleased with myself.

At the same time, the loss of my sense of humor haunted me. It left with the syndicate telling me SoCal and Knuckles was no longer relevant. I had grown very serious in the turmoil of the past months. I was determined to regain what I deemed a vital part of myself. I had a shelf full of books on drawing but found no answers there.

While at a store, I perused books on writing. I passed over the very clean, nearly new books, opting for the dog-eared ones that someone had actually used. Nestled among the romance-novel-formula books and the how-to-get-rich-writing books, was a small paperback, placed there just for me: *Snoopy's Guide to the Writing Life*. There were about three dozen writer's essays interspersed among dozens of Snoopy's *It was a dark and stormy night* strips. How appropriate. I sat down on the floor between the stacks and read much of it before I left.

By the end of the week, Snoopy and I were good friends. I took notes and reread passages. The authors wrote about how they started and how they worked. What I read was how they turned their passion and soul into ideas. They shared how they turned their ideas into words on the page. Sue Grafton advised me to listen to my own advice. Ed McBain taught me to express my intent in a title and read it when I lose my focus. Sidney Sheldon asks, "Is the idea worth writing about?" Each of the authors had something to say to me. That elusive notion I sought was no nearer, but I had new pathways to understanding it. I knew the path was there. All I had to do was walk until I met up with it. That was the first time that I came to view my art as a practice. That little book was a doorway to my understanding. I didn't know where it would lead, but I was moving.

In the studio, I had a new sense of anticipation. My drawing took on new meaning. I applied the writer's questions of audience, purpose, and genre to my trial-and-error approach. I thought less about outcome and freed myself up to greater experimentation. I worked with pastels, acrylics and watercolors. I went outside and sketched the house from different angles. I made a trip into the desert to draw landscape. I found an old box of crayons and played with them. It was the first sense of art as play that I'd had in years. Yet, there was something else. The answer came, not in the studio, but during conversation with Gen.

We were sitting in the kitchen sharing the remains of a bottle of very nice wine after a light Sunday supper. It's curious how many significant conversations occur in the kitchen. I finally got around to asking Gen about her meditation. The conversation wound its way to Buddhist practices in general and Zen Buddhism specifically.

She related the basic teachings of Buddhism, and told a curious story. "There's a practice, among Tibetan Buddhists. It's an activity. Actually, in the Western world it would be almost an oddity. When a young novice is tested, he sits on the ground; and the monks gather in a circle around him. They ask him questions. As he answers, they walk around him smiling and applauding. They join with him and encourage him. This event can continue for hours."

I said, "That is a far cry from Western questioning we experienced. Have you seen it?"

"I've only heard of it. One of my teachers told me about it. What I think I understand about the practice is it is not what the novice answers but how he answers."

"Meaning?"

"Is his answer the result of contemplation? Is it thoughtful, insightful, a development of personal understanding?"

"Go on."

"There are no right answers, Rocky. It is more that he answers the questions well, that is, well for him at his stage of enlightenment. The monks know he is as good as he knows how to be. They encourage him to be just that. The masters pose questions or at times statements that are paradoxical or enigmatic."

"Give me an example."

"I think I can." Gen paused for a bit. "There is a classic one that states you have to chase an ass to catch it, but you can't catch an ass by chasing it."

"Oh, that's illuminating…not."

"Absolutely. You're right, but the illumination is in the answer, not the question."

"I am not sure this is helping. I thought you were going to tell me about meditation."

"I am, Rocky. The answer is found in the meditation."

"Well, I'd have to meditate for a month of Sundays to come up with something on that."

"Exactly, now you are beginning to understand."

"I am beginning to understand nothing."

"That knowledge in itself would be considered progress."

"Are you messing with me?"

"Maybe a little."

"Stop it, and it would help if you dismantled the grin."

"Yes, Rocky." Still grinning, she continued, "There is a term in Zen Buddhism that describes these questions and statements. They are called *koans*."

"Cones?"

"No, koan."

"Cohan, like George M. Cohan?"

"No, Rocky, it's not Co-han, it's koan as in coe-anne."

"Ah, I get it: Conan, like Conan the Barbarian."

"Now, you stop it. You're the one messing with me. You know exactly what I'm saying."

"I confess. I do. Koan, as in Koan the Librarian."

"Thank you."

"Shazaam! That's it, Koan the Librarian. No, Gen, thank you. I have to go. Thank you, thank you, I know everything I need to know about Zen Buddhism. You are a great teacher. I need to go to the studio. I will pay you for the lesson tonight. Wow! I have to go to the studio. I said that already, didn't I?" I rushed out leaving a bewildered Gen at the table.

I sketched over the next few days. Ideas swelled in my imagination. I landed on a concept of punctuation marks as characters in a strip. Gen and I had conversations amid laughter, but I suspect she tired of my interruptions. I felt like my old self again. In truth, it was a new self I was experiencing. I had a meeting scheduled with Cisco, and I was excited to share my experience. I wondered if he would sense the change in me. In hindsight, that was silly.

* * *

With coffee in hand, Padre Cisco and I settled in to our respective chairs in the living room. The low drone of the swamp cooler was the only sound. The thick walls insulated the house against all else. The padre cocked his head and fixed his gaze on me.

"Might we sit a spell, Peter, and let the tension of the drive fall away a bit?"

I nodded assent. We sat drinking our coffee. I was thankful for the moment. Our cups empty, he said, "Let's get a refill. You can tell me about your new work."

I shook my head. *How does he do that?* We returned to our chairs. Putting my amazement aside, I started right in. "It has been an interesting and eventful month, Padre." I told him about my drawing, the trip to the bookstore, the conversation with Gen, and my illumination. I said that maybe it was an epiphany.

"How so" he asked.

"For the better part of a month I had the sense that I was on the verge of something. I couldn't put my finger on it. Then, all of a sudden, it was clear. It wasn't just that an idea for a strip emerged. The result was more inclusive. I have a greater sense of purpose. I am more purpose driven, intentional perhaps. In the past, I drew because I knew how to draw. Being an artist is what I prepared to be and enjoy. I drew comic strips as an occupation. I was good at it and enjoyed the recognition. My art paid me to do something I wanted to do. It was comfortable. I had an easy life.

"But work is more than that now, Padre. I can't quite describe it. It has to do with caring more about what I draw. My art has more purpose. It is audience driven. The source of an idea is intentional. I used to draw whatever came to mind. That isn't good enough anymore."

"I think you have described your experience very well. I can relate to what you are saying out of my own experience. At one point in my life, I thought I wanted to be a writer. Many people have that notion. In a way, I am a writer. I write my stories, but I just publish them orally. It is the way of many poets and storytellers."

He told me how he was busy gathering stories, writing them, and telling them. He developed a larder of stories for all occasions. He was going anywhere someone would invite him. Then came to a point when he was not proud of what he was doing. He said he knew he had to make some changes.

He said he didn't know how to go about changing. He searched the web for resources around Tucson and found a retreat on spirituality and work. He returned home with a new perspective and a new set of guidelines regarding his craft.

"The outcome of the weekend was that I identified three questions I needed to answer regarding any project I was to undertake."

"Tell me about that."

"I am about to do so; it is why I brought it up. You make a great sideman, Peter, my very own sideman."

"Thanks, Padre, though I am not sure I should be thanking you for that."

"I do have those moments. Again, I apologize." The brogue and the twinkle in is eye said otherwise. "So, Peter. The first question asks, 'Is the project worthy of me?' I consider the question 'Do I really want to do something just because I can do it?'

"Excuse me, Padre, but I just read that question. Sidney Sheldon posed the question in a book on writing."

"From what you have told me about your work, I am telling you something you already know. You said that work now is more than just being able to draw. That leads to the second question, 'Am I worthy of the project?' This includes questions about having the knowledge, skill, the time, the determination, and the willingness to persevere. Are there skills or areas of knowledge I need to develop even before I start? Equally important, do I have the will? The third question is 'Is the product worthy of the project and of me?' Essentially, I am asking myself am I proud of the product. I begin asking this before I reach the final product. These three questions have become my standards for decision-making about any task I consider undertaking."

"That is terrific advice, Padre. I want to use that."

"It sounds to me, Peter, that knowingly or not, you have taken yourself through the same terrain, and answered similar questions."

"Oh, without a doubt, Padre, though you have formalized the ideas. I just sort of mucked around and eventually found my way."

"I think you are underestimating your journey, Peter. You have traveled far in eight months. Do you remember Ram Dass?"

"Oh yes, Richard Alpert. He was one of Timothy Leary's colleagues. He was the guru of LSD. I was in college when he was popular. We all knew both of them."

"Ram Dass wrote that we cycle through three phases of life: retreat, preparation, and the marketplace. I think it was in *Be Here Now*. You have followed that cycle, Peter. You were in the marketplace for many years plying your craft. Your life changed, and you went into retreat. It was your 'Who am I, and what am I going to do?' phase. We began or conversation about that time. It was a period of rest, recovery, and reorientation. You began to do the inner work and to see life from alternate perspectives. Eventually, you morphed into preparation. That was around the period when you began walking, then running. There is a metaphor for your journey. You were preparing your body. You were still partially in retreat. You were asking, 'Who am I to be?' You began to move doing to being.

"The preparation stage probably began about the time you returned to the studio. You were drawing all those faces."

"Oh yes. That was a screwy time. I couldn't figure out what I was doing. I was just glad to be doing something."

"Now, you are re-entering the marketplace. You have a new strip idea to take to the market. You found an answer to he question of 'what am I going to do?' Next, you will be faced with 'what am I willing to give up?' That is a question for another time. For now, tell me about your insight, your epiphany as you termed it."

"I told you I left Gen sitting in the kitchen. When I got to the studio, I grabbed a black felt marker and made this quick sketch of Koan the Librarian. It was nothing more than an inverted V with some long squiggly lines signifying a beard, two dots for eyes, and two short lines for feet sticking out at the bottom. I wrote two tag lines on the back: Keeper of the Knowledge and Keeper of the Memories."

"Do you have it with you?"

"No, but I can show you." I drew a copy for him.

"May I have this?"

"Certainly, it is you."

"Me? It looks nothing like me."

"No, Padre, but he is you. You are a keeper of the knowledge. Not the data, but the larger knowledge, and you are also a collector of cultural memory. Those are elements of your stories and the understanding you convey."

"Well, I must say, Peter, I have now risen to the pinnacle of my professional career. I have been elevated to the status of comic strip icon. I am honored."

"Don't understate it, Padre. Soon you may be found in millions of homes across America, if only to wrap their fish headed to the trash."

"As I said, I am honored. Now, please return to your story."

"I will because the epiphany is on the horizon." I told him the process I went through generating the idea.

When I looked at my drawing, what I saw was not an inverted V or pyramid, but a caret – the editing mark used for an insertion. I named him Caret Top." I thought that would be a good strip title. Fortunately, my mind was running in overdrive. I progressed to drawing all the characters as punctuation marks. If Caret Top were the master, his disciples visiting him could be question marks. Lesser characters could be periods, commas, and exclamation points. That Caret Top is only an occasional insertion in their lives makes a caret the perfect symbol. "I progressed to the point when absurd bordered on profound. That's when a cartoonist goes beyond fun to absolute joy."

"I experience moments of joy, but not quite the way you describe. The metaphor of the caret is wonderful. The relationship between absurd and profound piques my interest. Keep going. I want hear the rest of it."

As the ideas streamed out, I realized that Caret Top was only a character in the strip. I fell thought of the title *Koanheads*. That's when I realized I was on to something. I had been concerned about losing my sense of humor. I knew I was being much too serious. Here was a way to address serious questions in a comical way. It was perfect. It was perfect for me in the place I was. It could be perfect for the folks who claim to be spiritual but not religious. It could appeal to people who are serious about their faith. Some of them struggle to lighten up. Koanheads could give them a different outlook.

"Padre, this strip idea could be the ministry of distraction, as you described months ago."

"Peter, that is epiphanous. I am impressed at your leaps, and I love how your mind works, how shapes and symbols connect to ideas and language for you. Is it always this way for you?"

"When I allow it to be, Padre."

Padre Cisco leaned back rubbing his chin and replied, "Ah, that is it, is it not?" His head dropped and tilted slightly. I have often wondered what intricate musings were taking place in his mind at those moments. I waited. He sat erect again and opened his eyes. "Excuse me, some distant connection rose in me. Keep going."

"It's not just about the intuitive leaps. It is, also, about the process. It's about all those stages, models, and ideas you shared along the way. It's about alternative perceptions, of how I see myself, and how I see the world. It is about presence in the moment, and it is about compassion. Without compassion, I now know I cannot see outside myself. Given all that, though, I still had to be willing to allow the ideas to come. I realized growth does start with willingness. In my case a lot had to transpire to get me to the point I was willing to listen, to look, and to open myself and to be able to change." I had talked on, and I realized that I was the audience for my own words.

"Your case is not just your case, Peter. All of us go through those retreat and preparatory stages. Perhaps it something we must do. Perhaps it just is the way it is."

I needed to say what I said. If for no other reason, I had to hear myself admit to my membership in the multitude. I slowly breathed out. My shoulders fell. I was lost, now I am found, and it t didn't happen without me knowing it. *Welcome back to the human race, Rocky Stellar. Welcome back into the marketplace.*

INTERLUDE

Beer

"He is a wise man who invented beer."
~ Plato

A year had passed since I visited Smitty. Gen encouraged me to go. I was hesitant to stop working now that something was emerging with my drawing. I had a full thermos of coffee, and for all my misgivings, I was ready for a road trip. I left at daybreak so the sun would be behind me. I timed the trip to arrive in San Diego between rush hours.

Once I get to the freeway, I don't have to concentrate much on the drive. I Take I-10 to Casa Grande, turn left onto I-8, and stop when I get to the ocean. I had the radio off. Only the road noise interrupted the quiet. Road trips are good thinking time. It wasn't until I passed Casa Grande that I actually left my work and Tucson behind.

My mind drifted to trips Gen and I had made. I thought about the endless conversations we had. I recall the surfing trips before the kids. I rummaged through trips when the kids were younger: Alex running up to us after his first experience with the ocean saying, "It's spoiled." He had not tasted salt water before. The kids' first surfing lessons on boogie boards under the tutelage and watchful eyes of Gen and Smitty. I made a rest stop in Gila Bend and stopped in Yuma to get gas before crossing into California. I traversed the sand dunes, thankful there was no wind, cruised through the farmland of the Imperial Valley, and wound my way into the mountains.

For all our differences, Smitty and I shared common experiences. After ASU, we went our separate ways but stayed in touch. We were best men at each other's weddings and best friends during each other's divorces. We each went on to successful careers. Gen blessed my life; Smitty never remarried. I think he came to know himself as a bachelor. Perhaps that is why he has invested himself in other people's kids. I know he is involved with a number of social services agencies that serve children, but he never talks about it. Morgan and Alex know him as Uncle Smitty. Alex once asked me if Smitty had a first name. I said, "Smitty," and he was satisfied with that.

Inattention on the mountain roads can be hazardous, and the memories came in snatches. Smitty came from a large Catholic family. His parents are gone, and his brothers and sisters are scattered. Occasionally, he spends holidays with us, but sometimes he just seems to disappear. We've tried to call him more than once around holidays. He didn't answer, or it seemed *wouldn't*. I know he has experienced some sort of change. At first, I wasn't sure if he was different, or I was. I thought that maybe we were just getting older. I eventually concluded it was Smitty but wasn't clear as to how he was different.

We share a love of sports. I played some beer league basketball after college, but we both drifted to sports such as surfing and cycling that at most happen in packs. It took only a few years for us to move from sport to activity. Smitty's blown knee limited his athletic endeavors. His size notwithstanding, the rickety knee was an even greater impediment to surfing, yet he persists.

Distances seem to get shorter after you make a trip numerous times. All I had before me was to cross Tecate Divide, and go over Crestwood and Lugana Summits. From there, it was all down hill. Traffic increased past Alpine, and I focused on driving, leaving my memories behind.

I arrived early afternoon and drove straight to Pacific Beach to meet Smitty. The temperature was in the mid-seventies. If the currents were right, the water would be warm. To a desert rat warm*ish* is a more accurate description. The spot we chose is officially Tourmaline Surfing Park, but the locals know it as Old Man's. Smitty was there when I arrived. He called out a booming "Rocky" and greeted me with a bodacious hug that only a large man can pull off in public. In spite of my height, I always feel like a little kid when he does that.

He smiled his big kid grin, and we exchanged amenities. We stood for a while on the low cliff and watched the movement of the tide. There would be plenty of time to talk. We changed into our wet suits. I waxed my board and we headed to the surf. We paddled out beyond the swells and waited.

"You know, Rocky, we've surfed this beach for forty years. Remember when we were groms; they call the newbies 'kooks' now. We were a pair with our size and clumsiness. I guess we still are, and we've finally lived into the name. We are old men on Old Man's Beach."

I chose to not argue the point. We talked about Gen and the kids, our beleaguered pro sports franchises, dismal political situations in Arizona and California, and he asked me about my drawing. I began to answer, but a swell worth pursuing cut short our conversation. We paddled to catch the break. The waves were coming in sets of five. When you haven't been surfing for a while, picking the right one is little better than a crapshoot. We spent a couple of hours, each of us had a few good rides, and we called it a day. The surf would be there.

"Let's get a beer, Rocky. We can go to the London's West End Pub up on Turquoise."

"What about T.D. Hayes?"

"It isn't there anymore."

"Mr. A's?"

"Gone."

"Hennessy's?"

"It's the Duck Dive now; it's not much different, but too far for me to walk.

We left our cars in the parking lot and walked up to the pub knowing there was little likelihood of getting parking places any closer than we already were.

It had a variety of foreign, domestic, and craft beers. Smitty got a Corona, and I opted for Arrogant Bastard Ale, a local classic.

"We'll have to try out a couple of the micro-breweries. Rocky, you wouldn't believe it; this town is a mecca for beer. I don't know why. I could balloon up if I weren't careful."

"Could? You seem to be living well."

"Thanks, Rocky. I left myself open to that. So, what's up with you? You sounded veritably ominous on a couple of phone calls we had. You doing better?"

During one call last winter, I'd complained about not being able to get going, being tired all the time, and becoming a couch potato. I could picture Smitty's head bobbing side to side as he said in a sing-song voice, "Well, Rocky, over here in

Southern California we refer to that as *depression*." Smitty's not one to pussyfoot; he leans to the two-by-four across the nose approach.

"It's been a journey, Smitty. It's been a struggle as well. Nine months later, I am finally coming out of it. 'Nine months later... coming out of it,' now there's a metaphor for you. Anyway, I am back in the studio and have an idea for a strip, but I have many unanswered questions. I think I lost sight of who I am. I know I did. I fell apart. I lost my job, and I fell apart. I've turned sixty. Crapola!"

"So bring me up to speed since the last time we talked."

"When was that?"

"Not long after you returned from seeing your folks. How are they?"

"They are as well as can be at their age. They are certainly challenged."

"Give them my best the next time you talk to them. They treated me like family when I was at your house." He paused turned his head aside. Turning back, he said, "So shoot."

"I'll give you the shorthand version. I felt washed up, dumped, overage, used up, and useless. For the first time in my adult life, I felt like a failure in my job, with my kids, Mary, and my parents. I rehashed my conversation with Gen about Morgan and my trip to Akron. A month or so after I got canned, Gen got me to go see Padre Cisco."

"Tell me about the padre."

"Gen and I met each other and him in a graduate class he taught at ASU. He was in the Social Science Department. The name he went by then was Dr. Frank O'Shaughnessy." I filled Smitty in on Padre Cisco's bio. "We've met and talked every few weeks since that time. He's given me a lot to think about and helped me alter my perspective on any number of things.

I got back into shape, read some books, and began the task of figuring out who I was and wanted to be." I started to recite the litany of topics with some of the details Padre Cisco and I had covered, but Smitty cut in.

"Who is that, Rocky?"

"Who is who?"

"Who you want to be."

"I want to be a better man." I told him about my conversation with Gen at the coffee house and the story of Jack Nicholson and Helen Hunt." Well, not exactly a better man, a more complete man I guess. It is still rather vague and amorphous."

"That's an understatement."

"You're doing a Gen on me, Smitty."

"You need another Genevieve in your life…Peter!"

"That's definitely a Gen move."

He replied, "I'm proud of myself for that one."

"If I may continue."

"Yes, please, do go on. I'm in rapt attention."

"I can tell." I paused and let Smitty have his moment. "I marvel at the padre. I don't want to be another Padre Cisco, but he has qualities I admire. He is interested in everything and everyone. He seems to have time for everything and everyone. Whatever he does, he does it purposefully, whether it is cooking, or gardening, or listening to me. He has a sense of presence about him that defines presence. He is present to all he does."

"And you're not?"

"Not the way he is."

"You are now."

"Well, this is different."

"Is it?"

"Now you've switched from Gen to Cisco."

"Have I?"

"Stop it! Just stop it. All three of you do this to me, throwing my hands in the air. You ask me to get all serious, then you zing me."

"Okay, I'll admit that last one was contrived. It was just payback for the comment about my living well. Up to that point, I was serious."

"Apology accepted."

"Oh, I'm not apologizing. You deserve everything I can throw at you. It's my calling."

"Then I can say you certainly fulfill your calling." We grinned at each other, enjoying the current byplay in years of mutual kidding.

"So Rocky, what's different?"

"That's a good question. Maybe it has to do with my intention. I am intentionally in this conversation. I am mindful of where I am, why I am here, and what I am doing. I am in the moment, but I know that there are similar times when I am not. It is as though it doesn't even occur to me. My mind wanders, or I think about what I am going to say next. I can appear to be there more than I am. That works until I realize later I missed the moment or the point. I've spent a lifetime of missed moments."

"I want to hear more about that, but I am feeling all grungy from the salt. I want to get a shower before dinner, and I have a couple of calls I need to make. I can do that in the car. Why don't you follow me? I can get us around the traffic. I've reserved a parking place for you and a temporary pass to the underground lot. There are a couple of vacant condos, and I know the manager. He's had me do a couple of things for him. Let's go."

* * *

We went to dinner at Tom Ham's Lighthouse. It is on the west end of Harbor Island off the north shore of San Diego Bay just a couple miles from Smitty's condo. The restaurant looks like a lighthouse but never was, and Harbor Island really isn't an island. Like its counterpart, Shelter Island, it's a long, one-street, man-made marina. Tom Ham's has good food and a great view of the city. The owners remodeled the restaurant since I was there years before. It has a chic, ultra-modern appeal now. My memory of it was mahogany and red brocade more appropriate to an old western bordello than to a restaurant. The hostess called us to dinner promptly, and we went upstairs. Our table was at a corner on the outside deck where we could watch the sunset and the city illuminate itself in response.

"Great seats, Smitty."

"I know the manager. I've done a couple of things for him."

"It seems you have done a couple of things for a number of people."

"I've been here for quite a few years."

"Yes, you have, though you've certainly lived all over the city."

"It took a while to find the right place and to be able to afford it. I am planted now."

"Gen and I love Tucson, but we are still getting used to it."

"It takes a while."

We sat for a bit, taking in the scene. Smitty and I can certainly fill the air space with chatter, but we are comfortable with silences.

"We watched the sunset during dinner at the Green Flash in P.B. a few years back."

"That's gone, too, Rocky. All the good restaurants in Pacific Beach and Mission Beach are either gone or turned into sports bars. P.B.'s not much of a family place anymore."

"You remember that dinner? You said something to me that I've never forgotten."

"Not particularly. What did I say? Was I erudite?"

"Not particularly." Smitty leaned back and covered his heart as though shot. He brought glances from our neighboring diners. A person of Smitty's girth is never unobtrusive. "It was poignant, however," I answered, ignoring him.

"Now I'm feeling the love."

I barged on, "I asked you how you came to be the way you are, mellow, go with the flow, and such. I thought you would say something about the beach life or the surfer mentality. Then I remembered you were like that as a kid. I think it is part of why we became friends. We were so different. I remembered that you had to convince the football coach that you could be violent enough to play defensive end."

"Oh yeah. That didn't work with coach Kush at ASU. He put me on the offensive line. I think that was part of what led to blowing out my knee. Defensive tackle is a rare back, full-head-of steam attack. The offensive position has a different skill set and some intricate footwork. I never got good at it. Anyway, go on with your story at the Flash."

"Your answer surprised me."

"So what did I say?"

"You said that you knew from the time you were young that big men didn't live very long, and you were going to enjoy every day while it lasted."

"I can hear myself saying that. I've said that to other people, but I don't anymore. Now for me it's more about living well and living in balance."

"You seem to have balance."

"Some areas, not others. That has not always been the case. It was my external demeanor as a kid. I spent years definitely out of balance, but it's not just about balance. It's also about harmony, and that is another topic altogether. I am learning both, and I had to learn life is about both. Is this what is bothering you?"

I sat silent for quiet for quite a while. "Perhaps."

"Have you more to say, or are you just inserting a Padre Cisco-ism?"

"More likely, I'm just buying time."

"Well, out with it, man. I can afford the dinner, but I can't afford to pay rent here."

"Hardly." I was still buying time. I wasn't sure I knew my own mind. Finally, I said, "It's part of it, but I think it has more to do with value. Does my life, or more explicitly, does my *work* have value."

"Well, Rocky, that's a classic question of men our age?"

"I am aware of that. I've been wrestling with what I'm told are all classic questions of men our age. You know this?"

"Of course I do. My blessing was that it came earlier in life for me. I think it was because I didn't have a woman like Gen in my life. I had to look elsewhere for reflection from someone else on my life. You have Gen, and now you have found your padre. I've had a couple of Padre Ciscos who've nurtured me for maybe ten or so years. Otherwise, I'd be an even bigger mess than you are."

"Ouch!"

"Well deserved."

The server interrupted us with our dinner.

Smitty had ordered red ale to go with his pan-seared salmon. I got blond ale to go with the saffron bouillabaisse made with main lobster, scallops, white fish, clams, and mussels. If I was to get only one fresh fish fix, I decided to maximize it. When nature created the Sonoran desert out of the ocean, fresh fish was one of the great losses.

"Let's take a time out, eat, and continue after dinner. I don't think you want to listen to me talk with my mouth full." Motioning to the feast before him, "I don't want to be distracted from this." We ate in relative silence, punctuated by tidbits of small talk and regular growls of pleasure. We reconvened only to exclaim our satisfaction. We ordered the apple-cinnamon bread pudding with caramel and vanilla ice cream and the cherry tart beer float with shortbread cookie. We shared them like a couple of teenagers on a first date and lauded our choices as equal to the main course. I knew I would pay for our gluttony the next day. It was a delight worth the agony. I sat back, savoring the meal, and delaying the future for just a while longer.

Breaking into the moment, Smitty said, "I've been thinking about your statement of wanting to be a 'completer' man, if I can use such a word. You saw *Saving Private Ryan*. You told me you went to see it in the theatre because you wanted to experience something of what your father must have experienced in Korea."

"You, too? Are you sure you don't know Padre Cisco? He talks about that movie."

"I know of him. Do you remember the final scene with an older Ryan and his family at the Normandy Cemetery?"

"Of course. The scene in which Ryan asks his wife to tell him he's been a good man."

"That's the one. It's a key point of the movie, but to me it's not the pivotal point in the story for Private Ryan."

"Okay, Smitty, my curiosity is aroused."

"Remember the scene when Captain Miller was dying and what he said to Private Ryan?"

"Yes the scene, not the dialogue."

"Leading up to it there was betting and conniving by the platoon to find out what job Captain Miller had before the war."

"Yes, but I couldn't tell you what his job was."

"Miller was a teacher, and his dying words to Ryan, his final lesson so to speak, was 'James, earn this…earn it.' This in a nutshell was for me a message equal to the final scene. The final scene hinged on Miller's statement. It was certainly poignant. It was about the outcome, which as portrayed, the director implied was a question. The earlier *dying-words* scene was about the process and the role people have in each other's lives to be teachers. Ryan's request at the end turned on that pivotal moment at Captain Miller's death. Now, I don't agree with Miller's statement, and I think it was wrong to lay that onus on Ryan; but that's another matter altogether. My take-away from the earlier scene is about the role and the process."

"So, tell me what you think is wrong about that."

"Ah crap, Rocky, I knew as soon as I said it you would go off on that tangent. This scene presents a major theological question for me, but we would need hours just for that. I'll respond to you, but this is just a digression, not the point."

"Okay, I'll accept that."

"Ryan was given a gift, a gift of life. Miller and his platoon gave Ryan the gift, but it was not a gift out of love. It was a gift out of duty. I'm not saying Miller didn't have love, but his act was one of duty, love for country. Given this, his parting words to Ryan were to exact a price, 'Earn it. James, Earn it.' It is not anyone's place, especially the donor, to ask the recipient to pay for a gift, or as in this case, earn it. A gift is free. That's what makes it a gift. It is only our place as a recipient of a gift to place a cost on it, which we often do. We label the cost worthiness. To do so is for us to miss the point that it was a gift. A gift has no strings attached. Can we leave it at that, and come back some other time?"

"Absolutely, but if this is not what we are talking about, what are we talking about?"

"I think, Rocky, we are talking about the questions Ryan, you, I, many, most, or all of us ask. We're talking about everything related to 'Am I a good man? Have I led a good life? Has my life been of value, or is my life of value? Is there some greater purpose in life? Do I need to respond to that? Do I need to change, alter my ways, come to myself, be a better man?' So, I'll put the elephant on the table, Rocky. Do you?"

"Do I what?"

Smitty gritted his teeth and slowly shook his head. He exhaled and in a soft voice said, "Oh come on, stop being a hard case." Returning to his normal voice, "You didn't come over here to sit and gaze upon my ravishing good looks. Move off the dime. Take a flying leap into the unknown. Do you feel the call to be a better man? I'll say it again. Do you?"

"I do."

"Hallelujah! I now pronounce you Rocky and Self. Mazel tov!" That got the attention of the other diners. "Of course, you want to be a better man. I know that; I just wanted to hear you say it. God bless it, Rocky. Everything you have said resonates a resounding yes! And yes, this is hard work. It's inner work, and you just did some of the hardest work of your life. You are on the journey. If you think you are on the journey, you are on the journey.

"Your nine-month metaphor this afternoon was highly apt. It just took losing your job and turning sixty to get you pregnant. Congratulations, Rocky, you have just given birth to a 6'5", 240lb self. Now all you have to do is raise your self into a full-fledged human being in the likeness you believe you are to emulate. You thought the birthing was hard. Wait for what comes next. Some of us, pointing at his head, have been saddled with a perennial teenager."

"Thanks, Smitty. That's inviting."

"Oh, it is. You get to parent yourself, and you know you don't want to be a single parent. It is too hard. You need help, and you know we all get along with a little help from our friends." He sat back, drained his beer, and said, "So there it is. Its out."

I was sure I was the center of attention of the entire restaurant. I knew they must be amazed at my ability to become shorter and taller at the same time. I hoped the beach environment masked the red that rose to my face. I said, "This must be what it is like for someone at AA to stand for the first time, and say hi, my name is Rocky, and I'm an alcoholic."

"Yes, Rocky, but that statement is followed by a chorus of friends and fellow pilgrims saying hi, Rocky. That's where the rest of us come in. We are your 'Hi, Rocky' chorus."

I sat back in my chair and exhaled deeply. A sense of catharsis fell over me. I was speechless, and Smitty allowed me to be so. I had dragged my feet in admitting what everyone around me saw. Now that I had said it aloud, I was taller. I sat there reveling in the moment. The diners at adjoining tables would see nothing different in me. They couldn't, but I could see a different me. I was present to myself.

Smitty brought me out of reverie when I heard him say, "Let's get out of this joint. I want to have another beer, but I'm driving. I have some Monks' Ale from a Benedictine Monastery in New Mexico that will set us right." I must have stood up and walked to the car. The next thing I remember is that we were sitting on Smitty's balcony on the eighteenth floor, looking out over the harbor, and drinking very stout beer.

Smitty lives in a high-rise condo in the Gaslamp Quarter overlooking San Diego Bay

He furnished it elegantly in a minimalist way. We sat for an hour or so, sipping our beers and enjoying the view. I was truly sipping. I can't imagine the double- and triple-strength versions Smitty told me they brewed. I asked him if there was a local distributer. He said, "No, I picked it up when I visited there." I was surprised, but too tired to pursue the thought. We revisited old times, retelling stories we both knew. I needed a break from the conversation. He was right when he said I didn't go over there for his ravishing good looks. At the same time, we have a lot of history of just shooting the bull for the pleasure of doing so.

I faded quickly, and went in to call Gen. I told her how appreciative I was for encouraging me to take the trip. I said that I might need a vacation from my vacation. We didn't talk long before she said, "Hang up, Rocky. You're falling asleep. I love you."

* * *

Smitty and I slept in. It must have been the natural sedative we'd ingested the night before. We had rolls and coffee on the deck. I didn't want to eat much because we were going for surfing.

The onshore breeze made sitting on the deck pleasant, but the wind pushing over the waves would make less than ideal conditions for surfing. I decided that was a good thing in my condition. We ate, put our boards in my car, and headed to Old Man's. The surf was quiet but better than expected. We both were ready to quit after a couple of hours.

We changed and headed to Seaforth Sport Fishery in the marina on Mission Bay. It has a fresh fish deli and with a walkup window. We ordered fish and chips and found a table outside.

Smitty and I sat in silence, taking in the scene around the marina. The boats' hulls creaked and groaned as they rubbed against their moorings. Seagulls flitted about, searching for handouts. Signs posted asked the diners not to feed the birds. The request drew only partial compliance from tourists, especially the children, who get few such opportunities. Marinas have their own smell, a combination of salt air, brackish water, and diesel fuel. Our perch had an overlay of fish frying. It was perfect.

An older couple, holding hands, strolled by in the measured steps of their companionship. In spite of the warm day, they both wore topcoats. He wore a fedora and carried a cane. A younger couple trailed them a short distance behind. Walking more briskly, they approached their elders, separated, and glanced over their shoulders as they passed. Rejoining, they clasped hands and slowed their pace. Smitty and I both saw it and exchanged smiles.

He broke the silence. "That moment and your story last night at The Flash of big men don't live very long reminded me of a statement of one of my mentors. We were discussing the idea of dying to one's self. He said in response to a question I had, 'Old wise men die many deaths on the road to wisdom.' We just saw one of those moments."

"Who did you see dying to himself?"

"Themselves! The younger couple of course."

"Not the old man?"

"No, Rocky, obviously, he has done that many times over. The young couple took each other's hand and slowed their pace.

They left a piece of old behavior, and possibly a piece of an old attitude, behind."

"Smitty, What you describe as obvious, I don't even see. I just saw a sweet moment. We look at the same things, but you see them differently. You ascribe greater meaning to them."

"I had a good mentor."

"Who was that?"

"He's a man that I met earlier in life when he was a business consultant. He worked with our company when we went through one of those repurposing periods. His name is Michael Lee, and he ..."

"Whoa, whoa, whoa, whoa! Michael Lee? Michael Francis Lee?"

"Yes, you know him?"

"No, Smitty, I don't know him, but I know *of* him. In fact, you're only the second person who has ever mentioned him and given veracity to his existence."

"I'm not sure what you mean. How do you know of him?"

"Padre Cisco grew up with him. They are friends. He quotes Michael Francis a lot. Until now, I've never been sure he was a real person, an alter ego, or a figment of the padre's imagination."

"Well, Rocky, Michael Lee is a real-life, living, breathing human being. In fact, he's very successful at being a human being. He was a highly sought-after business consultant in his earlier life. Now he serves as a spiritual director and is a mentor and guide to many men, including me. He is a bona fide second-half-of-life person. I would list him among the wisdom teachers of my life. Michael is a member of a group called Illuman. It is a group of men who are on the journey. He introduced me to it."

"So, Smitty, I want know how you came to know him in this later role. What is Illuman, and how did you become a part of it, but what I *really* want to know is why have you never talked about it? For as long as I've known, I've never heard about this part of your life."

"Probably guilty as charged. I think I've talked about it; you didn't hear me. At times the conversation diverted. At times, you diverted it. I don't want this to sound like this is all on you, Rocky. It is been a part of my life that has been discreet if not reserved. However, Rocky, you've been a lone wolf for much of your life. I left Akron to go to ASU to be part of a team. You left Akron to get out of Akron. You got to college and left your church behind. I hung in with mine. You're Jeremiah Johnson."

"Jeremiah Johnson! That's extreme."

"My work depends on other people. Your work is solitary. I know you and Gen are both working at home, but I'm talking about interaction with other people. I'm talking about being a part of a community. You don't go off to the mountains, but you don't go down to the towns either. We're different that way. It's not a condemnation; it just is. We were different as kids. I was Catholic and you were Protestant. We never talked about religion, much less faith or spirituality. We have been on different paths, but they are part of the same journey. These conversations are new arenas for us."

"But why didn't you ever bring it up before?"

"I guess I didn't think you had ears to hear."

"Well, Mr. Smith, I do now. Speak. Fess up. Spill the beans."

"Ooh, now I'm Mr. Smith. You're bringing the heavy-caliber ammunition. I'll have to think about where to start." Smitty sat for a bit. "Probably the car wash."

"The car wash?"

We heard our names called, and went to get our food. We sat back down and abandoned our earlier manners, eating and talking at the same time. The gulls began edging forward as though anticipating a reward. Smitty shooed them away with a thrust of his leg.

"The car wash," I repeated.

Smitty told me about an incident a few years ago. He was in Chula Vista to see a wealthy client. Chula Vista is a suburb south of San Diego. He was driving in circles when he passed a car wash. It wasn't a business, but a car wash held by a local group of family and friends. They had a sign about donating to their grandmother's funeral costs. He said, "It stopped me flat." He got angry. An image of a TV news story of the pauper's field in Phoenix popped into his head.

His car was clean, but he had it washed anyway. He asked the leader about the circumstances and learned the deceased was his mother. He said the man's name was José. He asked José where he went to church and if someone else could manage the carwash for a while. The church was just a few blocks away. Smitty called his client and told him where he was. Smitty asked if they could meet at the church.

The upshot of the meeting was that they arranged for the church to accept donations to cover the costs to José's family. They put a process in place to account for future similar needs in the parish. When Smitty and José returned to the carwash Smitty had what he called his "second revelation."

José called in the kids on the corner with the signs. He gathered his family and told them the news. He took a black magic marker, flipped over the signs, and wrote FREE CARWASH. He sent the kids back out to the street. José turned to Smitty and told him that they don't have money to donate, but they have time. "Time is what we will give." With a knowing smile he added, "But you know people, Mr. Smith. Some people will donate even to a free carwash." He told Smitty they would give the money they collected to the church fund. Smitty replied, "You're a wise man, José, and it's Smitty." They exchanged phone numbers, and Smitty drove off to see his client.

"I get it, Smitty, but I don't get it."

"You get what, but don't get what?"

"Why was that so important to you?"

"I want to answer that, Rocky, but I don't want to get pressed for time. I need to shower and get to my meeting. Let's go. We can continue in the car. After work we can try out one of the micro-breweries." We made the short drive in silence. I needed processing time.

* * *

Smitty went to his meeting, and I took a sketchpad and wandered about the Gaslamp district. I found a pub we might visit. I wound my way down to the bay past the convention center. I walked along the quay toward the pier where the harbor cruise boats moor and found a place to sit and sketch. The tourist crowds abate after Labor Day when children return to school. I had ample room to work. People tend to give artists a wide berth when they are working. They will rubberneck from a distance, but to get close it is like walking between a photographer and his subject. I needed the space and the time alone. My brain was bouncing between ideas for a strip, what was in front of me, and the conversations I'd been having. At four-thirty Smitty called telling me he was done.

We met at the Union Kitchen and Tap. It has a wide selection of draft beers and sandwiches. For all my yen for fish, I was ready to have simple food. We both got burgers. We acquitted ourselves well in expanding our horizons of the brewery fare. We caught up on our afternoons, and I reminded him that he was going to tell me why the carwash event was so important.

"Well, as Paul Harvey used to say, '…and now the rest of the story,' but this all came to me later."

He said that part of it was the twist on the parable of the Good Samaritan. The injured man by the side of the road was serving the others. He didn't see that coming. He was acting out of what he called a *this–is–a– good–deed–that–needs–to–be–done* moment. He was in his Beamer on his way to see the wealthy landlord, and he stopped off to take care of one of the 'least of these.' When José was healed he turned right around and became the Good Samaritan. That story is not in the Bible. Smitty said he was Private Ryan, not the old man Ryan but the young Ryan. He was the injured man by the side of the road, who Miller, in the role of the Samaritan, reaches out to one last time to try to help. He said, "I was getting messages that I was finally hearing."

Smitty said, "I acted out of anger. I didn't know why; I just did. I didn't learn why until after I did some of the inner work that each of us must do, but I was bothered about why anger rose in me."

"Are you saying this was about anger?"

"Yes, but it was more than that. I had a cocktail of emotions going: guilt and pride, anger and joy among them; but mostly I was embarrassed. My opulence and lifestyle in contrast to the scene I was witnessing embarrassed me. They were not conscious thoughts, but I know now they were part of what drove me to act."

"And this led to where you are now?"

"Not in so many words, Rocky. It set me to questioning."

He said he remembered getting home and feeling depleted. He sat and downed a couple of beers. He told me he was a pusher back then. The affable, loveable guy I knew existed only when he was off the clock. He said, "The high finance world is not a place for the timid." He likened it to playing football. When he was between the white lines, he was a different person. He could summon the rage. He sat and looked around at his surroundings, and the accumulation of toys. He asked the questions I've been asking. Is this it? Is this all there is? Is this what I have to show for what I am doing? Is this what I want to be about? It didn't lead anywhere, but it started the process. He said, "I began to recognize that I didn't want to be two different people."

"Wow, Smitty, I didn't know any of this."

"Of course not."

"Why didn't you tell me any of this?"

"It wasn't an epiphany. There were no lightning bolts. It was one event."

"But it led to a change in you."

"Rocky, I hear you seeking a direct answer, a formula. This is not, or at least it was not for me a point A to point B process. I didn't find the magic pill. My experience that day started the process. It even may have kick-started it, but change has been a slow shift over a long period. It takes learning, it takes practice, and it takes patience."

"So, where did it take you?"

"Well, it's going to take me home about now. I'm beat. Let's table this until tomorrow."

I wanted to hear the rest of the story, but I knew he was done. We paid our bill and walked home, making small talk.

The next morning we both drove to Old Man's for one more stint at in the ocean. Afterward, we met at the Bird Rock Coffee

House in La Jolla. We stood in line. There is always a line at Bird Rock. We found a table on the sidewalk and watched the parade of Porsches, Beamers, Ferraris, and Lamborghinis.

I said, "When we left off you were talking about where the carwash incident led you."

"It's a good thing you are keeping track of this. Give me a moment to recollect my own story." Grimacing, Smitty said, "I hesitate here, Rocky. I don't have this kind of conversation with many people. I wonder if you expect to get some insight. I have to say again that it was a slow emergence. It still is."

"I follow you. I don't have any expectations."

"There were a lot of fits and starts. I had questions without answers. I went through introspection, confusion, reading, wondering, and searching. I went down blind alleys. In the words of Johnny Lee, I was looking for love in all the wrong places. Eventually it took me to Michael Lee, or maybe it brought Michael Lee to me."

"I can't quite picture you as an urban cowboy."

"Trust me, Rocky, I wasn't."

The interchange brought a much needed round of laughter. This Smitty was all new to me, but I had a sense of anticipation as though this was why I was here.

"This is the part I've been waiting to hear, Smitty, you and Michael Lee. I have a hard time saying, Michael Lee; Padre Cisco's reference to him has always been Michael Francis or Michael Francis Lee. What was his part in this?"

"He told me that when I began getting serious about answering my questions, he started researching spirituality and such on the net. His church is small and doesn't offer much in the way of spiritual formation. He found a larger church that had contemplative prayer groups, classes, and a monthly one-day retreat. He enrolled on their mailing list and began attending some of their events. He still worships at his local parish, but it doesn't have the resources the larger churches have. Smitty said, "The resource challenge and the carwash experience later led me to use my experience in an arena of ministry I never expected, but that's another story...and I know you want the rest of this story."

"Yes, Smitty, Michael Francis Lee? What does this have to do with him?"

"About a year later, I received an email, and he was listed in the coming attractions section of the church newsletter. The contemplative life ministry at the church invited him as their fall retreat speaker. I hadn't gone to any of those days, but I went to that one."

"That's quite a coincidence."

"Perhaps it was simply the illusion of coincidence."

"You're being very spiritual now, Smitty. I'm going to get goose bumps."

"You are really having trouble with this, aren't you, Rocky?"

"I guess I am. My perceptions of you are all wonky. If you've heard the same stories I have, I'd say my ants are turning into water buffalo."

"I know that story. It's one of Michael Lee's. Where did you hear it? Oh, ...well of course, from Padre Cisco. Trust me, Rocky, your ants are ants, your buffalo are buffalo, and it is I who left you in the density of the rainforest."

"Okay, go on with Michael Lee."

"In keeping with your experience I'll refer to him as Michael Francis. Okay?"

"Got it."

He went to the retreat. After the first conference of the day, he reintroduced himself to Michael Francis. He was surprise Michael Francis remembered him. "At least he conveyed that he remembered me." Smitty asked him if he could have some time later. They talked for more than an hour. They caught up on their history since their earlier relationship. Michael Francis had a lot of questions. He suggested Smitty consider finding a spiritual director and talked about SDI, Spiritual Directors International and its on-line directory. He gave Smitty a couple of names. They exchanged contact information and left with a plan to talk again by phone.

Smitty attended his events when he was nearby and talked with him occasionally. After going it on his own with a couple of people, he did find a spiritual director, one of those Michael Francis suggested. Smitty said, "I would suggest the same for you. You can't keep driving over to see me to have someone to talk to, and I am definitely not a spiritual director."

"I'll look into it."

"Read about it on the SDI website, and talk to Padre Cisco. I'm sure he can steer you in the right direction."

"I would suspect so."

"Michael Francis introduced me to Illuman, and it's through that group we cemented our relationship."

"Illuman? What's that, Smitty?"

"It's a group of men with the common quest of the spiritual journey. It focuses on rituals related to men's rites of passage. It is getting too late to go into that, if you are going to get home before dark. Suffice it to say it is a community of men collectively dedicated to supporting each other in their individual journeys. We can talk more about that next time. Check it out. The Illuman website is very informative."

"I want to stay and talk more. I want to hear more about how what you have learned translates into daily life. I want to know the long-term outcome of your carwash experience. I sense that is part of it, but you are right about the drive home. I do need to get going."

Smitty said, "I'd say I want you to stay, but you know about fish and company. I am without a doubt sure that we have maintained our friendship for so long because we have adhered to that adage."

"That's always been a good rule of thumb, and a good note to leave on. It's been a great stay, and a great conversation, Smitty. I thank you for your support and your candor."

"Get going, Rocky, before I get all teary. It is embarrassing for people to watch a large man blubber."

I got one more cup of coffee and filled my thermos for the drive. With that we walked to our cars, hugged, and I left. I was anxious to see Gen talk with her.

Autumn

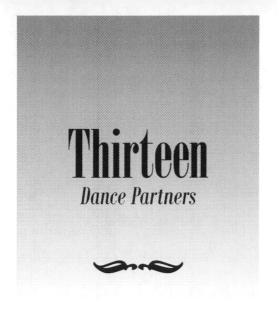

Thirteen
Dance Partners

"Abba, give me a word."
"Harmony, my son."
"How do I find harmony, Abba?"
"Balance, my son."
"How do I learn balance?"
"Harmony, my son."

I got back to Tucson before dark. I was glad that I went, but I was glad to be home. Gen welcomed me with her usual flourish. She didn't ask me about the drive. She knows the drive as well as I, and she's not one to belabor the obvious. We sat on the patio. She had snacks and a bottle of cabernet decanting. We had wine, and I devoured the cheese and crackers. I hadn't eaten only a sandwich in Yuma. I told her about the surfing and what a challenge is was, but that I didn't admit that to Smitty. I prattled on about the San Diego beer mecca and the fish.

Finally, Gen said, "So…Rocky?"

I can't say I was taken off guard, but I should have been prepared for her "So." I had just spent the previous six hours sequestered by my own thoughts, yet all I had to say in response was, "Which 'so' is that, Gen? The 'tell me about it so' or the 'what did you learn so'?"

"I'm hoping it's not the 'am I going to have to pry it out of you so.' Take your pick, Rocky."

"I'll stick with the first two." I recapped the trip, the surfing, and the conversations to cover the first 'so,' and then moved on to the second. I started to tell her about what I'd learned about Smitty, but she uncharacteristically interrupted.

"I don't mean to stop you, but I am. My question about what you learned was asking what you discovered about yourself, Rocky. I got the gist about Smitty from what you already told me. I am nearly as surprised as you, but I want to hear about you."

"This is too funny. At one point, I told Smitty that he was pulling a Gen on me, and now you are pulling a Smitty on me. Are you two in collusion? Is there no escape?"

"Certainly no collusion and definitely no escape. It's all about you right now."

"He called me a lone wolf and Jeremiah Johnson. I've never thought of myself as a loner. I'm a pretty social guy."

"Yes, you are, Rocky, when social comes to you, or I bring you to it; but you don't seek social situations out on your own. Jeremiah Johnson may be extreme, but I can understand Smitty characterizing you that way. He's a direct guy."

"Direct? I'd say blunt. *Extreme* was the word I used."

"Maybe so, but he made his point, didn't he?"

"You'll be gentler with me, I'm sure."

Gen answered, "I'll put my kid gloves on, Rocky" with a nod and a smile indicating quite the opposite.

I told her about the Mozel Tov conversation, and my sense of catharsis at Tom Ham's. I related that I recognized how long I'd been waffling, and it cued my memory to Padre Cisco's question the first time I went out there, "You have waffles for breakfast?" I finally got it. I had waffled even longer than I imagined. I laughed at myself for being such a dunce. I told her about Illuman, and Smitty's suggestion of seeing a spiritual director. I said that I had new questions for Padre Cisco. We cleared the table, went to bed, and Gen curled up into my arm.

I was anxious to see Padre Cisco, but I was more anxious to get back into the studio. I spent the morning reorienting myself in the project. I waited until the afternoon to call Padre Cisco. It was two weeks before we could meet.

The idea about the Koanheads was emerging. It involved "Koan the Librarian," a koan master, as a personified caret and other characters, the seekers, as question marks. The seekers would go to the library looking for answers only to get more questions in response. I progressed far enough in the two weeks that I thought I was ready to talk to my agent. I had three prototype strips completed. Two were black and white, four panel strips, and the other one was an eight- panel color version. I was jazzed by the idea.

I thought I could combine a business trip with a visit to the kids. I called Arnie, but Marcia, his secretary, said he and his wife were leaving on vacation to Europe in a week. I decided to go anyway and called both kids. I talked with Alex and arranged to meet for coffee. I left a message on Morgan's phone but did not hear back from her. After two days and two more calls without a response, I called Alex and said I needed to reschedule the trip. I wanted to see both the kids, but I needed to see Morgan.

Wen I was finally over my peevishness, I called Arnie and set a date to meet the first week of November. I called Alex, and we found a suitable time for both of us to connect. Morgan's phone went straight to voice mail, and I left a message with my itinerary asking her to call me. She didn't. I wondered if she was avoiding me. A litany of *choice* words ran through my mind. I thought of what I was going to say when I saw her. Then "Don't rehearse tomorrow's problems," jumped into my mind and nudged my other thoughts aside. *That's what Mary was saying. Well, Rocky, you're slow, but maybe there's hope for you yet.* I still didn't know who Sarah Young was. I did know any progress depended on me. I would just have to keep after her. I decided to give it a couple of days and call her again.

Gen and I were both busy. We had time together before breakfast, quick lunches, and long dinners. We ate out more, returning home to have a glass of wine together. Other than my complaining about Morgan, our conversation ran the gamut of subjects, and on and off about the year. We talked more about our feelings toward the events than the events themselves. The intimacy in our relationship returned. I felt good to be in rhythm again. I thought about rhythm and wondered about its relationship to balance and harmony.

* * *

Padre Cisco greeted me in the driveway. The day was a typical autumn day that reminds me why I put up with the monsoon season. Late September has cloudless skies, cool mornings, warm afternoons, and pleasant evenings. We sat in the Adirondacks on the veranda with coffee in hand. The sun peeked through the ramada, creating silhouettes of ladders on the walls. A peace settled over me in the afternoon stillness. Breaking the silence I said, "It's been a month or so since we have talked. It's been busy. I'm glad to be busy and productive again, but "I've missed this."

"That is good to hear. You had quite a dry spell. How was your trip?"

I said, "Well," slowing nodding my head to punctuate my feeling. I recapped the visit with Smitty, telling the padre about the discussions Smitty and I had. I told him that many questions arose in me. I let him in on my awakening to his waffle remark from the first time we met. He laughed and actually slapped his knee. I don't sneak up on him as often as he does on me. I told him about the connection between Michael Francis Lee and Smitty. I covered Smitty's suggestion to find a spiritual director and wondering about the relationship between rhythm, balance, and harmony. "It seems, Padre, the more answers I seek the more questions I have."

"That is a good place to be, Peter. Ranier Rilke would be happy for you. I don't have many answers, but two things arise. Life is all about the questions, and being in the conversation is the way into the questions. I have learned that though I could be an institutional dropout, the questions remained, and I needed to stay in the conversation. If we are not in the conversation, we are only into ourselves. That is a place of little stimulation for growth, much less change. Being in the conversation is a key to personal movement. Is that not what we have spent nearly a year doing, Peter, holding conversation?"

"We certainly have, Padre, but sometimes I think I am just going in circles."

"That reminds me of Eric's swimming story. He did not know how poignant he was." Padre Cisco leaned his head back and closed his eyes. After a moment he continued, "You are in a circle, Peter; that is the beauty of it: always a new beginning. Wherever we arrive, we are always at a new beginning. Perhaps there are three things to which I might have answers."

"You are two up on me, Padre. The one thing I know is I have more questions."

"Absolutely. Take the ultimate question: Who or what is God? As soon as we answer that, our concept of God is changed, and that creates new questions about the nature of God. It is a circle. It is a hora."

"Hora, Padre?"

"Yes, it is a circle dance. You remember *Hava Nigila*?"

"Okay."

"Richard Rohr wrote a book about his understanding of God called *The Divine Dance*. He used the image of a circle dance as a metaphor for God. He also used a rubber band. That one made me laugh. Rohr is expansive in his thinking, no pun intended."

"I'm never sure about the no pun intended part, Padre, but I can see what you mean about always being back to the beginning. Once I make the complete circle, I come back to a place I've been. The circle dance certainly describes my predicament."

"Join the club, Peter. It is a large club, the universal predicament."

We stopped, got up and poured fresh coffee, then stood talking in the kitchen.

"Peter, you said you always come back to a place you have already been. That is true, but because of your experiences, you come to that place with a different perspective. Perhaps your definition of that place has changed. We have been there before, and we are not the same. It is like waking up each day and knowing it is a new beginning."

"In essence you are saying that regardless of the answer, returning generates new questions."

"Exactly, Peter." He paused. "I want to hear your other questions, but you mentioned rhythm. Let me explore that for a moment." We returned to the veranda and sat. "I have not spent as much consideration on rhythm as on balance and harmony, but I can hardly think they are not related. Is the tide related to the ocean or the moon to the tide? Are our circadian clocks related to the sun, moon, seasons, or length of days? The late John O'Donohue, an Irish poet and mystic, links rhythm to a sense of destiny. He wrote that when you awaken your sense of destiny, you find your rhythm, which is the secret key to balance and belonging. He uses the term *dynamic equilibrium*. I think everything may be related in ways that we can hardly imagine, much less understand."

""Like many people, Padre, I have those moments of being connected to all things, the cosmic consciousness or whatever people call it. When I catch a good wave and ride it well, I have that feeling.

"That is an apt analogy. I have been pondering the relationship of balance and harmony to movement and shift."

"Okay?"

"I connect those ideas to Judith Favor's *oceanic consciousness*. I will tell you about her. Bear with me on this. I am still in the process of sorting it out myself."

"Lead on, Macduff."

"Lead on, Macduff. Sometimes you just crack me up, Rocky," grinning and shaking his head. "Anyway, these thoughts began in the early eighties when I read Ken Keyes's *The Hundredth Monkey*."

The padre related the gist of Keyes's book, based on the concept of *shift*. It was a study of monkeys on a Japanese island in the 1950s. Scientists were dropping sweet potatoes for the monkeys. The potatoes got sandy, but one young monkey learned to wash them in the stream. The monkey taught her mother and her companions, who taught their mothers. Most of the monkeys were soon following suit. When the number of monkeys washing their potatoes reached some tipping point, euphemistically the hundredth monkey, all the monkeys began washing the potatoes. He said, "Then the unexpected happened. A shift occurred. Monkeys on other islands began washing potatoes."

He called it *collective consciousness*. He related a popular PowerPoint called Shift Happens that went viral on the web and the book *The Tipping Point*. Both publications promoted the idea that at some point when enough people think or act in a certain way, a shift occurs. Most people start thinking or acting the same way.

He said he began to look at the idea from a personal standpoint like a circus performer spinning plates. No sooner would he get one plate spinning than others were wobbling or crashing. Life out was out of balance. Since he wasn't able to keep all the plates spinning, he was never satisfied. He said, "I realized I was seeking the wrong thing, balance not harmony." Balance requires that you pay as much attention to the things you are not doing as to the one thing you are doing. To achieve balance he was continually distracted. "Harmony can be found in paying attention to that one thing you are doing, but at the expense of balance."

"I've experience the same thing, Padre, but I've never put those labels to it. When I was in the studio working on the strip, I was content. Nothing else entered my mind. I've always thought my life was in balance, but it may have more a case of harmony. I will need to think more about that."

"You might want to add this piece to your thoughts." He described going to the opposite extreme. I seeking harmony he could be content doing one thing in spite of all the other things that were at that moment left undone. He said he was nearing the tipping point to harmony, convinced that if he remained in harmony, balance would sort itself out. That point never came. There was something missing. He settled on the notion that balance or harmony at the expense of the other was at best half a loaf. He said, "Balance and harmony are dance partners."

"Padre, my first thought was 'hand and glove,' but that concept has a sense of primary and secondary facets. ' Dance partners' has a greater sense of equality to it. I like that."

Please, do not quote me on this. I am still working with it. It is just a notion. I need to sit with the idea for a while."

"Then you can imagine my dilemma, Padre. To me this is like one of those year-end, giant crossword puzzles in the Sunday newspaper."

"We are a people of words, but you are blessed, Rocky. You are, also, a man of pictures. I can imagine that your dreams are very vivid."

I threw up my hand as a stop sign. "Please, don't even begin to go there. That is mishmash beyond comprehension. You spoke earlier of Judith Favor," I said, wanting to change the subject.

"Ah, yes, Judith Favor. Judith is a spiritual director, a writer, and contemplative. She tells of sitting on a bluff on the Oregon coast at sunset. As a young woman, she was a professional balloonist until a fiery crash. She was sort of a modern-day Amelia Earhart or Georgia O'Keefe."

"I can identify with Georgia O'Keefe, Padre. She was a bit of a dare-devil, zooming about on her motorcycle in her leathers and goggles."

"She was an independent woman," he answered in his non-judgmental way. "Judith told a group of us that when she was a small girl, each evening her grandmother would sit on a bench overlooking the ocean. Judith has this voice like Julia Child's and is a low-talker, in the Seinfeld vernacular. She is difficult for me to hear. I am never sure I have her stories straight. You might notice, Peter, when I can I sit with the light at my back. Hearing gets harder as we get older; it helps to see the speaker. You speak clearly and loud enough that it isn't a problem, but it still helps to be able to see you speak."

The story she told the padre was that one evening she asked her grandmother if she could sit with her. Her grandmother replied that she could if she would be perfectly quiet. Judith said that after many evenings of watching the setting sun, she developed what she described as an oceanic consciousness. The padre said that he loves the concept with its connotation of wholeness, but he thought there was another piece to her story. He related it to the musician Sting.

Sting described a similar experience with a shaman in the rain forest. Brazil. He said he would go each evening with a shaman to a hillside. They would sit silently and watch the sun go down. Sunrise and sunset are the times that you can look directly at the sun. At those times, your eyes can absorb lithium from the sun. Lithium is a requirement of our bodies and serves as an anti-depressant. It helps us have a sense of wellbeing. Padre Cisco said, "Hence, we have the source of Sting's song and album, *Lithium Sunset*."

"That is so cool. I love learning the background to songs. It enhances their meaning."

"What strikes me, Peter, is that I wonder if the effects lithium had on Judith tempered her experience in silence and stillness. In the same way, I wonder if pausing daily to sit in stillness and silence to watch the sun go down mediated Sting's experience with the lithium effects of the sunset. Perhaps it is never all of one thing but some of both."

"Not to divert you, but you like Sting?"

"Yes, I do. I like the thought that goes into his music. I like the fact that he still produces music with real instruments rather than synthesizers. I am not against that, though. I certainly like Manheim Steamroller, and their music is full of digital sound. I just appreciate the effort Sting puts into his music."

"I like his music, too."

"Peter, I think our ADD just took over."

"We did get onto a tangent."

He waited for a moment and returned to the discussion. "I appreciate the effort Judith puts into her writing and her life. Judith's concept of oceanic consciousness resonates with the concept of movement and shift. It was not an epiphanous experience with her grandmother that altered her consciousness. It was because she had repeated experiences. Sting says the same thing. They both practiced silence, stillness, awareness or consciousness over a long period, and movement developed. Out of the repetitions, shift happened. I suspect they were not actually aware of it until they looked back. Again, these are just notions. I am speculating a lot here. For Judith, her experiences were as a child, while Sting was an adult. That might make a difference in his level of consciousness. Perhaps those two are spiritual dance partners. That would be a sight."

"Perhaps you are man of pictures as well, Padre."

"Perhaps."

"Well, Padre, the *perhaps* I am considering in my own life is perhaps I am experiencing movement. It seems like it's been a long haul. I am aware of changes. I know I am looking at things from a different, if not new, perspective. It certainly has been full of fits and starts."

"Movement is just that. The tide rises and ebbs. If we were to use the music metaphor, life is a symphony of many movements. The Greek derivation of the word means 'concord of sound.' The modern use of the word connotes a particular four-movement form of classical music, though with variations. In the symphony of life, there can be as much dissonance as concordance. Life seldom occurs according to form. Fanfares, adagios, sonatas, scherzo, allegros all emerge in their own time. The music of life repeats and alternates throughout each of our own symphonies. There are as many variations as there are questions."

"I have to laugh, Padre. Sometimes I'm not sure whether your metaphors clarify or confound my thinking. I imagine, though, that I'm not alone in that."

"As I said earlier, Peter, you are not alone. It is large, this club called human beings; and beyond that, to be sure, you are also not alone."

"That's just it, Padre, in this journey thing I feel alone."

"How so?"

"But for you, Smitty, and Jen, I am alone. It's of my own making. Smitty called me a lone wolf and Jeremiah Johnson. He's right. I've lived a solitary life for a long time."

Padre Cisco sat, waiting for me to continue, but I didn't have any elaboration. It was as simple as Smitty had described. Finally, he learned forward with his elbows on his knees, and said, "To a certain extent, that is the way it is. You make your own journey. It is your life to discover. At the same time, it is not a good idea to go it alone. It is not healthy. You need help, guidance, and emotional support. The spiritual journey is an inner one, but it needs spiritual guides and spiritual friends. It is a community effort. Allow me to come back to that in a few moments."

I nodded.

"So tell me, what else is on your docket?"

"Morgan seems to be always on my docket. She continues to frustrate me, but that's not what we're here to talk about."

"We can talk about anything you deem important, Peter."

"It's important, but I need to work it out for myself. Give me a moment." I had to stop and think for a moment, recalling what we had or had not discussed. Padre Cisco waited as he always does with his eyes fixed firmly on me. "Smitty suggested I should consider seeing a spiritual director. I know nothing about what that is. He, also, talked briefly about a group called Illuman. The phrase 'ears to hear' has come up more than once, and I would like to hear more about Michael Francis Lee. Right now, that seems to be the extent of my list."

"Perhaps, rather than going right to those topics, I could interest you in an alternative experience that might shed some light for you. I meet regularly, about quarterly, with a small group of men for the purpose of sharing our lives in mutual support. Two of them are out of town, but Michael Francis will be there along with a couple of others I have known for many years. We would like you to join us. It is two weeks from today. We commit ourselves to this gathering and to connecting with each other at least once a month. For most of us, it is weekly."

"I would be honored, Padre. Is it okay with your friends?"

"Absolutely, Peter. I would not invite anyone without the group's concurrence. Michael Francis suggested inviting Smitty, as well. Would you check with him? I look forward to meeting him."

"I know he wants to meet you, Padre. I'll call him to check, then confirm with you."

"I must warn you, Peter, this is a group of men of faith. Most of us are Christians, though we are not limited by that."

"That won't scare me off, Padre."

"I did not think it would, but I do not like to blindside people."

"Oh, right, Padre, like you never do that in our conversations."

"Well yes, there is that," he said, grinning. "We meet about five and have dinner about six. We seek to have good conversation over a good meal. Hoover, one of our members, has a restaurateur friend who comps a room and the meal for us. Sometimes we designate a topic. This time, we chose community. We thought that would be germane for you. The group has followers of Saint Benedict of Nursia, Saint Francis of Assisi, and Saint John of Inglewood. They like to talk about community."

"Well, Padre, I can use all the help I can get on this community piece. I'm familiar with Benedict and Francis but not Saint John of Inglewood."

"I am surprised, Peter. I thought you would know Saint John. He had a complete sense of community, though he called it team. John Wooden, that is."

"Speaking of blindsiding, you may not have blindsided me, but you snuck up on me again, Padre. I don't know how I keep letting you do that to me."

"You told me you thought you were getting too serious. I just try to do my part."

We shared the moment. Padre Cisco stood and reached out to give me a hand up. We stood for a moment shaking hands, and he said, "This is good. We should have quite a gathering. I think you will appreciate what these men have to offer. Would you like to pray with me?"

Surprised at my willingness, I said, "Yes, I would, Padre."

We stood there in silence. After a couple of minutes, he said, "Amen," and then in his brogue added, "May the road rise to meet you, may the wind be always at your back, and may

you be an hour in heaven before the devil knows you are dead."
With a leprechaun's grin, he said, "I got you with that one, did
I not?" and ended with "I will walk you around, my friend."

I called Smitty on my way home. His reply was "Yes,
Michael Francis called me. I'll send you my flight information
and arrival time. See you then, Aloha," and he hung up. I
thought about how terse in ending conversations both these
men could be. It has never bothered me with Smitty. I just
always took it for how he is. His phone cell phone-outgoing
message is, "Speak at the beep." I've always wondered how his
clients responded to that.

On the way, home I found myself humming *Lithium Sunset*.
I realized how often I feel contented driving home from the
Padre's. *It's a far cry from my first visit. Maybe I am in a shift.*

Fourteen
The Seven Wise Men

"Abba, give me a word."
"Community, my son."
"What of community, Abba?"
"Leaves of gold grow on many trees."
"Where are these trees, Abba?"
"They must be planted."

I picked up Smitty at the airport, and we stopped at a coffee kiosk then drove to the restaurant.

"I have been looking forward to this evening, Rocky. Meeting Padre Cisco is high on the list. I've been wanting to talk in person with Michael Francis for a while."

"The interest is mutual, Smitty, but I'm a bit nervous."

"Nervous? You? Why?"

"You have experience with this sort of thing. It's new to me. I accepted Padre Cisco's invitation, but I may have acted out of the enthusiasm of the moment. I'm not sure I belong in this group."

"Perhaps that's what you're here to learn, Rocky."

"I *am* here to learn. I am sure of that."

"For a long time, I thought I had to go find a community. When I asked Michael Francis about the difficulty of that, he told me I might need to create my own. I asked how I do that, and he said we gather it one person at a time. Perhaps that is what Padre Cisco has done. I am curious about how this group came to be."

"Michael Francis and Padre Cisco have been friends since boyhood, though you know that. Two of the men Padre Cisco met at a retreat. I am not sure about the others."

"Rocky, my question is more about what draws them together than how they met. What draws them together, and what keeps them together?"

"I have the same questions."

We drove the short distance in silence. I had difficulty concentrating on driving.

When we arrived, the others had already gathered. Padre Cisco greeted us at the door. There were four men in addition to the padre and Michael Francis. We were in a small informal banquet room with a round table set for eight to one side. There were additional groupings of lounge chairs though everyone but Thomas was standing. A self-serve bar stood at the side of the room opposite the dining table. I wasn't sure whether I should sit or stand. *When in Rome...* I sided with the majority.

We spent an hour in greeting and conversation. Smitty introduced me to Michael Francis. He greeted me as though we had known each other for years. I confessed my question of his existence. Through a broad smile, he assured me that he was not a mirage. He is the tall, slightly stooped, Albert Einstein minus the mustache character that Padre Cisco portrayed. His half-frame glasses tethered to strap perched on the end of his nose. He asked about Gen and our children by name, which surprised me. His aura of amiability was all that Padre Cisco had described. I withdrew, knowing Smitty wanted time with him. Michael Francis drew in Padre Cisco. They spent much of the hour together with the intermittent inclusion of the others.

I met Gordon next. He dwarfed even Smitty. He is a former a football player with the girth, shoulders, and neck of a lineman. In his forties, he looked like he could still play. I learned that he progressed as far as the taxi squad on a couple of pro teams. He was wearing a golf shirt with a Wildcats emblem on it. When I asked if he played at the University of Arizona he answered, "No, but when in Rome don't be a Goth. Gordon is the fleet manager of a local car dealer. I liked his creative play on the adage. Apparently, he was not fleet of foot as a player. His teammates nicknamed him Flash. Enrique joined us. He is a chaplain in a recovery center. Enrique is short, round, bald, and about my age.

Hoover, the only Asian in the group, is a small as Gordon is large. He is the retired owner of a market and told me that he has dabbled in land. I learned from Padre Cisco that he has owned significant portions of downtown Tucson over the years. Hoover's father named him for President Hoover. He has brothers Roosevelt, Washington, Lincoln, and Truman.

In a lull, I went over to sit with Thomas. Before I sat, he reached out to shake my hand and with the other offered me his wine glass. He asked me if I would refill it for him. "Red, please. With a twinkle he said, "I can have a second glass; I'm not driving. I came with Hoover. I don't drive at night anymore." I thought of having a glass with him. I looked over at Smitty and saw he had wine. I stuck with coffee. I was driving.

Thomas is a tall, thin black man, likely in his eighties, but with a smooth face belying his age. He has closely cropped, short, salt and pepper hair. He was primly dressed wearing polished loafers, smartly creased gray slacks, and a navy blue cardigan sweater. He told me he and Padre Cisco met as teachers before the padre went to the university. Thomas was a basketball coach, and I assumed the St. John reference was to him. He had a quiet mien about him. In fact, all the men there seemed to have quiet dispositions. Tonight, even Smitty was relatively so.

A distinguishing characteristic of all of the conversations was that each of the men in one way or another asked about my family, my life, and particularly about my journey. Most curious among their questions was Hoover's.

He asked, "How's yer bones?"

"My bones?" I replied, wondering what he meant.

He said, "Well, if I were a Buddhist I might inquire as to your state of mind. As a Christian, I might ask about your soul. Among some Native Americans, the question would be how are your bones? I like the concept; it seems all encompassing. It's a variation of asking how you are doing. It is more than that though. It asks about your well-being."

I told him, "My bones are growing."

He accepted that with a laugh and said, "Nice answer."

Thomas was the most direct. He simply said, "Tell me your story, Rocky. What brought you to this place and time?" I gave him my bio brief. In turn, he gave me the thumbnail sketch of his own journey and his relationship with the others. Every man in the room wanted to know my story and listened intently as though there was no one else in the room. In an off moment before we sat for dinner, I asked Smitty for his impressions. They were similar to mine. He said they were consistent with his experiences around the men of Illuman and men he had met on retreats.

Toward six, the group began moving to the table. Padre Cisco asked me to sit next to him. As I sat down, I whispered, "Thanks, I can use the added security."

He replied, "Really? I would not have expected that."

"That's because you're not the one with expectations, Padre." Somehow, my small joke helped me relax.

Smitty and Michael Francis were across from us. Gordon and Thomas were to my right and Enrique and Hoover to Padre Cisco's left. Padre Cisco gained our attention and said, "Before we start, may we take a moment to give thanks? I asked Thomas to offer prayer."

Thomas gave thanks for the food and those who prepared it through the entire distribution chain back to the farmers who grew it. He gave thanks for the presence of each of the men and for the evening's leadership of Michael Francis. He ended with "and all God's children said…"

"Amen," came the collective response.

Padre Cisco acted as moderator. He asked if we could sit for a while in the peace of silence, seeking wisdom of speech and discerning hearts. After five minutes, he said, "Peace be with you," and we replied in unison "and also with you." The food servers obviously knew the protocol because they began serving the salads.

"I think we have had check-in unless anyone wants to apprise us of anything." The padre paused. Hearing no response, he said, "The focus of our conversation tonight is on community. The guiding question is what do we know about community that can serve to aid us in our daily lives." He stopped and folded his hands. "You might find this an amusing question from a man who spends most of his time in seclusion."

"We can now award the prize for the understatement of the evening," Gordon interjected, drawing nods and smiles of affirmation from the others.

Padre Cisco continued, "In my own stead I must say that though I do not get out among them often, I still feel responsible to be in the world. I have asked Michael Francis, who is often out among 'em, to open with some thoughts to provide a framework for our conversation. Before he begins, I want to share a bit of our process for Rocky and Smitty. We refer to conversation, but actually what we have is time to share. Our house rule is the golden rule. We take turns sharing ideas on a topic with little comment. We keep it simple: one speaks the rest listen. We do not engage in cross talk, and we do not challenge ideas except to challenge ourselves in our own understanding. Would anyone like to add to that?" Padre Cisco waited for comment. There were no additions. "Take us into it, Michael Francis."

"Thank you, Cisco. It is always a joy to be here. To see Smitty again and meet Rocky are special blessings. I haven't seen most of you since the last time we met. I am thankful for the array of electronic media that helps us stay in touch. I have been traveling too much and gone too long. It is good to be back. Thank you all for entrusting the context of the conversation to me. The idea of community is at the heart of our relationships, and we cannot be too vigilant in keeping it at the forefront of our attention.

"I will be brief." His comment drew a collective throat clearing and eye contact among the group. With his hands folded in his lap, he leaned forward. "To continue, *gentlemen*, as a follower of the Rule of Benedict, if I were to say that Benedict was all about community, I would be understating the case. He was all about community in the way that business is all about location, life is eighty percent about showing up, and attitude is everything. Community, like anything else, is never all about one thing, but for Benedict it was the context for all relationship. A man asked Benedict about life as a hermit versus life in community. He replied, 'Whose feet would the hermit wash?' That says it all to me."

Michael Francis sat back, took off his glasses, and shook his head sideways. "In Rocky's vernacular, I am painting with broad strokes." He said that community has no single definition, and the nexus of community can be any common element: religion, ethnicity, culture, age, gender, language, or topical mutual interest, as examples. The question is not so much what brings people together but what *binds* them together. The question of how we find communities of support was another concern. He suggested we might find the answers to both questions in the same place.

Michael Francis continued by sharing his own study. "In exploring ideas for *Dance Partners*, I've looked at the relationship between belonging and membership. I have heard Tomas quote his pastor as saying, 'If you think you belong, then you do.' We, also, can have an illusion of community. We can be members of a community but not belong. Does either of these scenarios represent your experience?"

He said the group's work with people on the frontiers of society brought some of the members together. It may be part of what binds the group together. Ideas worth considering might be the scale at which a community operates and the sustainability of the group. He asked if there were other factors we could identify? He paused and put his glasses on. "Perhaps that is enough to get us started. May we take a couple of minutes and allow our thoughts to rise. When you are ready, just jump in."

The group fell into stillness. I was not sure what I was thinking. I lowered my eyes and pushed my salad around my plate. I knew I was there as a listener, not a contributor. There were seven wise men gathered to do that.

Enrique severed the silence, saying, "Each of us, with the notable exception of MF, has at various times in our lives lived on both side of the tracks."

Michael Francis broke in, "Oh yes, I grew up in Eloy's Nob Hill district. What is this? Is it my turn in the dunk tank? I know I am violating house rules, as are all of you. Am I going to need to take you guys outside one by one, or must I just expect you to gang up on me?"

"That latter would be our preference, Michael Francis," came a quiet reply from Thomas.

"Okay, just as long as I know how it's going to be," he said, unable to maintain his aura of indignation.

Thomas interjected, "You have been gone from us for too long, Michael Francis. We just want you to know we still love you. We will stop now." I was feeling more comfortable by the minute. I thought these men knew how to take life and each other with a grain of salt. They enjoyed each other. I thought that must be one of the elements of successful community.

Enrique began again. "MF, to echo Thomas' remark, we will mind our manners, now." With sheepish grins, nodding heads gave their collective assent. "Considering what MF said about factors that bind people together, Hispanic culture in the United States is formed at the center of many of them. We share nationality, language, cultural heritage, and often religion. All four of those are part of my identity as a Mexican-American.

"I am a third-generation immigrant," Enrique continued, glancing at Smitty and me. I think he was letting us in on what the others already knew. "My generation was Americanized. As such, we were not encouraged to learn Spanish. I grew up learning Spanglish from my friends. It was an impediment to inclusion in the community. Though later I learned differently, I thought I had to learn Spanish to gain full entry into the community. I was embarrassed. I covered it by saying I wanted to learn *good Spanish* so I could be a reporter on television."

Enrique went on to say that language is a cornerstone of community. Every community has its own language. It can be the latest jargon, idioms, or the language of the liturgy of the church. Professions have their own technical language. Social strata and cultural communities have their own enunciation. Trying to talk to a group of teenagers and will immediately let you know that it is more than your age that divides you from them.

The group fell silent, I think reflecting on Enrique's words, as I was. I thought back to my conversation with Smitty when he mentioned that as kids we didn't talk about religion. There was an unspoken divide between us that I had never recognized.

Smitty broke the silence. I'm sure my head must have snapped in his direction. I thought my role there was to listen, and I expected he would feel the same. Smitty said, "My younger brother, Bill, was considered the gray sheep of the family. He raised his children in the church, but he did not take an active role. When his son, Bill Jr., married a Greek girl, Bill Jr. converted."

Smitty told us when Bill Jr. and his wife's children were baptized in the Greek Orthodox Church, the godparents not only adopted the children into their family, but Bill Jr., his wife, and his brother and sister-in-law as well. Eventually, his brother and his wife converted to orthodoxy and embraced the culture as well as the religion. His brother has studied Greek since that time. "My brother says the same thing you said, Enrique. The lack of facility with the language was a barrier. In spite of their nationality and their name, the Greek community considers the entire Bill Smith family as Greeks. They are not double-hyphenated Americans."

The conversation fell to sidebar dialogue while the waiters cleared the salad dishes and served the main course. Again, Enrique restarted things. "I want to add one more point, and then maybe others can expand the thought. When I spoke about language, I said I learned differently later. While I think it is integral to community, I also think cultural heritage may be even more important. Could it be the traditions passed from generation to generation that give reality to our identity? When I meet a young Hispanic boy or girl, I address them in idiom. I say mijo or mija. It's not just a language thing. Their elders traditionally call them that. It is more about them relating to me than me to them. I don't have the same feeling or need to address Anglo kids the same way. It wouldn't fit."

Once again, there was a pause in the conversation. I realized it was part of the "house rules," though it was more than that. The group seemed to assume time for silence. These men demonstrated active listening. There was no hurry in the conversation. They gave over airtime to reflection. Then I heard the "perhaps" of Padre Cisco.

"Perhaps I could enter a twist on your thought, Enrique." I expected an interjection from someone to the effect of "that certainly would be natural for you." The banter was over. The only responses were the slight re-ordering of postures to turn toward him and some hurried bites of roast beef or potatoes. "Perhaps we could look at the idea of tradition from the point of view of how it is transmitted." He paused. I wasn't sure if he was allowing for comment or just thinking.

"Are you referring to story, Cisco?" Thomas asked.

"I am, as you would expect from me. Tradition is transmitted generationally through story, but you know that. However, in the context of community and what binds people together perhaps story has a larger role. As we hear the stories, we become participants in them. The theologian Martin Buber said he could not have a significant conversation with someone whose story he had not heard. I think his point was that as we share our stories we begin to create a common story. I wonder if sharing a common story is what binds us together. Common and community have the same root. I think we might pause here and finish our meal. I imagine we all have things we want to discuss. Heads nodded and multiple conversations ensued."

Gordon leaned over and asked, "Where are you from, Rocky?"

I was thinking about what Padre Cisco had just said. I thought he had labeled Martin Buber as a theologian for my benefit. I imagined the other men would know who he is. I realized Gordon has spoken to me. "I'm sorry Gordon. My mind was still on Padre Cisco's comments. What did you say?"

"I asked where you are from."

"Oh, Akron, Ohio."

"I meant where is your family from?"

"Oh. They likely came from Italy, Gordon. We're not entirely sure. There were Stellas, Stellis, Stelinis, and other variations in the Bologna area, but there were also people of similar names from Croatia. Stellar appears to be an Americanization of the name. Why do you ask?"

"I have not heard your name before. Our name often expresses something of our heritage. Do you know much about your ancestry?"

"Not much past my grandfather. He was Peter as well. The traditions and history of our family began with him. My grandparents died when I was young. I never really knew them."

"Peter?"

"Yes, my given name is Peter. Rocky is after Rocky Colavito, the baseball player."

I asked Gordon the same questions, learning about his history back to Wales. We talked about our families, and I shared with him my growing sense of need for connecting with other people, particularly men. That was the second time I was surprised that evening. I don't know if I was aware of my feeling until I labeled it aloud. As the waiters were clearing the table and bringing desert and coffee, Michael Francis called us back together. "Does anyone want to add to Enrique, Smitty, or Cisco's thoughts?"

Padre Cisco said, "Thomas, Dr. Thurman likely had something to say about this. Would you share that?"

I looked at the men around the table, and they were all nodding in agreement. *I'm out of my league in this room.* I didn't know who Dr. Thurman was, though when I got home I looked him up on the web. I learned that Howard Thurman had been one of the most noted philosophers, theologians, and civil rights activists of his time. He authored twenty books, was an advocate of radical non-violence, and spent time with Mahatma Gandhi. He was a mentor to many civil rights leaders of the sixties, including Martin Luther King, Jr., the son of a classmate at Morehouse College where Thurman was valedictorian.

"I would love to, Cisco." After a pause, Thomas said, "Dr. Thurman wrote, '…it was upon the anvil of the Jewish community's relations with Rome that Jesus hammered out the vital content of his concept of love for one's enemy.' Thomas said, "Community is always about love or *should* always be about love. Love expresses itself through humility. In fact, I do not think love can exist outside an attitude of humility." He paused again. "Also, I must preface my remarks that any discussion of community needs to consider inclusion versus exclusion."

Thomas spoke communities by their very purpose and makeup being either inclusive or exclusive. He grew up in a time in which the dominant white community was exclusive. His school years were spent in segregated schools. He went to Booker T. Washington Elementary School and George Washington Carver High School in Phoenix. He graduated in 1953, the year Arizona passed the desegregation ruling, a year before Brown v. Topeka. In 1954, then-Governor Howard Pyle wrote a letter commending Arizona's early move to desegregate and described it as being entirely without incident of any kind. Thomas said he thought that was certainly an overstatement. "As Dr. Thurman so eloquently described, we learned humility at an early age, but sadly, we also learned the necessity of false humility. I tell you this so that you understand the context I grew up in. I do not see the world in that context, today, but there is no escaping it entirely."

Thomas related that Dr. Thurman's wrote about love and community many times. He wrote about exclusivity in the relations between the Romans and the Jews. The community accused Jews who made friends with Romans of fraternizing, which took the "who is my neighbor" question to a new dimension. He said neighborliness is nonspatial; it is qualitative. This is the love-ethic, central to Jesus' teaching, at work. To love Romans was to de-classify them as enemies. That took great risk. He said that most people of different races or stations in life operate in the *mood of the exception*. They do not apply their understanding of an individual to the group as in "I have a friend who is a Jew," or "you know those Catholics, present company excepted..."

Thomas said that Dr. Thurman was conscious of developing an attitude of respect for personality as a skill. The Buddhist would use the word mindfulness as in we need to become mindful of respect for personality. It is mindfulness that brings down the walls between classes, races, religions, the strong and the week, the rich and the poor, and the possessors and the possessed. In general, it eliminates the barriers between those that have and those who are in need.

Thomas concluded with, "I did not begin to learn this until much later in life. Early on, I was just young and angry. Anger was my defense, and it created my barriers. It was you, Cisco, who lived in my mood of the exception, and it was through you or with you, again in those later years, that I began to decompose the barriers."

"Thank you, Thomas, I have no doubt you have contributed more to my understanding that I to yours." Turning to Michael Francis, Padre Cisco said, "Perhaps you could center us again."

"Perhaps," he said with a bobbing of his head and a shy smile. "One thing Thomas said that caught my attention was the relationship between love and humility. Fifteen hundred years ago, Benedict wrote about this. Benedict's Rule has seventy-four chapters, but only two are long enough for the reader to consider them chapters. The longest is on humility. Benedict divides attaining humility into twelve steps. In such a short treatise, the length of a section attests to its importance.

"As an aside, the word *rule* is not the word as we use it today. The title can put people off. The word does not come from the Latin *legis*, meaning law. That is how we think of rule. It comes from *reglas*, which literally means railing, bannister, or guidepost. The *Rule of Benedict* is a guide to assist us in living in community, not a set of rules. Benedict had no chapter on love. It may have been too obvious to write about separately. With that in mind, might we consider this relationship between love and humility?"

After a time, eyes and heads turned toward Hoover. The group must have detected some change indicating he had something to say. "Thomas spoke of humility and its cousin false humility. Perhaps respect is the third leg of the stool that, also, bears humility and love. I come from a culture imbued with a long history of false humility. Kow-towing was an expectation." Hoover said that throughout history in most cultures, some form of bowing to one's superiors was an expectation. Possibly, what may have first been a ritual of respect between equals became a symbol of station between un-equals.

Rituals as signs of respect are based on humility. They are ways we honor one another. A man taking his hat off in the presence of a woman, lifting it in passing, or even touching the brim is a sign of respect. "Maybe only American cowboys and pro golfers do that any longer." That drew a chuckle from the group. This is more than just courtesy. Such a ritual is an outward sign of equality. Warriors of earlier centuries shook hands, guaranteeing the other's safety. This became a ritual of respect. "I don't know if current practices of fist, elbow, or chest bumping carry the same connotation." That brought forth another collective chuckle. Monks walk with their heads bowed but raise them and bow to their fellows in passing. Bowing or nodding to another person, even waving are rituals indicating we recognize other as equals.

The Hindu *Namaste* recognizes the light and god in others. The Dali Lama, a man of high station and great respect, bows to touch his forehead to another. Men open doors and stand back allowing others to pass through first. The mutual kiss on the cheek connotes affection but also equality. These rituals of respect connote humility. "This does not include the kissy-kissy of the Hollywood types who are in reality rivals or the A-frame hug of teenage girls." That statement along with Hoover's brief demonstrations drew a sustained laugh.

"Rituals like these are communal practices that are inclusive. So perhaps one way to determine a group's inclusivity would be to examine its member's practices of greeting and recognition. Do members of a given community have actions and a body language of humility that demonstrates that all are welcome?"

Without pause Gordon interjected, "For men of Smitty's and my size it is difficult to have a body language of humility. Even with our heads bowed we are looking down at the rest of you." This brought uproar from the rest of us. Smitty simply raised his hands and shrugged his shoulders in acquiescence. Michael Francis said, "Why don't we take a break for a few minutes? The group dispersed, and Smitty and Gordon found each other. The rest congregated or took the opportunity to find the facilities. I refreshed my coffee and joined Hoover and Michael Francis. Hoover told us of the difficulties of prejudice while growing up in Tucson, which at that time was still a small town. Then he asked, "How's yer bones now, Rocky?"

"My bones are groaning, Hoover," laughing at myself.

"Ah, Rocky, perhaps that is even a better answer. How is that your bones are groaning?"

"I feel a little bit out of my league here, Hoover. Actually, I am far out of my league. You men are way down a path I have barely begun."

"Possibly, that is merely an illusion."

"An illusion?"

"It only may appear that we are further on some path. You are hearing what we know. We are obviously not talking about what we don't know. Everyone in the room knows that is vastly greater. What may be the most common bond between us is our common understanding of how little each of us knows. We simply share what perspective we have at the time hoping to enhance all of our understanding."

I appreciated what Hoover was saying, but I wondered if it could be that simple. Michael Francis caught our eyes. He extended an open hand toward the table inviting us back. The rest of the group saw our return and ended their conversations. Michael Francis asked if we had other aspects of community to explore. Padre Cisco leaned back and then forward, and the circle of men gave him their attention.

"In the spring, Peter and I spent time discussing resolution and reconciliation, and how reconciliation ultimately occurs in community. For me that is an important part of the function of community. To an extent, willingness to reconcile differences defines its members' commitment. Christian communities, as Benedict and Francis described, are the home court on which we refine our ability to practice the teachings of Jesus. That practice begins with commitment.

"Perhaps it is more a balance between individuals and community. Community and its members hold a symbiotic relationship. Benedict calls it *mutual obedience*. Hoover described practices that overtly demonstrate mutual obedience. This community of men thankfully has few instances of the need for reconciliation. Perhaps our very attention to mutual obedience minimizes that need."

Enrique spoke up. "I'd like to add to that idea." The eyes and bodies shifted toward him. "I've always struggled with Benedict's focus on obedience; it seemed almost to the point of obsession. Recently, my view changed." Enrique told us of a monthly e-letter he receives from Elizabeth Rechter. She is the Executive Director of Stillpoint, The Center for Christian Spirituality located in Pasadena. She wrote about the story of Samuel and God's call to him in the night. Elizabeth wrote that she decided to check the Hebrew meaning of the name Samuel. His name, shma', shem-ah´ El, in Hebrew means *hears God*. It made her cry. She said the word in Hebrew for *hear* is the same word for *obey*. To hear God, to listen to God, is what it means to obey God. She went on to say the beginning of any journey with God, will be to hear God. "To echo Cisco, perhaps we not only listen to each other, but we hear each other."

After another period of reflection, I was surprised to hear my own voice. "Among these various characteristics of inclusive communities, what do you think is most important in binding people together?"

Michael Francis looked around the circle a couple of times. "I think I can answer that. All of them are important. Benedict emphasizes obedience. Cisco might say story. You heard from Enrique and Thomas. Smitty's thoughts you probably know. Hoover spoke of the three legged of respect, humility and love. If your question were to be answered in a word, perhaps it is commitment. We all have what Dr. Thurman called an attitude of respect for personality." We each have made a commitment to that attitude. He paused and looked around the circle.

After a few moments, Thomas said, "Might I add one thought to that, Michael Francis?"

"Please."

"I could not agree with you more. I would describe that commitment as a *covenant*. We have a covenant of respect. The covenant is our commitment to bind ourselves in relationship. We allow each other to hold each of us responsible for our part in mutual obedience. We practice respect among ourselves. We offer the same respect to others: men, women, children, the aged, the impoverished, the marginalized, and all life. All people are our neighbors, and all things are connected."

"Thank you, Thomas. That is a beautiful description. Covenant aptly describes the extent of our commitment. "Michael Francis eyed the group again then said, "This may be a good place to stop. It is about as summative as we would ever be in this collection of divergent thinkers." That brought smiles, head nods, and laughs from the group. "Again, it was great to be among you. Cisco, I assume it is in your hands to gather us again." Cisco nodded. Michael Francis said, "Thomas?"

Thomas asked us to stand, and he offered the prayer of St. Francis of Assisi. We responded with a collective "Amen."

We said our goodbyes. I lingered. Gordon offered me his card and invited me to call him if I wanted to get together or just to talk. I thanked each of the men for inviting me to share the evening. I checked in with Padre Cisco and set a date to meet. Smitty gathered me up and we left. While I hadn't been sure of my place there, I didn't want to leave. I still had questions. A teacher was knocking at the door.

* * *

I put my questions aside when we arrived home. I received my usual though abbreviated reception from Gen as she rushed to greet Smitty. He enshrouded her in a long hug. Their affection, even love, for each other is equal to that for me. It is part of our bond. An insight flashed. *I am living this evening's conversation. Ultimately, it is love that binds us together. We are a community of three.* I imagined that if I told Padre Cisco about the moment, he would say, "Where two or three are gathered together, there am I." It was true. The clarity of it awed me. I wedged myself between Gen and Smitty and relished the group hug. We stood there together in the entry for longer than I ever would have imagined.

Gen had a dozen questions for Smitty. I went to open a bottle of wine. I puttered in the kitchen, giving them time together. I returned with the wine and went back for cheese and bread. I don't know why I thought we needed more food after the salad, the main course, and the to-die-for chocolate mousse. We didn't. Smitty and Gen needed more time.

I laid out the food, and we sat in the kitchen. I listened to their chatter until I finally called out in my best Desi impersonation, "Lucy, I'm home."

"Oh, Rocky's here, Gen," came the reply with the two of them giggling like school kids.

"Hi, Rocky. Did you miss me?" Gen said, carrying the charade a step further.

"I always miss you, Gen, but I'm starting to miss the big guy a little less."

"You'll miss me when I'm gone," Smitty said.

"So?" Gen interjected. Her meaning was clear. It was the 'tell me about it' so.

I began, and Smitty added his twists as I went along. We told her about the setting, the progression of the evening, each of the men, and their contributions. When we got to Thomas, I said, "As I was listening to him I realized that while I was aware of his race and his age, I did not connect them to the context of his life. When he shared that piece of his story I began to hear him in a different way. The padre often talks of context. I am starting to get it."

Smitty said, "His mood of the exception concept resonated with me, reminding me of the carwash story. Did Rocky tell you about that, Gen?"

"He did, Smitty, though I know we both have questions about where that led you."

"That's a story for another time."

There's more to that story than Smitty is telling us. He's holding something back. He's right, though. Tonight is worthy of our single focus. Smitty related the crux of the mood of the exception to Gen and went on to Enrique's letter from his friend.

I said, "By the way, Smitty, who was this Dr. Thurman? Everyone but me knew about him. That was one of those moments of feeling I was out of it."

"There is little reason for you to have known about him. He was a black theologian at Howard University and Boston University. He was well known in the religious community." Smitty changed the subject. "I don't know about you, Rocky, but I was as glad as Enrique to hear that interpretation of the word *obey*. As a Catholic, obedience has been a lifelong bittersweet challenge."

"I felt the same way about the word *rule*. Michael Francis' interpretation put it in a better light for me. I got a kick out of Enrique calling him MF."

"I asked Gordon about that afterward, and he said Enrique always calls him that. He said it comes from something in their history. It seems so out of character to call him that."

I told them about Gordon's question about my name and heritage. Then Gen had one of her moments.

"I was so happy when we got married, Rocky. Stellar was such an upgrade from Bullwinkle."

I said, "Oh, please."

"It was so much more heavenly, so galactic. Our name is of such cosmic proportions. Our heritage is surely with the Roman gods and goddesses."

"Are you finished?"

"I am." She flashed mischievous grin.

Smitty said, "Please do go on. I love these parts. I don't get to do this in my life."

"Don't encourage her."

"Oh, Rocky," they both responded as though they had rehearsed it." It gave us all a good laugh.

"Since you two are in cahoots, I'm declaring a return to sanity." I expected a "that's insane" from a least one of them, but all I got was Gen signing thumbs up. "What I want to tell you, Gen, is that Smitty and I shared some common experiences tonight; but one of the things that amazed me was the openness of these men. Either before or after the discussion, each of them gave me his phone number and offered to talk, or meet, or asked if I would like him to call me. They were so generous. I've not been around men who reach out like that."

Smitty said, "I had similar experiences."

Gen interjected, "It's an invitation to the circle, Rocky. It's a circle of friendship. There is a community there willing to adopt you. The ball is in your court. What are you going to do?"

That's what is unsettling me. "I'm not sure. The invitation is an honor for sure, but it makes me nervous. These men are so far beyond me. I became aware of how pointed the conversation was. It wasn't stilted; in fact, it was very organic. Yet, it was measured. None of the men went on at length about anything. They just put an idea out there and let us interpret it. We were at a round table. There were no sides to the conversation. There was no questioning, no conclusions. I'm not sure I have anything to contribute in that environment."

Smitty challenged me. "If you weren't good at arithmetic, would you avoid math class?"

"That's not the same."

"It certainly is, but you are missing the point, Rocky. They didn't invite you to a class or even a discussion. Men who care about you have invited you into spiritual friendship. What you have to contribute is you, your experience, and your personality.

You heard the reference to Thomas' pastor's statement that if you think you belong you do."

"Isn't that the point of this discussion, whether or not I think I belong?"

"Yes and no, Rocky. The belonging is not about membership. It is about your willingness to commit. The offer is one of mutual invitation. That's the covenant Thomas described. These men have invited you into their lives. The only question remaining is whether you are willing to invite them into yours. There's no alpha male in this pack, but you can remain a lone wolf if you want to."

With that, we broke to get Smitty settled in for the night. I think Gen and Smitty knew they needed to leave the proverbial ball in my court. Gen went to bed, and I went to Google to check out Howard Thurman.

Gen got up the next morning and fixed breakfast. I love it when she gets domestic. I think she wanted to remind Smitty of what it could be if he had a woman in is life. I've never shared with her the many women that Smitty has had in his life over the years. I couldn't imagine she was under the illusion that his current monkish ways had led him to celibacy. The thought conjured a range of amusing images of this giant monk padding about in obedient humility. I thought I would do a strip for him. I could call it *Kung fu Smitty*.

We sat in the kitchen while Gen worked. Memories of mornings in the kitchen before school with Smitty rose up. I shared the thought with Smitty, and we traveled the memory lane of our youth. We talked about coming in from shoveling the snow off the driveway, and Mom would shut the kitchen door and turn on the stove to warm us up. I thought about how crazy it seemed to have soup for breakfast.

Gen said, "I don't remember hearing that story before."

Smitty laughed, and said, "Neither do I."

He got up to help her serve the meal. We drove the byways of our common past and rehashed the previous evening until it was time to go to the airport. Gen expressed chagrin at the brevity of his trip and that she would miss him. He said, "Of course. Who wouldn't?" The obedient humility image took a hit on that remark. I grabbed his bag and went for the car while they said goodbye.

We were hardly out of the driveway when Smitty said, "Have you made a decision?" He didn't say "any decisions." He is never that circumspect.

I was my usual ambivalent self. "If you are asking what am I going to do, I can say yes and no. Yes, I am going to talk with Padre Cisco again. No to all the other choices."

"Am I seeing shadows lurking about, Rocky?"

"Shadows?"

"Yes, psychological shadows."

I said, "Oh, those shadows. Perhaps." I waited, hoping Smitty would fill the void, but he was better than I was at the game of silent chicken. I swerved first. "I've been worried about when that would come up."

"Well, it's up. To quote your lovely bride, 'So?'"

"You aren't going to let this go, are you?"

"No, I don't have much time with you. I want to give you my best."

"I appreciate that. The question of shadows has been dogging me, but I don't know what to do about it. I don't know how to deal with them. Give me some direction here."

"This is not my field. It's a job for the pros. You might talk to a psychologist." Smitty paused, shaking his head. "Why did I even say that? Lone wolves don't visit head bangers. Maybe seeing a spiritual director would serve you. Let me think a moment."

I waited, and he said, "When I can't identify what's going on, I read. You might check out Jim Clark. He's at St. John's Seminary in Camarillo. He writes about rituals as a way of healing. He's working on a new book; I think it's about the common roots of pain and suffering. I was at a men's seminar. I remember him saying the number one source of pain is father loss. We've both experienced that. It might be something to talk about with the padre."

We approached the turn-off for the airport, and I said, "I'll do that, thanks, Smitty, and thanks for coming over, and thanks for your input. Gen was so glad to see you." I wanted to close out the subject of shadows. "I'll keep you apprised." I knew that was an overstatement. We arrived at the departure curb. I got out to retrieve Smitty's bag, and we gave each other a hug. We shook hands, and then he headed toward the gate, leaving his advice behind. It went home with me.

I called Dad on my way home. I was eager to talk to him about the experience I just had, and I wanted to talk baseball. The Indians had a great season. They had a phenomenal win streak toward the end. It was something like thirty games. They reached the World Series losing to the Cubs in seven games, eight to seven in ten innings. We talked a lot more baseball than we did about the previous evening's dinner. We both got a good laugh when he ended the call with "Wait 'till next year."

Fifteen
Follow the Water

"Abba, teach me of water."
"It stands and goes, moves and flows."
"Abba, how do I flow with it?"
"Get in, my son."

I headed to San Francisco to see Morgan, Alex, and Arnie, my agent. I was in good spirits and great anticipation. I returned in discord. The airline canceled my flight. I got a seat on the next flight out through Reno, but it couldn't land because of fog. The plane diverted to Salt Lake City. I got a call from Morgan. *Now she calls.* My ego wanted to send her to voicemail. That would serve her right. I pressed the "Accept" button.

She was at the airport and angry with me for not calling her with the change of schedule. She was right, but I couldn't abide with her attitude. She had stiffed me too many times. She said the airlines shouldn't be allowed to cancel flights. She said she knew she should have checked the flight status. I decided she was mad at herself. I tried to set a time with her, but she said she had to prepare for exams. I wanted to talk longer, but she said she needed to go. She said we could talk at Thanksgiving. She assured me she would be home for the holiday. That was little consolation for my mood.

By the time I arrived in San Francisco, I was three hours late and had to reschedule with Arnie. Our meeting turned out to be one more disappointment. Arnie was not nearly as enthusiastic about the strip as I was. He said that he didn't think it would work for general readership. "Too subtle, too oblique, and too esoteric" was his exact phrase. He said he might be able to peddle it to some trade journals in the world of spirituality and religion. I blew my top at the word "peddle." I felt my national standing as a cartoonist was above having to peddle my strips. Nothing in our conversation went well after that. We cut it short. The only upside was that I gained some time before my date with Alex.

We met for coffee and chatted about life in law school and the Bay area, Pac12 sports, and everything but the weather. He had fallen in love with the law. He said that he is interested in water law. He spoke of surface water designation, water resource law, riparian rights, rights of prior appropriation, and other legalistic terms. I knew the words but not their meaning. He talked of representing native communities in their battles to reclaim their water rights.

"Do you, have any idea, Dad, how long people have been working to get their water rights back?"

"Not really. Should I?"

"Up to a hundred years and there's hardly any reason you would know. Maybe that's part of the problem. This kind of exploitation doesn't get the press. The only time it's in the news is when there is a court opinion rendered on some suit."

"I don't see or hear many of those.

"That's what I think I might be able to do something about, Dad. It's why I took the public relations – public policy dual major."

His zeal impressed me, and I wondered how long he would be able to sustain it along with his altruism. We talked about the current political climate in Arizona and the country and his take on its effect on his current interest.

"How did your meeting go with your agent?"

"Don't ask."

"That good, huh? But I did ask?"

"It was a disaster, Alex. Arnie thought my idea wouldn't sell. I thought I was on to something. I had one of those creative insights I used to experience. I'm not giving up on the idea, but I'll have to figure out the market or how to adapt it. It will come. How are you classes going?" I wanted to change the subject.

He gave me the lowdown on his projects and the rigors of keeping up with the demands. I asked about Morgan. He didn't have any more up-to-date knowledge about her than I had. He said he'd tried to get together with her a couple of times recently, but she's buried in her studies. After the second refill, we had closed out the major topics. Alex said he had better get going. I gave him a hug for Gen, and he told me to kiss her for him. We parted, voicing our anticipation of the Thanksgiving visit.

I called the airline, changed my flight, called Gen, and headed to the airport.

I got home late. Gen had waited up for me. All that I had worked through in recent months came to a stop. I slouched through the room and went to the kitchen. I opened a beer. Gen poured a wine, and I poured out my whine on her. I railed about Morgan and her double standard. I railed about Arnie and what I thought was a cavalier attitude toward my effort.

I talked. She listened. Finally, she said, " Rocky, I know what you would say to me. Patience, Gen."

"I want to do something. Morgan and I just don't seem to be able to get on the same page. I want to fix it. Maybe I just want to throttle her."

"One thing I know, Rocky, is that I don't want to do anything that causes the kids to have anything they will regret. Your Richard Rohr writes about the first and second halves of spiritual life. It seems as though there are first and second halves of family life as well. We spend the first half of our lives trying to get over our parents and the second half of life trying to get over our kids. They have enough on their own to manage without us adding to it. I think this is one of those times we just have to be patient and let nature take its course."

I said, "I don't want to be patient. Mother Nature? I'll allow for her. I'm not sure how willing I am to wait for Morgan's nature to take its course. I'm not sure I'll live that long."

"There's something else, isn't there?"

How does she know that? It's like talking to Padre Cisco. Am I that transparent? "Why do you ask?"

"Rocky?"

"There is, Gen; but how do you know?"

"I'll tell you later. Right now, I want to hear what's bothering you."

I wanted to hear what she saw or heard. I wanted to talk about anything but what I had come to realize. It was on the flight home. Because of my height, I fly first class. I had a seat and my thoughts to myself. I wasn't in a mood to be pleasant.

"On the way home I came to a realization."

"Uh huh."

"I've been deluding myself."

"Okay."

"For all the talk with you and Padre Cisco, all the reading, and all the trial and error work in the studio; when I finally got myself going I went right back to where I had been."

"What do you mean?"

"I created another strip. I was excited about it. I still am, but it is still just another strip. I haven't done anything new; that is, new to me. I fell back on skills I already I had."

"So you're saying you're not satisfied with that?"

"During my first visit with the padre, he told me a story about pebbles. Many things he has said came to mind. The padre and I had quite a discussion in my head." I paused, closed my eyes gathering those thoughts, and then went on. "During one of my first visits, he said there was a time after he left the university that he thought he wanted to throw one more pebble into the pond. He thought he wanted to see how many ripples he could make. Eventually, he learned that he was not to be the thrower, but to be the pebble. I think I am beginning to understand what he meant."

"I can tell you, Rocky, I have *no idea* on this one."

"I thought I was going a new direction, but I wasn't even going in a different direction. I was only trying to recreate something I had lost. I was trying to prove I could do it again. I wanted to see how many ripples I could make. No, more than that, I wanted waves."

"Are you telling me that's not what you want to do anymore?"

"No, I think I am saying I that to be the pebble I have to give up wanting to be the wave maker." I paused to think about what I just said.

"Keep going, please."

"Remember that day the padre and I hiked out into the desert?"

"Yes."

"We talked about retiring, change, and the like. We talked about what it means to be an artist. I used the term 'working artist.' Near the end of that conversation, he told me of a question his priest posed to the congregation. "Can you give up what you know to discover what you don't know?' That moment has stuck with me because I remember asking myself that question. Padre Cisco said it is the entry question to the second half of life."

I stopped. I knew I hadn't been willing to answer it. Gen waited. Her eyes focused directly on mine. It was not only the entry question; it was the central question to everything I had been experiencing. My lone wolf attitude, my displeasure with Morgan, a life out of balance, and lack of harmony drive my unwillingness to give up a life in art, as I knew it. Blood rushed to my head. I closed my eyes again and took deep breaths.

"I don't remember when it was, but Padre Cisco talked about 'dying to myself' and 'death as an embarkation.' At the time, neither idea made any sense to me. They do now. Dying to myself is giving up what I know. Death as an embarkation is entry in to discovering what I don't know.

"Okay."

"Sometime, early in my life I lost my focus. For nearly forty years, I virtually fixated on comic strips. I moved from being an artist to being a cartoonist. When people would ask me what I do, I'd say artist. Then I would correct what I said with 'really, I'm a cartoonist.' It dominated my life. I lost sight of having an artful life because I was fixated on being a *working artist*.

Except for a quiet "H-m-m" Gen just listened.

"If I'm going to have any chance at a future in art, I have to give up the notion of being a cartoonist. I have to let it die. It's holding me back. Not only is it holding me back in art but in the rest of my life as well. I love that Dad and I have found reconciliation. The same goes for my relationship with Mary. I know it has affected us. I have hopes for Morgan and me. I have not been able to enjoy what has transpired or to live the fruits of it because of SoCal and Knuckles. They've held me hostage. I've been paying the ransom for years in all the angst I've held on to. I want to be released."

Gen said, "So." It was that empathetic, two-syllable version. She sat smiling at me. "I love you, Rocky Stellar."

"I know you do, and that's what makes this all worthwhile."

"Thank you."

"However!"

"Uh oh."

If people knock on our door asking about my great idea for a strip, I'll talk to them. Short of that, it's in the archives."

"Fair enough. I thought you were really going to hit me we something there."

"I am. I love you, too, Gen. I love you for walking with me throughout this journey. I love you for listening to me. I love you for the woman you are."

"Thank you."

"Okay, it's your turn. How did you know I was bothered?"

"Oh, usually you get that way off in the distance look. When it's about your art, you want to fix something. When you were younger you would find something around the house to fix, or you would putter with the car. Sometimes, you would repaint a room. Tonight, you just said it outright about your relationship with Morgan. 'I want to fix it.' It's not rocket science. I've lived with you for a long time."

I am transparent. "I certainly won't be playing poker with you anymore."

We ended on a good laugh, and my mood ended better than we started. At least by that point I was able to be in the mood. We went to bed.

* * *

On a clear, warm November afternoon, I drove out to Padre Cisco's house. To say that in the Southwest is almost redundant. Most November afternoons are clear and warm. The desert trees were just beginning to turn. The air was dry and had lost its morning crispness. As usual, the padre met me out front and invited me into his palms-open greeting. We walked around to the veranda, got coffee from the kitchen, and sat down. I was glad to be there. I had a lot I wanted to ask and to discuss. We sat for a while in silence until the padre broke the silence with his typical "And how is it with you, Peter?"

"I am well, Padre. Et su?"

"Tambien, the same, Peter."

I related the events of my days since our dinner together, the offers of each of the men, and my misgivings about life in relationship to a community. I shared the trip to San Francisco, my conversation with Gen, and the resolution I had found.

He was excited for me. He reminded me of Thomas' statement about not letting his experiences define him. "It sounds as though you are experiencing a shift. You are redefining yourself, Peter." We toasted my awakening, clinking our coffee cups together. I bemoaned how long it had taken me to get there.

He replied simply, "The tortoise and the hare, Peter, the tortoise and the hare."

"The problem, Padre, is that I am the tortoise."

"Perhaps that is not a problem at all, Peter. Perhaps it is a blessing. Life builds on relationships. Relationships take time.

They build on shared experiences and shared story. Building a relationship takes repetitions, and repetitions take time and effort. You have a maturing relationship with Smitty because of the time and energy you both put into it. Out of all the kids with whom you grew up, you and Smitty chose each other. You spent time fostering that choice. You developed a common story. Perhaps being the tortoise is a good thing."

I related the conversation with Smitty on the way to the airport, and reminded him of the discussion about shadows we'd had in the spring. I asked him to give me the short course on shadow selves.

Padre Cisco said, "All of Smitty's suggestions are appropriate paths to take," and then he went off on his typical tangent. "A favorite quote of mine is from John O'Donohue. He writes, 'I would love to live as the river flows, carried by the surprise of its own unfolding." I was hoping there would be more, but Padre Cisco sat back and allowed me to absorb it.

After what I thought was a courteous pause, I said, "I need you to give me something more here, Padre."

"What more do you want?"

"Something more concrete."

He sat and I waited. After a minute or so he said, "When I get flummoxed with myself, Mo-ma reminds me of the first time we went tubing on the Salt River. I was a gawky ten or so years old in one of those growth spurts. Well, that obviously never went very far." He laughed at himself.

When they got into the water everyone but the padre immediately began floating down the river. He was still back in the shallows of the takeoff point. He climbed into the tube but dug his heels into the streambed, unwilling to give up control to the current. They all had to paddle against the current to get to the bank. His brothers went back to the start and eased him into the river. They held onto him and pulled him along. His parents and Mo-ma got back in when they saw him approaching. "We all floated in tandem until I said they could let go. It is one of the most gracious moments with my brothers in my childhood memories."

"That is a great gift, Padre, to learn that freedom so young."

"Peter, it was not something I learned; it was just an introduction. I have had many repetitions of that day throughout my life. I remember a day in my mid-thirties when we took the kids to the water park. They had a great time on the slides. I awakened the next day, and every muscle in my body barked at me. I had spent all energy trying to control my rate of descent for fear of flying off the slide. The source of my fear that day was that I was on my own. I had no guide, no support system. I had no brothers there to come and guide me into the flow."

"I can hardly imagine you as that person."

"I am not that person today. You have never met him before now. Eventually, he died. A person an inch closer to me in the now emerged. Peter, the reason why I can see the lone wolf, as Smitty calls you, I was a lone wolf. At some point, I recognized my own vulnerability. I realized I could not go it alone."

"What did you do?"

"I sought out the brothers. They are everywhere. We just have to learn to recognize them. They are theologians."

"Theologians, Padre?"

"Yes, historically a theologian was a person to whom God was known. It meant literally 'one who knows God.' Today's meaning is more about a professional who can describe God and has an understanding of god stuff. There are people, books, and music all around us who have had glimpses of God."

"People and books I understand, but not music. How so?"

"I grew up in the folk music era; much of it was social protest music. They were writing and singing about the world as it could be or should be. Some of the music was commentary. Pete Seger, Peter, Paul and Mary, The Kingston Trio, Woody Guthrie and his son Arlo were prominent. They and many others sang about how society might reform and serve those who Jesus called 'the least of these.'"

"I understand the social protest part but not the theology part. Can you give me an example?"

"Well, of course I can. You know we only bring up things in conversation we want to discuss. That is why we have to remind ourselves to be the student, not the teacher. If we only hear ourselves, we live in danger of believing only what we are saying. However, I digress. An example. Ah yes! *Desert Pete*. *Desert Pete* was an early guide to my understanding of life."

"Who was Desert Pete? What did he sing?"

"*Desert Pete* was not a singer; he was the song. It was a Kingston Trio recording. I do not remember the verses but for one line. They sang of a man in the desert who is without water and finds a pump. He thinks it may be a mirage but finds a note with a jar of water. The writer of the note tells him not to drink the water but to use it to prime the pump. Padre Cisco sang the chorus in his quiet rendition: *you've got to prime the pump, you must have faith and believe / you've got to give of yourself 'fore you're worthy to receive*. The chorus ended with the instruction to leave the bottle full for others. The song was about love, risk, trust, thinking of others before you, humility, living in concert and harmony with others, and likely as many more ideas. *Desert Pete* was great theology. I believed it when I heard it. I still do, though I have different understanding of lines like '*fore you're worthy to receive*.'"

"Wow, Padre, that gives me a different appreciation of popular music."

"All music, Peter, has a theology behind it, though that may be stretching the point a bit. Certainly classical, jazz, blues, and rock do. I struggle with the grunge and acid rock, though hard rock and hip-hop have powerful statements about life in them. Songwriters' lyrics express their worldview, their theology. We are all theologians in the same way that we are all spiritual. We just do not necessarily know how to practice our spirituality. We all practice theology, but we do not necessarily know we are doing it. We are all theologians in that we are constantly redefining our worldview. We do not necessarily recognize it as theology." Padre Cisco paused, then said, "That was a mouthful."

I said, "For me it's a *brainful*. I remember talking with Gen not long after you and I began our conversations. I described myself as 'spiritual but not religious.' I remember saying that I didn't know what that even meant."

"Have your ever listened to Leonard Cohen?"

"No."

"Listen to him on YouTube, and go read his lyrics. He was one of the great jazz–folk theologians of our day."

"So where do I start, Padre?"

"You started a long time ago, probably when you left home. It just took some minor inconveniences like losing your job and approaching a milestone age to heighten your awareness of your own spirituality. Those events brought you here, but, as I said to you before, this is just a wayside stop on your journey. 'Where do I start?' might not be the question. Perhaps it is 'Where do I go next?' An attorney, John McQuiston, wrote a modern-day paraphrase of the *Rule of Benedict* titled *Always We Begin Again*.

In the great circle of understanding 'always we begin again.' Perhaps the question is 'how do I begin again?'"

I said, "If I am at the beginning, then how do I begin again?"

"Only you can decide. If I were to suggest, I would say pick a metaphor and follow where it leads. We understand our spirituality through seeing the world in metaphor. One of mine comes from Cohen's *Anthem, There is a crack in everything / that's how the light gets in.*"

"I am a visual person more than a literary one, Padre. I can visualize the crack."

"Yes, but you are other things as well. You are a very kinesthetic person. You are a surfer. You have a surfer's sense for rhythm, balance, harmony, ebb, and flow. If I must, I would say follow the water."

"Follow the water?"

"Yes, as a social scientist I taught my students to follow the water. Water is the life-blood, if you will, of all civilization. Moving from a society of hunters and gatherers depends on a source of water to farm. Culture develops as enough food as a few grow to sustain the many. Others then develop the arts, spiritual observances, and creative endeavors of utility. Water links people in a thousand ways. Until airplanes, transportation followed the water. The development of industry was linked to water, power, etc."

"I get that part, Padre, but how does that relate to my challenges?"

"O'Donohue says if your heart is hardened, give yourself the gift of your inner wellspring. Gradually the water will soften the clay of your heart. You are ready to receive love. He says the hidden love within you makes you independent and readies you to come close to the other. I think he is referring to God, but I think he is also referring to our relationships with people. He defines this closeness as intimacy, affinity, and belonging. I relate that to the sense of belonging Thomas' pastor spoke of."

"I'm listening, Padre, but I'm not sure I am hearing. However, I think this means I finally have the ears to hear notion."

"That is terrific! Self-awareness is a window into your soul. Voicing our awareness is opening the blinds to let light fall on the shadows. In ancient times, they would have called it 'being possessed by a demon.' Speaking of ancient times, a couple of conversations back we talked about balance, harmony, and rhythm. I mentioned O'Donohue's dynamic equilibrium. Do you remember that conversation?"

"I do."

"He may be someone whose writing would speak to you, Peter. O'Donohue says our sense of rhythm is ancient. All life came from the ocean. Each of us comes from the waters of the womb. The ebb and flow of the tides are alive in the ebb and flow of our breathing. He says, and I quote him here, 'To be spiritual is to be in rhythm.' That idea resonates with me.

"Perhaps because I live in the desert, I am drawn to water metaphors. Perhaps it is more than that. Perhaps it is Judith Favor's oceanic consciousness. The seashore draws many of us. Perhaps watching and listening to the tide allows us to reach down into the primal rhythm that abides in each of us. Oh, Peter, I am perhaps-ing excessively. Your question about rhythm the last time we met sent me into an exploration, which sent me back to John O'Donohue. That is always a treat, but he also sends me to wondering."

"You, Padre, are the John O'Donohue in my life. When you don't outright vex me, you at least set me to wondering. This isn't easy."

"No, the path on what we call the journey is not easy. Your statement caused a thought to rise in my memory. Oh, that is just too funny. Sometimes, I scare the blarney right out of myself." He laughed at some private joke he was hearing. "I am sorry, Peter, you will get it in a moment. I was thinking of Norman Maclean's novel *A River Runs Through It*. Do you know the movie?"

"I do, and I'll just have to trust you on the joke, Padre."

"Thank you for that. Norman, the older son and the narrator of the story, said, 'My father was very sure about certain matters pertaining to the universe. To him, all good things – trout as well as eternal salvation – came by grace; and grace comes by art; and art does not come easy.' As an artist, you know this, Peter."

"That is understatedly true."

"The more famous quote from the story is...Wait, I need some help with this." He got up and pulled a book from the shelf. He took out a single sheet and returned the book. Sitting back down, he unfolded the paper, wiped his glasses on his shirt, put them back on, and read, 'Like many fly fishermen in western Montana where the summer days are almost Arctic in length, I often do not start fishing until the cool of the evening. Then in the Arctic half-light of the canyon, all existence fades to a being with my soul and memories and the sounds of the Big Blackfoot River and a four-count rhythm and the hope that a fish will rise.'"

Ah, there's his glee.

"Eventually, all things merge into one, and a river runs through it. The river was cut by the world's great flood and runs over rocks from the basement of time. On some of those rocks are timeless raindrops. Under the rocks are the words, and some of the words are theirs. I am haunted by waters.' I do not know if Norman Maclean's father understood 'all good things...come by grace; and grace comes by art; and art does not come easy,' but Norman did. He was a theologian. He had a theology as deep as the basement of time."

"So, Padre, you are saying movies, like books, and music, and art have theology. *A River Runs Through It* has theology? *Saving Private Ryan* and even *Groundhog Day* have theology?"

"Yes, Peter, but more than that, I am saying they *are* theology in that they are an *expression of theology*. Think of the *Star Wars* movies. They are modern classics of theology. How the screenwriters and the director have the actors play their roles is those characters' spirituality. The acting is an expression of the writer's theology. The composer of the score, and particularly the film editors, add nuances to that expression. They appeal to all our senses. You can hardly think of *Apocalypse Now* without hearing Robert Duval's 'I love the smell of napalm in the morning' and thinking you *can* smell it. Movies are powerful expressions of how people see our world."

"So, what about the actors? Are they just acting out the writers' and directors' theology?"

"This is one of those yes and no answers, Peter. Yes, they have a responsibility to the writers and to the directors, and let's not forget the producers who are paying them. However, as actors they adopt the personality of their character. They have their own view of how that character would act or respond to any give situation. That is why there can be creative conflict on movie sets. The actors bring their own spirituality to the scene and have their own understanding of each character's spirituality and of his or her theology. In a serious movie with serious people, who are aware of their own interpretations, satisfying everyone's interpretation is a tough task."

"So, again, my spirituality is nothing more than how I act out my personal theology, and my theology is nothing more than how I see the world. Yes?"

"Yes, and yes but."

"But?"

"Yes, but the nothing more part is perhaps an understatement. Our spirituality expresses our awareness of the significance of all things, all actions, and all decisions. The awareness of this significance of all things leads us to ask the important questions of life. I think I would define our spirituality as our consciousness or mindfulness of trying to live out the answers to questions we consider most significant in life. Spirituality is about focusing more on our eulogy than our résumé. On the other hand, Mo-ma reminds me that our mother taught us not to be so heavenly minded that we are no earthly good. Keep everything in balance, Peter."

"I'm working on that, Padre."

"We are all on the journey. We need to recognize our spirituality can be anywhere on a continuum from immature to wisdom. Some of us are aware, and some not. Some of us are mindful of that awareness, and some are not. Some of us are mindful of the significance of the universal questions, and some are not. Our spirituality is the expression of our awareness of our place on the journey that is common to all."

Laughing at my own predicament, I said, "Padre, when I said I needed more, I had no idea how much more I was going to get."

"I did unload on you, Peter."

"And I am thankful for it."

"I almost hesitate to say it, but there is one more piece. Do you have time?"

"Time is what I have, again laughing at the reason for it."

"You said earlier that you described yourself to Gen as spiritual but not religious; and you did not know what that even meant." I nodded. "There are many people in today's world who make the same statement. Many others are deeply spiritual in that they know what they mean and at the same time are not religious. Please, bear with me; this might take a bit of time."

"Go for it; I think I have ears to hear."

"Thank you. I once told you I try to be an unteacher and that I think teacher can a subterfuge for preacher, which to me can be a proselytizer. There is a lot of proselytizing in the world today. I imagine there are people who say to others they are spiritual but not religious to ward off the proselytizers. I am with them that. I, also, think among them are spiritual people, who, as you said about yourself, do not know what that means. Okay so far?"

"I'm with you."

"I am going slow here because I don't want to misspeak." He paused in his own thoughts. "The very fact they claim to be spiritual means they are. Awareness of the journey means they are on the journey; but to be on the journey does not mean they are on the path. I say *the path*, singular, even though I believe there are many paths. Each of us travels our own path. As I was when I was in the river, they are experiencing the journey. Their awareness is the indicator. Mindfulness shines the light on their paths. Mindfulness expresses the idea of practices. We talked about mindfulness in our discussion on practice. We have to remember all people are at different places on their journey. Those that are aware of their place are on their path."

"That seems to make sense to me."

"We, also, talked more recently about the challenges of the journey and the challenge of traveling alone. Go back to

James Finley's find your teaching, practice, and community. Community supports teaching and practice. Communities that foster spiritual growth are an essential source of acceptance and support.

"Spirituality entails knowledge or assurance that there are answers to our questions, but the answers often lead to deeper questions. If God is larger than anything we can imagine, then there are questions to which we can find no answers. As Rilke reminds us, some questions are so large that the only assurance we have is that we can some day live into the answers. It helps to be able to live into a community of spiritual support."

"That *was* a lot, Padre. Did you record it? Could you write in down for me? When we first started, I was aware I was simply wandering. Now I am aware that our talks have created more wondering than I am sure I can hold on to."

"An Imam friend would say that the heavens open, and some valleys retain more water than others."

"That's exactly what I am talking about. Now *I* am the one who is going to say we should quit. The 'now' meaning quit while I am almost even."

Padre Cisco smiled broadly and told me to pass along to Gen his wishes for a Happy Thanksgiving. I returned the salutation, we said our goodbyes, and I drove home.

INTERLUDE

Wine

"I cook with wine; sometimes I even add it to the food."
~ W.C. Fields

Gen was so excited to see the kids that she hugged them all the way to the car. Alex sat in the front with me, and Gen and Morgan chattered in the back. Looking in the mirror I asked, "How is school going, Morgan?"

"Oh, it's fine, Dad." Her tone was dismissive. *How's school going? Really? You can be such a putz, Rocky. How banal can you get?*

"You two look so good," Gen chimed in filling the dead space. "Tired, but good. It's the first time I've seen you without a tan, Morgan."

"Maybe they could install tanning lamps in the study carrels in the library, Mom. I'm not getting much time at the beach."

Alex turned to look back over the seat. "How are you two?"

"We are very well. Life is good. We're both busy though I don't think our busy is anything like yours. Your dad and I are so glad you could come."

"So are we," Alex said. "Morgan and I talked on the way about how long it's been."

There's the understatement of the year. I was glad to see them, but I was edgy. *Right now you need to keep you mouth shut and not say something you'll regret. Focus on the effort they made to come.*

Gen said, "You kids know we wanted to go see your grandparents this holiday. We still want to do that. We need to do it. Your schedules make that more challenging. Before you leave, let's make sure we talk about how we might be able to fit a trip in. My word, you've just gotten here, and I'm talking about before you leave."

"Oh yes, Mom. Alex and I talked about that, too. We haven't seen them since graduation. We want to do that."

Gen turned and said something to Morgan, and they giggled. Alex asked me about my work. The twenty-minute drive passed in an instant. It was near midnight when we got home. Both kids showed the effects of the lives of graduate students in high-pressure fields. There was scant time before they were both ready for bed.

Gen and I went to bed but lay awake talking. We drank too much coffee waiting for the kids' arrival.

"So, Gen."

"So, Rocky?"

"They're here, finally. I've waited; well we've waited for this day for quite a while. It came and went in the blink of an eye, and I must wait again."

"Wait for what, Rocky"

"The talk."

"The talk? You're way past the talk, Rocky."

"Not *that* talk," which gave me a chuckle. "The talk about us, Morgan and me. It's something I need to get off my chest, out in the open."

"Will that help?"

"Yes, I've been carrying this for a long time."

"I mean will it help *Morgan*."

"Morgan seems to be taking care of Morgan just fine."

"Rocky!"

"I know, Gen. I'm sorry. I just…never mind; I was just venting."

"It's okay. Better that you vent here, now. I am thinking of the two monks and two wolves stories you told me. It is clear which monk you are. Maybe the question is which wolf are you feeding. Maybe it's not something you need to say to get off your chest but something deeper down. Perhaps, it's something you need to say out of your heart."

"You are right, Gen. She's just been so frustrating."

"And you haven't been, I guess."

"I thought I've been doing pretty well. I thought I've been very patient with her."

"You have, Rocky, but maybe it's not Morgan that is the subject of forgiveness here."

"What are you saying?"

"You and Cisco talked a lot about resolution and reconciliation, and forgiveness and compassion. Morgan may not need forgiveness, but Morgan does need compassion. We've talked about who's to blame before. I think from what you shared with me, until you truly resolve that with yourself, you will struggle to find reconciliation with Morgan. You will continue to harbor anger, or as you call it, frustration."

"You're right Gen, but…"

"Wait, Rocky."

"Wait for what?"

"Wait to say what you were going to say."

"Why?"

"Because there's a good chance that what comes after 'but' is explanation, and explanation is often a justification for our feelings."

"But! I want her to know what my feelings are."

"I know you do, Rocky, but she can't. She hasn't lived your experiences. You need to find another approach. Remember the first time you went to see Padre Cisco?"

"Yes."

"What did he talk about?"

"He told a story about an insurance salesman. It was about being present to others."

"Maybe that is what you have to do."

"What kind of approach is that?"

"I didn't say *I* need to find another approach. You have to find a way, and I know you will because you love her, Rocky, and compassion rises out of love."

"Smitty reminded me of that when he talked about Captain Miller and Private Ryan. Remember that?"

"I do."

"Maybe you could have this conversation with Morgan. You would be a lot better at it; or I could fly Smitty over."

"You made your bed of nails. You get to lie on it."

"You could lie on top of me and whisper directions into my ear."

"Rocky, if I am going to lie on top of you, it's going to be in this bed. I'm happy to give you directions if you want, but I don't think you need them."

"Let's find out."

* * *

Thanksgiving morning, Gen arose early to start the turkey. She went to great lengths to recreate our traditional holiday experience in a place we knew the kids did not perceive as home. Whether intentionally or not, they were both very gracious not referring to that fact.

Morgan got up early and came to the kitchen for coffee. She greeted Gen and me with hugs. She offered to help Gen fix the meal. Gen asked Morgan to get the cranberries from the pantry to put into the refrigerator to chill. She couldn't find any, and Gen realized she had forgotten to buy them. She asked if I would go to the store. I was glad to have a reason to get out of way and give the two of them time together. On my way out Gen told me a package had arrived, and she put it in my office.

Alex slept until noon and managed to rouse himself for in time for dinner. I showed up to make the gravy, and gave Alex a combo demonstration in turkey carving and soup making. The roaster was clean and the broth simmering when we sat down to dinner.

After the last of the cups and pie plates made their way to the dishwasher, I remembered the package that had come. Thinking it might be something Alex and Morgan had sent, I went to check. To my surprise, it was from Mary. I opened the box and found an envelope taped to a wrapped box inside. The plain card inside read 'Rocky, years ago when I was clearing out the basement I found the contents of this box. I think this is a good time for you to have them. Enjoy the game. Love, Mary.' I opened the box and found two baseball gloves and a well-worn ball. At that moment, I understood what *taken aback* means. I had to sit down.

I sat there cradling the gloves and ball and cried. Streams of memory flooded my mind. I put my glove on and tossed the ball into it repeatedly. I traded it for Dad's and did the same. I don't know how long I sat there. I wanted to call Mary to tell her what a wonderful gift she had sent, but I knew I needed to compose myself.

I went the bathroom to rinse my face. Back in the office, I collected the gloves and ball, and card; and took them to the kitchen. Gen and the kids were sitting at the table talking. I showed them my gift and read Mary's card. I began to regale them with stories of playing catch with my father, half-expecting one of the kids to say, "Yeah, Dad, you've told us before." That day, they just listened. After a dutiful time Alex said, "C'mon, Dad, let's not just talk about it. Let's do it." The two of us went out back to play.

We tossed the ball back and forth in silence with only the slap of the ball on leather or an occasional grunt from me. After a few repetitions, Alex started with baseball chatter. "C'mon Big Guy, pitch it in here. Just throw strikes, pitcher. Give me some smoke." I told him the only smoke I had left was a lazy plume blown away by the wind. We laughed and chattered, taking turns in the rhythm of the ball the way we did when he was young. It was like that with my dad when I was young.

"Alex, I want to share something with you."

"Okay."

"I left home forty years ago. That's nearly twice as long as you are old. From the time you can remember how many times a year did we see or talk to your grandparents?"

"A few. They would come visit. We would go to Akron every couple of years. We talked on holidays."

"So, maybe a half dozen times per year."

"Probably."

"I can tell you I made the connection even fewer times each year before you kids were born. The price you paid was that I did not nurture in you kids a sense of relationship with your family. I'm speaking about your whole family. That was my fault, not your mothers."

"What are you getting at, Dad?"

I caught the ball, held it, and walked over to Alex. "I need to stop to be able to talk."

"Okay."

"After I came back from seeing your grandparents over Memorial Day weekend, I realized how little I had done to sustain, much lest foster, the relationship with them. I didn't stay connected with them or with your Aunt Mary. That meant you kids weren't connected either.

"I've never thought I missed out. I have to admit, though, I don't know them very well. I can't say that I think of them much other than on birthdays and holidays."

"That's my point, Alex. Your mother said something to me after my trip to see you. She said that we don't want to put you kids in a position you will have anything to regret. I hope I haven't done that, but I do think I created the conditions that it could happen."

"How so?"

"That's just about how I handled things. It doesn't matter. What does matter is it not your fault. It you ever feel the need to question what you did or didn't do. If there is blame, it is mine. I regret decisions I've made that kept our family from remaining connected. I don't want you to make the same mistake. I didn't work at it. I learned that too late. I can't change that or even make up for it, but I can change me."

"Don't count yourself short, Dad. Morgan and I turned out fairly well."

"Yes you have, but that's not what I'm saying. I am talking about being intentional. I'm saying I can be intentional about maintaining connection. I'm asking you to do the same. It's part of maintaining balance in life, and it's about living a life you won't look back on with regret."

"I hear you, Dad, and I'll take what you've said to heart."

"Thank you. So let's throw a few more balls before my arm wears completely out." About the time I was feeling the effects of overusing my pitching arm, Morgan appeared.

"Can I play?"

"Sure," Alex and I replied.

Alex held out his glove and said, "Here, Sis, I need use the restroom."

I almost said, "I wonder why people call bathrooms *restrooms* when they are in someone else's house." I realized I didn't want to imply they weren't in their own house.

Alex handed Dad's glove to Morgan. It was too large for her so we traded. We tossed the ball for a while, and she said, "I remember watching you and Alex toss. I asked you why I couldn't play, and you said, 'Of course you can. Do you want to?' I told you, 'No.' I don't know why. I really did want to play. Do you remember that?"

"I can't say that I do. How old were you?"

"Maybe ten. Do you remember what happened the next day?

"Tell me."

"When I came home from school a brand new baseball glove with a red bow and a card hung on the knob of the back door. You knew what I really wanted. All four of us went out in the yard and played catch. You don't remember that."

"Now I do."

"It was spring, and the days were getting longer. After dinner, Alex and I went back out and threw until I couldn't any more. The next day, I woke up and my arm hurt so much I cried. I couldn't lift it."

"It must have hurt. You were not one to cry much."

"No, I wasn't, but I cried that day."

"Well, Sweetheart, I'm going to be crying tomorrow if I don't stop. Let's sit."

"Let me run to the ladies room. I'll be right back."

There it is again, *ladies room*. "I'll get us a couple of waters." I returned and stood on the patio gathering myself. *All right, Rocky, be present.* I said it a dozen times, and then I said *Help me be present.*

Morgan came out, and we sat at the table across from each other. She talked about school, her roommates, and living in Berkeley. I couldn't tell you what I said.

Finally, I said, "Morgan, you know I want you to have a joyous, full, long life."

"Of course I do."

"I just worry about you. I want you to be safe. I want to protect you."

"I know you do, Dad, but you don't have to protect me. I'm a big girl. I'm out there, on my own daily having to make big-girl decisions. You simply can't be there for all the moments."

"But I would like to be."

"That may be true, Dad, but that's only what *you* want. It isn't necessarily what I want. You have to trust me. You have to trust that you did your job. You and Mom taught Alex and me to be independent. We are independent, and you get to reap the reward of what you taught us. Part of that comes at a cost."

"It can be a pretty high price tag, Morgan. We feel, or I should say *I* feel, you don't want me in your life."

"I can't control that. As John Travolta in the movie *Michael* said, 'That's not my area.' You have to figure that piece out. I recognize the tension between us, and I have to learn to do my part to move past that. I know that I've been uncooperative at times. I know I can do better. I will. Trust me. I love you. You are the last person in the world I would want to hurt. Well, maybe the second to last...or third person. There is Mom, and there is a man I've met. No, no, no, Dad, I'm just kidding; but there is a man. It's too soon, and I have too much to do to get serious, but he could be the one. We'll see."

"What's his name?"

"Anthony."

"Tell me about him."

"He's handsome and tall, taller than me. He's kind, creative, and funny. He's a musician and helps support his tuition with local gigs. He's in business school studying management and marketing. He wants to go into the business side of music and entertainment."

"So you like him?"

"Of course I like him. You're too funny, Dad, and don't ask me the next question. It's much too late to have *the talk*."

"I look forward to meeting him."

"We'll see."

"I can only assume he will be an upgrade over some of the iconic bad boys you gravitated to in high school."

"Don't go there, Dad; you never liked any of my boyfriends in high school."

"Yes, Morgan. In the back of my mind I can hear myself saying 'Yes, Gen.' Can we return to the discussion?"

"What were we talking about?"

"Now, you're imitating your mother."

She grinned at me. "She would say that's a good thing. She'd say I am too much like you. However, to be serious again..."

"Thank you."

"Your feelings about my independence don't always match up with reality. The reality is you want me to be independent, but you treat me as if I'm still Daddy's little girl. I will always be Daddy's little girl, but I need to make my life on my own. It isn't that I don't need you. It is that I need to learn to depend on myself, and I learn that by depending on myself.

"You're the one who taught us this. You are the one who said we don't learn to make decisions by making decisions. You said we learn to make decisions by accepting and taking responsibility for the consequences of our decisions. That's a direct quote, Dad, and you are stuck with it. I am making my own decisions, and I am accepting the consequences."

"I may be stuck with my own words, but I don't have to like it."

"Just another case of tough love, Dad."

"I feel so useless in that scenario. I feel like I don't even get to be the sidekick character in the strip."

"Do you remember the time Alex asked you the baseball question in the driveway?"

"Vaguely. How do you know of this?"

"Multiple ways, Dad, but Alex told me."

"Refresh my memory."

"We were about seven or eight. Alex was playing peewee baseball, and he asked you if he could quit. Remember now?"

"Not exactly."

"You asked him, 'Who decided to play?' He said that wasn't an answer and repeated *can I* quit baseball. You did the broken record thing with him. He told me afterward that was when he learned he was in charge of his own life. At eight, he knew that. I remember thinking he was so much more mature than I was."

"So, how does that relate to you?"

"Ice skating, Dad?"

"Oh yes, you were dead set on being an ice skater. You were going to be the next Sarah Hughes. You even had your hair cut like her. It was shades of the past and Dorothy Hamill."

"Then you also remember it was a pipe dream. I quit. I remember telling myself it was because I started too late; but more than that, I remember it was okay for me to quit."

"You knew that?"

"I did. I knew if it was okay for Alex to decide keep playing, it was okay for me to quit. What's good for the goose is good for the gander. I learned I could be in charge of my life, too. You didn't give me as much leeway, though, as you gave Alex."

"Morgan, I thought it was my job to protect you."

"It was, and you did; and you taught us how to take care of ourselves."

"But what about the time I didn't. I still feel like I let you down."

"Time for more tough love, Dad. Let it go. Let it go. Let it go. You've been carrying this around for ten years. It's been an elephant hovering over us for too long. It wasn't your fault; it was mine. I ignored the symptoms. Today, I would say that I didn't listen to my body. I was as driven about school then as I am today. I wasn't going to miss school. I thought I was indestructible. All kids do. I was in my 'I don't need you' phase. You didn't know because I didn't let you know. I was better at hiding my feelings by then."

"But..."

"C'mon, Dad, no more buts about it. It happened. I survived, and good came out of it."

"There's more to it, Morgan, but wait. What do you mean by 'good came out of it'?"

"It was the first time I knew I wanted to be a doctor. I didn't like my doctors. They talked to you and Mom about me. They didn't talk to me. I wondered if that's how they treated Alice. Remember her. She had cancer and lost all her hair."

"Yes, I remember her."

"She was dealing with serious stuff, adult stuff. I wondered if they treated her as though she didn't have any say in her own treatment. Later I, also, realized I was bothered that doctors only show up after someone gets sick. That's great. We need that. I realized I wanted to be a doctor who would take care of people by teaching them how to take care of themselves. I don't want to just treat their illnesses. I want to help people to keep from getting sick, and teach them how to listen to their own bodies. I want to work with children. I want kids to know their doctor values their thoughts and their feelings and treats them like real people."

"Morgan, that is such a great mission in life." I realized I almost said "ministry in life" and was aware my attitude toward work was changing. Her work *would* be a ministry. "I am so happy for you. Having that sense of mission must make your studies more significant for you."

"So, Dad, does that mean you now understand why I am so monomaniac about school?"

"It does. I know about monomania; I have a long history. Let me go back to the 'there's more to it' part. There's another side to what you call your reality. Earlier, you said there's a price to pay for teaching you and Alex to be independent. You're right; there is. My father didn't teach me that; he only conceived of my life in the plant. I grabbed it on my own, and I held onto it tenaciously. He paid the price, but so did I. We pay a price with each choice we make. In choosing one thing we give up another."

"What are you talking about, Dad?"

"Like you and Alex, I left home right after high school. For me it was a week after I graduated. However, I didn't just leave home; I left home *behind*. Smitty recently called me a lone wolf. I was, and I have been a lone wolf since I was eighteen. I've paid a price, and I'm okay with that. What I'm not okay with, and I didn't realize until recently, is the collateral damage. My mother, Mary, my friends, and you kids paid the price as well."

"How did we pay a price?"

"In a moment. You want more water?"

"No, I'm good. I want to hear this."

Okay, she's listening. Don't blow it. Give her your heart. I thought about the conversation I'd just held with Alex. *Maybe it was a rehearsal. If it was, then this is prime time.* I took a deep breath. I retold my side of that talk starting from "I left home forty years ago," and walked her through the same questions, the same concerns, her mother's wisdom, and to my admission and my intention. "I don't want you to suffer regret, Sweetheart."

"I appreciate that, Dad. Do you know that's the second time today you've called me Sweetheart. It's nice to hear."

"You are a sweetheart. You are my sweetheart, and don't you forget it. So you hear what I am telling you?"

"I do, Dad. I get it."

"There's one more part to get. Okay? You remember Padre Cisco?"

'Yes."

"Padre Cisco told me two stories, one about two monks and another about two wolves." I shared mangled versions of the stories with her. "I can tell you I have been the grousing monk heading down the road, and the wolf I've fed has not been the one full of compassion. I carried what I perceived as failure. Don't misunderstand me. It wasn't always conscious. But when

I became aware of it, I realized I carried a great sense of guilt, and you paid an additional price."

"Me?"

"Yes, Morgan, I projected my guilt onto you. I chose to see you as angry with me so I could react to that. It made it okay for me to be angry with you. I chose to cast my blame for myself for not protecting you onto you. Moreover, it was an overlay to the unrecognized guilt of not nurturing family relationships. Life is all about relationships."

Morgan sat back, stared wide-eyed at me, and said, "Wow! I didn't know."

"Now it's my turn to say 'you couldn't have known.' I can't say I even knew until I just said it. I apologize for the way I've been. I am sorry."

"You don't have to apologize, Dad."

"Oh, yes I do, if not to you, then for me. I don't want to forget this, but I want it to be as much in my past as it is in yours. I want to learn from it, and I want you to learn from it. Your aunt Mary and I have patched things up, no, *more* than patched up, we have reconciled. Your mother held us together. Your granddad and I have found peace between us, and your grandmother has never had an angry bone in her body. However, I missed years of relationship that could have been so much better, and that spilled over onto them, and to you and Alex. You missed out, too."

"I am glad to hear that. No, that didn't sound right. I am happy that you, Mary, Grandma, and Granddad are feeling good about each other."

"Thank you." I paused and let that settle, then continued. "The bottom line here, Morgan, is I see the same thing happening to you. Your life is about achievement right now. That's good; it's more than good, but you need to temper achievement or whatever you chase with balance. You can have it all, but you do not find everything in one thing. It is found in balance, and an important part of that balance is relationships."

"Let me add one quick piece to this. You are living in a world of noise, and it is getting noisier. Relationships build on conversation. For all of the technology available to us, it seems that conversation is becoming more difficult to have. If you, I, and all of us are not intentional about it, conversation will not occur, and our relationships will be diminished."

"So then you won't get so bent out of shape when I don't return your phone calls right away?"

"You are being your mother again. You can quit."

"Okay."

"Of course I'm going to get bent out of shape, but I'll build in a grace period. Sometimes I just need to know you are okay. Call and leave a message. If I see it's you, I won't answer it so you don't have to worry about getting into a long discussion. Let me know when you will have some time. Tell me to pick up. Whatever works for you? However...and it's a great big however."

"I can it see it coming, Dad. You're going to hit me with the big O."

"The big O?"

"Yeah, O as in onus."

"You're right, Morgan, I am. Remember your peevish attitude when you called me in Salt Lake City? Don't answer. I know you do. Well, the phone works in both directions. For someone who had returned no phone calls, you were hard on me. You know that gander and goose thing. Well you're the gander in this one. Just take on the big O."

"I'll be more diligent, Dad. You know I love you. I'm just very self-absorbed right now."

"Morgan, I don't think there's any right now about it."

"I just threw the self-absorbed thing in for fun. Quit while you're ahead, Dad."

I did. We hugged, and laughed, and wiped the tears from our eyes until Morgan said, "Let's go back and join the world again. You and Mom take a break. Alex and I will finish cleaning up."

I went to my office and called Mary to share my surprise and my joy with her. She was her ever-effusive self. "Oh Rocky, that was so much fun. I wish I could have been there to see you open the package."

"Well Sis, you have been witness to a blubbering lump of clay. I never would have dreamed of such a thing." I told her about the game of catch, the kids, and the day. She said Mom and Dad had come for dinner and filled me in on their doings. We talked until Gen came into the room and I handed the phone to her. I called Mom and Dad on the landline and held the same conversation plus baseball talk. Dad again ended the call with "Wait 'till next year," only this time his voice had a more optimism in it. Gen and I compared news, and I told her I thought Dad's tone was more about life than just the Indians' prospects. She agreed based on what she heard from Mary.

We got wine and sat on the patio to resume our conversation. I said, "Morgan and I got time to talk."

"I saw that, Rocky. How did it go?"

"Do you know Morgan has a boyfriend?"

"Of course."

"Why am I the last to know?"

"Dads are always the last to know. How did it go?"

"Morgan is sounding more like you every time we talk."

"I see. It went well then."

"Better than I imagined." Her remark was not lost on me. I had a few minutes alone on the patio. I remembered our conversation last night. I told myself to be present. I said it like a dozen times. Then I said, 'Help me be present.' I think I prayed if that's what prayer is because I was present, and that's what made the difference. It's not the first time I've been present. I am present to you lots of times, but it was the first time I had a sense of being aware of it, of being *intentionally* present."

"That's wonderful, Rocky. That's a huge chunk of awareness."

"I feel the same way, though I have to tell you, Gen, I am a little embarrassed."

"Embarrassed? You, Rocky, why?"

"Well, at least I think I *should* be embarrassed. I was worried about how it would go. I thought I would need to loosen up Morgan. We didn't exactly switch roles, but she was an adult in the conversation. She has an amazing grasp of her reality. I wish I had known at her age what she knows. Life would have been easier."

"I doubt that."

"At least it would have been more intentional."

"That could be true. Maybe you were present for her for longer than you realize."

"Perhaps. I'll have to think about that."

"Why are you so surprised by her? You raised her. I should say we raised her to be what the woman she is."

"Morgan reminded me of that, and she said raising her to be independent comes with a price. Boy, was she right about that."

"So, Rocky, do you feel you have resolution?"

"I do, and more than that I feel we are reconciled. We had very different perceptions of the past. Hers was the more accurate one."

"Does that mean you are going to quit beating yourself up about it?"

"I'm not sure I'm willing to go that far. I don't know what I'd do with all my free time."

"That's good to hear. I was afraid you were going to be lurking about bothering me."

"I like lurking about and bothering you, Gen."

"That sounds more like the Rocky I know. Perhaps you have reconciled."

Friday, Alex and Morgan said they had studying to do. I said that I hadn't seen them bring any books. They both alluded to my status in the fogey generation, each telling me their texts were on an iPad. I readily accepted their teasing and let them do it. We went out to dinner and talked together late into the evening. Saturday morning, Gen and I reluctantly took them to the airport, saying goodbye amid a torrent of tears. I couldn't help but smile to know they were making their way into the world with ideals and dreams intact. Gen cried and I smiled all the way home.

Winter

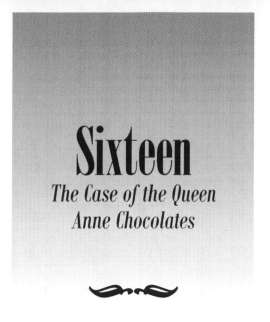

Sixteen
The Case of the Queen Anne Chocolates

"Abba, give me a word."
"Giving, my son."
"As in it is more blessed to give than to receive?"
"Sometimes, my son, it is more blessed to receive than to give."

A week after Thanksgiving, I drove out to Padre Cisco's for what I thought would be the last time. It wasn't that I didn't need to see him anymore. I knew I had only begun on my path. I knew there was much he could teach me. Perhaps I was afraid I had come to depend on him for guidance, and it was time to fly the nest.

We sat silently in the living room. I attended to the impending "lasts" around me. I scanned the room, taking in the furnishings as I had my first time just over a year ago. I breathed in the aroma of mesquite from the beehive fireplace. I savored the fresh coffee. I listened to the silence the thick adobe walls and isolated location create. I had only just arrived, and I was missing my visits already. I thought that maybe Padre Cisco was reading into my mind because we sat for longer than usual. "Peter, how is… No, that doesn't sound right anymore. Perhaps it is time I called you Rocky, and you dropped the Padre."

He did know. I don't know he knew, but he did. "Perhaps we should, Cisco."

Cisco said, "You've come far, Pilgrim."

"Feels like far."

"Were it worth the trouble?"

"Huh, what trouble?"

We played out that brief scene from *Jeremiah Johnson* between Bear Claw Chris Lapp and Jeremiah. It would just have been too much if he had delivered Del LaGue's line, "Maybe you best go down to a town. Get out of these mountains." Jeremiah's response was, "I've been to a town." I wouldn't have been able to deliver the line honestly. I knew it was time I went to a town. *Smitty made that allusion when we talked. I missed it. Well, Rocky, you said you missed many moments by not being present. Perhaps sometimes we just miss them. Tune in, Rocky, or you miss this one.*

I heard Padre Cisco say, "Rocky, let me begin again. How is it with you?"

"I am well, Cisco. All is well." I gave him a thumbnail sketch of the holiday weekend and filled him in on my conversation with Morgan going back to the San Francisco trip.

"You have let go of that part of your past then?

"I have."

"It seems I am to become part of your past."

"In this context perhaps, but not totally. How do you know these things?"

"I told you once, I am a practiced observer of the human condition. I am still a social science guy at heart. Your mood, your attention gave you away. I would not recommend you take up poker playing for a living."

"I learned that from Gen. Obviously, my tells are worse than a spaghetti western."

"That is too funny. I love the movie allusion."

"In your honor, Cisco, but I can only claim unconscious competence."

"Thank you just the same."

We sat for a few moments and he continued.

"You have let go of a lot of this year: Morgan, Mary, your dad, your loss of syndication, perhaps some of your old self. You were holding on to a lot. The Buddhists call it grasping."

"It seems that should be self-evident, Padre, ah excuse me, Cisco. It's hard to break old habits. I sense grasping has much more to it than its literal sense."

"Perhaps. You can decide. There is a children's story widely used in schools called *Where the Red Fern Grows*. Do you know it?"

"Yes, but it was after my time in school. The kids read it in fourth or fifth grade."

"It is a boy and his dogs story. The part I am referencing is early in the book."

He told me that Billy had two coonhound pups he wanted to train. He needed to catch a coon for the pelt, but had no dogs to tree the coon. Billy found a log with a hole in it. He placed a shiny trinket in the hole and drove nails on an angle into the hole and leaves. A coon came along and reached in to grab the trinket. The trap has caught the coon. The only way the coon could escape was to release the trinket. As long as the coon holds onto the trinket, its fist is too large to slip past the nails. "It is an almost iconic scene of grasping. It is not quite as iconic as *you have to go to the mattresses* or *life is like a box of chocolates*, but it is close." He shook his head laughing at himself. "Billy's solution is a great metaphor for how we live so much of our lives."

"So let me take a go at this. We talked about pain and suffering when you told the story of the two monks. One monk had the physical pain from carrying the woman across the river, but the other monk had emotional suffering because he held onto the event. That would mean that though the pain the raccoon experienced was expected, grasping the trinket caused the suffering it experienced. So, we cause our own suffering because of our inability to let go of the events."

"I should say it so well, Rocky. There are some corollaries. Pain and suffering bring with them lessons. The first is suffering ends when we release the events, and ending the suffering opens us to the lessons. The second is pain or suffering themselves open us to the lessons and what we learn allows us to end the suffering. The third is that not all lessons come with pain and suffering. Some lessons grow out of joyous moments and become joyous memories."

"I have a feeling, Cisco, you have one of those memories to share."

"I do, and I have been blessed to have it return each Thanksgiving for over ten years."

"Let's hear it."

"We need fresh coffee. This is a full cup story."

"I'll get it." I took his cup and got the refills. There was a twinkle in his eyes and a smile on his face. "I must warn you. This story has a twist to it. He took a drink, relaxed back into his chair, and set his cup on the bucket.

"Thanksgiving passed, and the Christmas season was in full swing. This was ten years ago." He unleashed his brogue for the occasion. He was in full story-telling mode. "Lights festooned the neighborhood. Stores, filled with Christmas trappings, were abuzz. I meandered through a drug store." He was illustrating the story with his hands as much as telling it.

I passed through the candy aisle. Bags and boxes of samplers, assortments, clusters, fudge, and chocolate-covered everything filled the shelves to the edges. I saw the Queen Annes. They incited riot in my memory.

"Since I was a small boy, I gave my dad a pound of chocolate-covered cherries at Christmas. For the first time in nearly half a century, I would not repeat the annual ritual. Dad's birthday, celebrated posthumously, had just passed. My emotions, full as the store shelves, spilled over. All those years of sustaining a tradition, all the wrapping paper, yards of ribbon, bows, gift tags, and transparent tape used to excess, came unraveled in my memory. I remember walking to the corner market to use my allowance to buy his special present. Later, I had proceeds from odd jobs in the neighborhood to cover the cost.

"There were years when my father smoked a pipe that I gave him a pound of Prince Albert tobacco, but I still got him the Queen Annes. As I grew older and he grew beyond the pipe, I enjoyed watching him open that box of candy as much as when I was a child. He knew what was in the box. There were years I thought, as many youngsters do, that it was cool to disguise it in a variety of packages. Some years, I put it in multiple boxes just to prolong his fun and my joy. He always feigned surprise and thanked me profusely for my thoughtfulness. Eventually, I was able to afford more. I still gave him the cherries if just for the nostalgic gesture of an era gone by. What a wonderful memory of him I had uncovered.

"It was not until the previous Christmas after my mother passed and I especially wanted to sustain tradition that Dad, in his quiet, offhand way finally disclosed to me the unimaginable.

"'You know, Francisco, I never liked Queen Anne chocolates.'

"'What?' I was flabbergasted. 'What did you do with them?'

"'Your mother ate them.'

"Mom had eaten them all. It never occurred to me that in all that time I had never seen Dad eat any of the candy. Why hadn't he told me? Then I realized I had solved the case of the Queen Anne chocolates. For once receiving was more blessed than giving. Not until that moment did I know how much joy he actually had all those years. He had fun allowing me the pleasure of giving my gift to him. What a hoot!

"For nearly fifty years my father would happily accept a gift for which he had no taste. Year after year, he would graciously open the same gift just to sow the seeds of joy in the heart of a small boy regardless of his age.

"The torch had passed to my children, who began giving me the candy. Just the same, I bought a box of Queen Annes. I savored each one."

"Oh Cisco, what a wonderful memory."

"It is a memory I hold dearly, and it is a lesson that I hold onto as well. Sometimes it *is* more blessed to receive than to give."

"I bought my dad chocolate for Christmas. I wonder how many of us share your story."

"I have had many people share similar memories with me. For some it was candy, others gaudy Christmas socks, ties that light up, or fruitcake in a can."

"Oh, yes, the dreaded fruitcake."

"However, this story has a 'the rest of the story' twist to it."

"The plot thickens?"

"It does. The rest of the story is in those cans of Prince Albert. I remember going to the corner store asking for a pound of tobacco. That was in the days when storekeepers could sell tobacco to take home to their fathers. I could not remember what brand my father bought. I told Mr. Garcia it was one of those English guys, and he gave me the Prince Albert. I later learned my father smoked Sir Walter Raleigh. He abhorred Prince Albert. I have vague memories of seeing Prince Albert cans around, but I think he dumped it and replaced it with his brand. He doubled down on me."

"What a revelation."

"I've learned that part of living is sharing the burden, but it is also sharing the joy. We are good at serving, but not so at allowing service. My father taught me that at times we could serve others by allowing others to serve us. Thomas talked about that last month when he said communities are bound together by sharing the joys and the burdens."

"I must say, Padre, and I use the title with respect. You have been a mentor; I'll not say *teacher* and offend you. You are a spiritual friend in the truest sense. The burden shared was mine, and you bore it with me. I am grateful. John O'Donohue would call you an *anam cara*." I wanted to say more, but he was becoming embarrassed.

"Rocky, I hold great anticipation for the quality of your journey. The least of what you have been is a burden. I have no doubt our future association will bring great joy."

With that, he saw me out for the last time. I reached the bend in the road and took a final glance in the mirror. I saw him standing there in his usual pose, bidding farewell and welcoming me at the same time. I made the turn and drove out of sight; but I knew we would meet again. I was in the conversation.

The End
and
The Beginning

EPILOGUE

The Other Man

"Now you know the rest of the story."
~ Paul Harvey

Gen and I occasionally visit with Cisco at his storytelling events. I continue to see him at the gatherings of the wise men. Through them, I have met others. Each has his story to tell, which has led to many significant discussions. Enrique and I have spent time together, and his story is equal to that of Cisco. Perhaps his story and mine will become our story. Through Enrique, I made a contact in the Illuman group, and registered to attend a "Male Rights Of Passage" retreat.

Smitty is Smitty, and our story unfolds and refolds. Morgan and I have grown closer. She actually calls every other now and then. Her relationship with Anthony is blossoming. I definitely missed the window for *the talk*. Gen and I travel to the Bay as often as Alex and Morgan allow the intrusion. We booked flights for all of us to go to Akron in the spring.

I read that each new chapter in our story begins with risk. My life in art continues to be a risk. My experimentation has broadened beyond comic strips. As a kindness to myself, I call it an exploration, which is a euphemism for I haven't produced anything someone wants to buy. My life in writing has been an even greater risk. I have no illusions about setting expectations. I live in anticipation that someone who reads this will want to join the conversation.

I set out to tell the stories of Padre Cisco. In doing so, I discovered the unfolding story of Rocky Stellar. I didn't expect that Cisco's story and my story would become our story. I learned we do not author our stories alone. I've made the circle back to the beginning, knowing that always we begin again. It is like savoring a fresh cup of coffee.

ACKNOWLEDGEMENTS

I thank my wife, Becky, the *anam cara* in my life. She was my first reader. With grace and mercy in her heart she would say, "Perhaps you might consider…" about the words with which I had already fallen in love. *Padre Cisco* is a better story and a better book because of you.

I thank Chris Noël for his editing prowess. Ron Schmidt and Melinda Worth Popham, I thank you for reading renditions of unpolished manuscript and for abiding with my incessant questions and arguments.

Thank you, Ravi Verma and Christopher McCauley, my desert fathers in a journey that led to *Padre Cisco*.

My Walk to Emmaus brothers, John Paterson, Mike Gallagher, Tom Salt, and Jim Moser listened to the moments in the learning curve of my spiritual journey for twelve years, and for the last three accepted without criticism my presumption that I could be a novelist.

Thank you, Manny Fimbres for bringing Padre Cisco to visual life in your painting. I am indebted to Iyanla Vanzant, who I have never met. Reading her admonition, "If it is not your story to tell, you don't tell it," guided me to fulfill a primary task of story telling.

Thank you, Henry Rojas, for your spiritual friendship and years of illuminating conversation.

WHO AND WHAT IS REAL?

This is a work of fiction, and the characters do not represent any persons living or dead. However, some of the people and organizations mentioned or quoted in the book are real. Following is a list of the real people and groups in *Padre Cisco: Conversations with a Desert Father*.

The *Cursillo* movement began in the United States in Waco, TX, in 1957 as a movement among Catholics. Within a few years, it spread to other denominations as *Walk to Emmaus, Three Day, Tres Dios,* and *The Great Banquet. Cursillo* is a registered trademark of the National Cursillo Center in Jarrell, TX. https://www.natl-cursillo.org/resource-center/ Walk to Emmaus is a trademark of The Upper Room of the General Board of Discipleship of the United Methodist Church. http://emmaus.upperroom.org

Illuman is a men's group founded by Fr. Richard Rohr, also, the founder and core faculty member of the Center for Action and Contemplation in Albuquerque, NM. https://www. illuman.org

Stillpoint is an open and inclusive community that prepares deeply grounded spiritual directors, and to live together into a deeper contemplative life of faith, spiritual practice, and action. https://www.stillpointca.org

The movies, songs, poems, books and authors quoted are all real except for Michael Francis Lee and *Dance Partners*.

Au, Wilkie; Noreen Cannon. Urgings of the Heart: A Spirituality of Integration.

Bolz-Weber, Nadia. Accidental Saints: Finding God in All the Wrong People. The Crown Publishing Group.

Boyle, Gregory. Tattoos on the Heart: The Power of Boundless Compassion. Free Press.

Brown, Brené. Daring Greatly: How the Courage to Be Vulnerable Transforms the Way We Live, Love, Parent, and Lead. Penguin Publishing Group.

Cacciatore, Marianna. Being There for Someone in Grief: Essential Lessons for Supporting Someone Grieving from Death, Loss and Trauma. Raku Press.

Clarke, Jim. Creating Rituals: A New Way of Healing of Everyday Life. Paulist Press.

Dass, Ram. Be Here Now. HarperCollins.

Hanh, Thich Nhat. Living Buddha, Living Christ 10th Anniversary Edition. Penguin Publishing Group.

Kushner, Rabbi Lawrence. Jewish Spirituality: A Brief Introduction for Christians. Turner Publishing Company.

Lama, Dalai. The Book of Joy: Lasting Happiness in a Changing World. Penguin Publishing Group.

Lewis, C. S. Surprised by Joy: The Shape of My Early Life. Houghton Mifflin Harcourt.

O'Donohue, John. Anam Cara: A Book of Celtic Wisdom. HarperCollins.

Rilke, Ranier Maria Rilke. Letters to a Young Poet. W.W. Norton & Company.

Rohr, Richard. Falling Upward: A Spirituality for the Two Halves of Life. Wiley.

Rupp O.S.M., Joyce. The Cup of Our Life: A Guide to Spiritual Growth. Ave Maria Press.

Thurman, Howard. Jesus and the Disinherited. Beacon Press.

Young, Sarah. Jesus Calling: Enjoying Peace in His Presence. Thomas Nelson.